THE DROVERS

OUTLAWS

JOHN D. BROWN

BLACK
SWORD
BOOKS

GET EXCLUSIVE CONTENT!

Join John's newsletter to stay up-to-date with new releases and receive exclusive bonus content.

www.johndbrown.com

To Nellie.

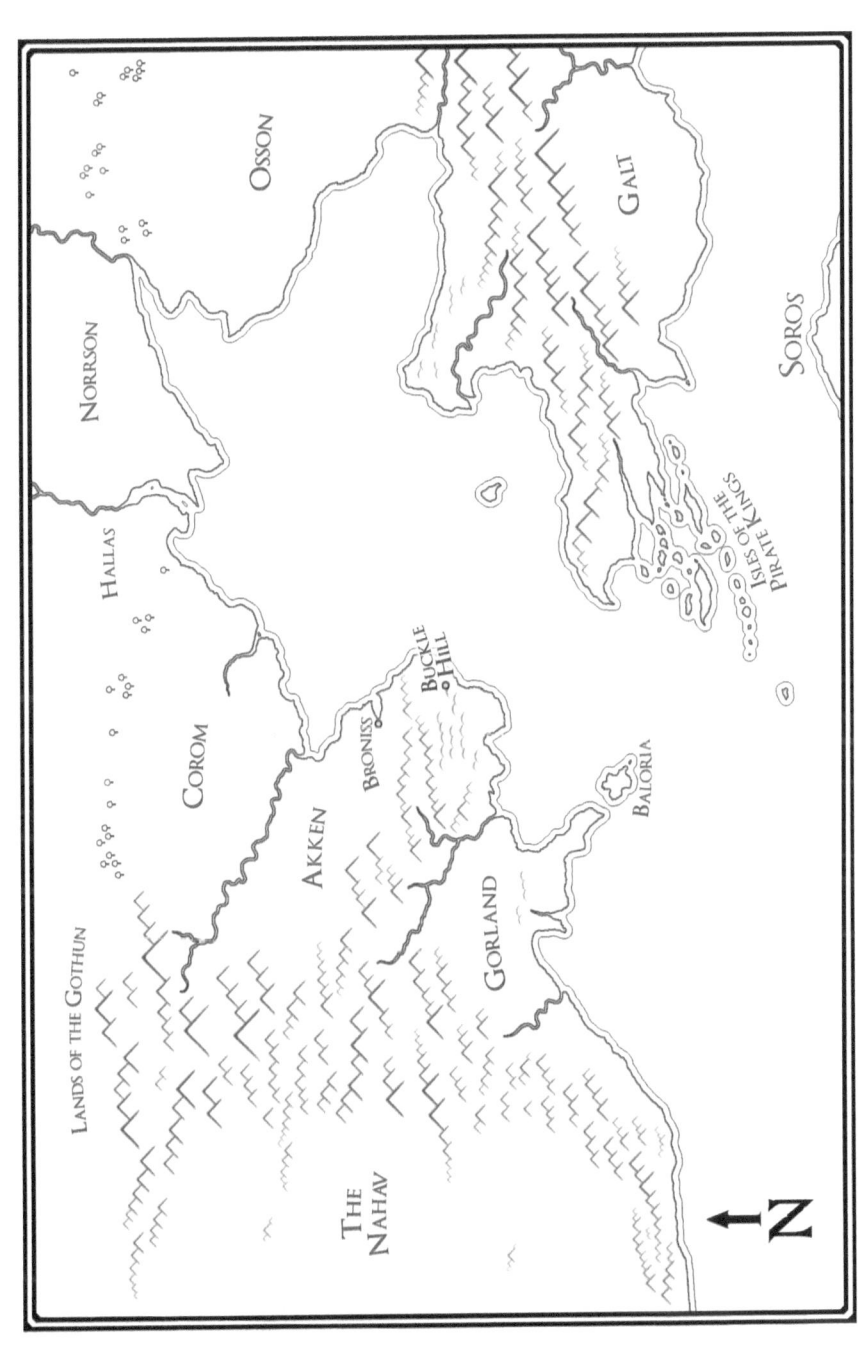

PROLOGUE

THE GUARD PEGGED the three men as problems as soon as they rode up.

The first man was a big, meaty fellow with a full beard. The next was bald and skinny. The third had outlined his eyes with kohl. It was a fashion in the south to do that. And the guard supposed there was nothing wrong with it, but what was a Southerner doing way up here? Especially one that looked like he'd not only rob his grandmother, but all his nieces and nephews as well.

The guard moved a bit closer to the money box. There was quite a bit of coin being collected here, and these louts weren't going to get a penny of it. Not while he was around.

"Would you look at that," the tailor's son said. "A Southerner."

The tailor's son was wearing an uppity hat with a big fancy feather in it. He removed his hat, ran his hand through his hair, and put his hat back on. He was one of six from Pencoy's lands that had been assigned to protect the money. Everyone wanted to see the body of the korrog and hear the tale of the battle that had taken place just a few days ago on this very field. And they could for a price.

"They've come a long way," the tailor's son said. "I told you, didn't I? They're going to come from all over."

"He didn't come from the South," the guard said.

"But—"

"It's only been a few days," the guard continued. "Not enough time for the news to travel that far. Certainly not enough time for anyone there to make the ride."

"They could have come by boat."

"Maybe. But if they did, they'd have to be fools. Who would risk the Osson ships raiding off the coast?"

And if they were seamen, where did they get the horses? And what kind of seaman went touring around the countryside and left his ship unguarded against an attack? No, these weren't seamen. They were trouble.

The three men tied their horses to the split-rail fence post and walked over to the greeter's wagon. The woman there welcomed them and gave them a cup of sweet well water from the water barrel and directed them to the food tables. The girls at the tables removed the fly cloths to reveal meat pies, cheese, and honey cakes. There were also roasted nuts there and fresh apricots. The woman at the cook fire next to the table removed the lid from the pottage and gave it a stir to show how deliciously thick it was and allow the aroma to fill the men's nostrils.

The men surveyed all that was displayed, and the guard watched them closely to make sure they didn't filch a crumb, for that food had been earning them all a lot of copper as well. It seemed the thrill of hearing the tale and seeing the beast produced large appetites and loose purses.

And it appeared that was no different with these three, for after a bit of haggling, the man with kohl eyes bought cheese and meat pies and divvied them up with his companions. And then the three of them sauntered over to where a guide was waiting.

Kohl Eyes pointed out into the field behind the guard. "That great lump out there in the field—is that it?"

The guide, an older man who carved fabulous toys, said, "Oh, yes indeed. A beast most fearsome. You can see its wicked teeth, the size of which will astound you. And then there are the talons and claws. The terrible eyes. You will see its very blood on the grass round about."

"How do we know it isn't pig's blood?" the big hairy one asked.

"Oh, no, there were no pigs here. No, you'll see it is quite authentic."

"How much?" Kohl eye asked.

"How much blood?" the woodcarver asked. "Plenty, I can assure you. Why, the ground is black with it."

"No, how much for the tour?"

The woodcarver smiled at his mistake. "Oh dear. How silly of me. I see now. I see. It's one birdseye to see the sight of a lifetime. A monster from legend. But not only that. I will tell you the tale of the battle. I will walk you to the camp where you will see one of the spears that was snapped in the fight. You'll hike up to the hill where you can see one of the arrows that struck the largest of the three creatures. You'll see exactly where it fell when the creature ripped it out of its wing. It will be as if you were there with the roaring and trumpeting splitting the sky, and the drover and his little band scurrying about and fighting for their lives. And then you will come down from the hill and view the sky terror up close. Everyone who stands next to it is amazed. And it costs one mere birdseye per person."

Two other guides were here. Both were out with other groups. One was on the hill talking to three families from Woodstrife. The other was leading a man and his three daughters to the beast. And it was true that all who saw the creature were amazed. The guard himself was still amazed even after hearing the tale and seeing the sights multiple times.

Kohl Eye bit into his meat pie and chewed. "And this was two days ago?"

"Two days ago, just as the sun was sinking in the west, the first of the creatures appeared. I will show you the very rock upon which it landed and the scratch marks it left there."

"You said there were three of them?"

"Indeed, indeed. Three terrors. And as your guide, I will tell you about each one of them."

"When did the drover leave?" Kohl Eye asked.

The woodcarver smiled. "Oh, immediately after the battle, good sir. We gave him a wagon and mule. And a good sturdy pony."

"We heard he was traveling north."

"They headed for the coast, to join up with an escort that would lead them safely to Broniss and the Queen."

It was a lie, of course. The drover had not gone to the coast. Two crews of Osson scum had landed there and made a camp up one of the inlets along the coast road. Reports claimed they were around a hundred or hundred and fifty strong. That was a nice-sized war band, and the fact that they were there had everyone on edge, for it meant Gallas the Bloody, king of Osson, was truly coming to bring their blessed Corwenna, mage queen of Akken, to heel. Gallas, the pig, was coming to slaughter her and all who supported her. If the drover went that way, he'd be killed and his cattle stolen.

So he'd taken the road west toward Gorland, which was madness if you asked the guard. The wildmen of Gorland were no friends of Akken. Plus a stretch of that road ran close to the blight. Nobody in their right mind would go that way, but the drover had insisted.

There had been brutal-looking runes on the largest korrog. Marks of a wolf mage. Marks that would give any man the shivers. It was probably some filth cooked up by Osson wizards. Either way, news of such black arts had to be taken to the mage queen. And quickly. And so the drover had left to do just that.

He'd asked the villagers to tell everyone he took the coast road. He was worried that brigands might steal the carcass of the korrog he took with him, for the body of such a creature could bring profit just as the one here did. Great profits. He'd also been worried about his cattle. And so the villagers had agreed. Although the guard didn't know how long the secret could be kept.

"How many men were with the drover?" the bald skinny one asked.

The guard narrowed his eyes, becoming wary of their intentions.

"Well, that is the thing," the woodcarver said. "That's part of what makes the events here so miraculous. There were five boys, although one was bigger than most men. Five boys, one dog, a cook, and the headman. You will thrill when you hear about their courage. And you will feel sorrow, for two of our neighbors came to help and met a terrible end. The money we collect here goes to support their families who, as you can imagine, are disconsolate with grief."

"To the coast, you say?" Kohl Eye asked. "But Osson has taken the coast road. And Pencoy's down in Dob's Port, so who was their escort?"

4

These three were asking a lot of questions about the drover. The guard's suspicions rose.

The woodcarver smiled. "Oh, I don't know those details. Although I did hear Lord Pencoy arranged for the cattle to be pastured by one of the villages between here and Larkin-on-the-Rye. So they could be there."

That was another lie.

"Maybe we'll just go talk to them," the big hairy one said. "Hear the story right from the source."

"You may indeed," the woodcarver said. "You may indeed. But I say, why not do both? There's nothing to compare to hearing the story at the very site of the battle. There's nothing like seeing the creature where it fell."

The woodcarver was smooth as butter, but the guard wanted to steer the conversation away from the drover. His little band had no escort. Nothing but one cattle dog for protection. And if the wrong sort went after them, well, that drover might find himself hard pressed indeed.

Of course, that crew of men and boys had killed two korrogs and driven off a third, so maybe they could take care of themselves. It wasn't any of the guard's business. And it certainly wasn't the business of these three louts. Besides, there were others coming down the road to hear the tale, and he didn't want these three souring their experience.

The guard said, "So do you three want to see the sights and hear the tale, or would you like to move along?"

"Oh, we'll see it," said Kohl Eye and held three birdseyes out to the tailor's son. "We wouldn't miss this for the world."

"You won't regret it," the woodcarver said. "I promise you. Now, come with me to see where they made their camp. They told us they had seen something three times on three different nights in the sky. They thought it merely a fancy. But on the morning, before they arrived here, they awoke to find that something had dragged a heifer and two year-lings out of the large paddock next to where they had camped. Right from under their noses.

"Can you imagine? What power must a creature possess to do that? Well, they followed the blood trail and found that not only had it killed the cattle and eaten their choicest parts, but it had also scuffed grass and dirt onto them. You know what that means, of course. You can imagine the shock and horror the little band must have felt upon seeing such a sight, knowing the creature could, at any moment, return to its kills. They immediately broke camp and hurried the cattle here, hoping to find safety."

The woodcarver continued walking and talking. The three men ate their meat pies and followed him out into the field.

The guard turned to the short arrowsmith who'd brought two of his bulldogs for added security. "When those three come off the hill to go view the beast, make sure you meet them there with your dogs. Keep an eye on them. Do not let them pluck even a hair from the beast's body."

The arrowsmith patted one of the bulldog's head. "We'll be happy to keep them honest, we will."

The guard nodded and thought about sending someone to go with the woodcarver. The woodcarver was smooth, but he also liked to talk. And talking sometimes led even the most circumspect to blab about things they shouldn't.

He was about to send someone when then the tailor's son spoke up. "Now, look at that crew!"

The guard looked down the road. There was crowd of at least thirty people heading this way. Men, women, children, and a few dogs, all come to see the spectacle.

"Did I tell you?" the tailor's son asked.

The guard rolled his eyes. "Are you going to say with every donkey, dog, and rat that comes round that bend?"

"I'm just saying."

This crowd looked friendly, but there were a few young boys among them. Odds were some of them would be tempted to filch some food off the tables. And maybe some of the others would try to sneak in without paying.

The guard looked out at the woodcarver and the three men. They were almost halfway to the campsite. Surely, the woodcarver wouldn't let anything slip. And it didn't matter anyway—with such a crowd, the guard needed all eyes and hands here.

1

PIE

T HE FIRST THING to disappear was Caswal's hand pie.

Ferran and the others were two days farther down the road from where they'd waited for Pencoy's escort and battled the korrogs. Two days closer to the blight.

They'd herded the cattle into a pasture, parked the wagon with the carcass of the huge korrog on it, and gone another thirty yards to an old campsite that backed up on the woods. The campsite was overgrown and clearly hadn't been used in some time. The pasture fence and water ditch were a bit ramshackle as well, and so Borros put them to work.

Ferran would have normally been assigned to water the cattle with Winwalom, his best friend in the world. But Winwalom had been injured in the fight with the korrog and was in no shape to wield a spade. Instead, he was over by the wagon, tying his long hair up on his head so he could help Lagash preprare the meal.

Lagash himself was a mystery to Ferran. He was a dark Sorosian who'd been a warrior, maybe part of the most elite band in his country, but now he was just a cook. What kind of warrior elected to cook meals for a foreign drover? And why had he come across the sea? None of the boys knew. However, Ferran did know Lagash could cook. Although cooking might not be the right word, for what that man did with pottage could surely make a king warble like a bird of joy.

With Winwalom helping Lagash, Ferran and Ranoc had been assigned to clear the ditch that was supposed to bring water to the pasture. Ranoc was rangy. And brave. Borros had called him reckless. And Ferran supposed that was true. Ranoc had a wicked scar on his neck from one summer when he'd repeatedly tried to ride a mad bull bareback. But he'd also been the one to jump up on the korrog's back, knife in hand. Furthermore, he was an excellent shot with his sling. Having him close gave Ferran comfort, for they were getting close to the blight, and who knew what might come barreling out of the woods in this place?

Caswal—the cruel, the coward, the pig-brained, the turd with hairy warts—and Krov, the massive woodsman's son with a patch over his eye were helping Borros chop trees to repair the fencing.

Ferran and Ranoc finished clearing the ditch and getting the water to flow, then walked back to the cook fire. Lagash liked to make his fires in a hole in the ground that was connected to another hole about a foot away.

Two bars had been laid across the mouth of the hole. On those bars sat a wide, black cooking pot. But the scent that wafted on the breeze was not pottage. It was something that smelled of baked crust mixed with something sweet. Ferran's mouth began to water.

"What is that smell?" Ranoc asked Lagash.

"I promised you raisin pies for standing guard that last night back at that vale. Well, I'm delivering on my promise."

And then he shouted to the others to come get them while they were hot.

Both Ranoc and Ferran took in another big whiff of the aroma and made small groans of anticipation. Surely a wonder was in that pot.

Lagash removed the heavy lid and revealed the miracle. And Ferran corrected himself. It was not one miracle, but seven. Seven large hand pies. They were golden brown and crusty. Steam wafted up from a little halfmoon cut into the top of each pie. Lagash unsheathed his knife that had a fox inlaid with silver in its hilt and used it to separate the pies from the surface of the black pot and hand the pies out to the boys.

Caswal and Krov arrived and made sounds of delight as they took their pies. But then Borros called them back out to the pasture to fix some shoddy work.

Ferran's pie was warm in his hands and fragrant. He took the pie back to a nice, grassy spot next to a tree, then sat down and leaned against the trunk. The pie felt heavy. He blew on it, then took a bite of one corner and blinked in shocked delight.

By the queen's lovely eyes! He held the pie up and looked at it. It couldn't have been that good. He took another bite. But the second bite was even better than the first. Crusty, but not hard. Sweet but not cloying. Familiar, but surprising. And all of it warm and urging his mouth to rejoice.

He licked his lips and decided he was not going to rush this. There would be no gobbling. He was going to make this pleasure last as long as possible. And so he took the smallest of bites, savoring each delicious crumb of the crust and blend of flavors in the filling.

There was flour, lard, salt, water, raisins, some devilish Sorosian spice, nuts, and who knew what else. It was divine. Every bite soothed, and he decided he must learn how to make these so that he could bake a batch for his mother and sister. Before they left this world, they needed a bite of such a pie.

Ferran took another bite, savored it, and felt the soothing pleasure start in his mouth and then wash through the rest of his body. He sighed and thought someone should write an ode to this pie. He continued to nibble and savor.

And then Caswal started bellowing.

"Hey!" he demanded. "Who took my pie!"

Ferran looked over. Caswal was standing next to his pack, which he'd set against a tree.

"I put it right here," Caswal said angrily, pointing at his sack. "Who took it?"

Winwalom, Ranoc, and Lagash had finished their pies and were licking their fingers. They shrugged. Krov and Borros had just begun to eat theirs. Ferran still had a third of his pie left. He shrugged as well, but Caswal narrowed his eyes at him.

"You," he said. "That's my pie!"

"No, this is mine," Ferran said.

Caswal threw down his pack and marched toward Ferran.

Ferran rose and backed away. "No, this is mine. Ask them."

"Give it to me," Caswal demanded.

Ferran scampered back. "It's not your pie."

Caswal lunged at him.

Ferran darted past Lagash and Winwalom. "Tell him it's not his pie."

"Get back here," Caswal ordered.

Ferran was not going to let Caswal anywhere close to his pie and began to run out toward the field.

"Stop," Borros commanded. Borros was a large figure. He was balding and had a dark beard with streaks of gray in it, but he was by no means an old man. He was weathered muscle, sinew, and scars. Furthermore, he'd been a grimsman and warrior and who knew what else. Borros was one of the anointed, one of those who could ingest the power of earthmeal to wield whatever might and grace the mages had worked into the runes they'd put upon him. And Ferran dared not disobey him. Not outrightly.

And so Ferran stopped running, but continued to walk to keep ahead of Caswal.

"I said stop. Both of you."

Ferran stopped and took another nibble of his beloved pie.

"Is that his pie?" Borros asked.

"No sir," Ferran said. "I went. I sat. I've been taking little bites. There's wizardry in this pastry, I'm telling you. I've never had anything like it. And I don't know what happened to his pie because I've been too busy savoring mine."

Borros grunted and turned to Caswal. "Where did you put it?"

"In my pack. And then I closed it."

"Maybe some critter got into it," Winwalom said.

"There was no critter," Caswal said. "Not unless it knows how to open a pack, steal a pie, and then close the pack up again."

"Well, it wasn't me," Ferran said.

Borros looked at Lagash for some insight, but he just shrugged. "I was over here, making dinner."

"That leaves only him," Caswal said, pointing at Ferran.

Borros turned his gaze on Ferran.

"I did not take his pie," Ferran said. "Maybe it fell down into the bottom of his pack. Maybe he ate it."

"I didn't," Caswal said.

"I didn't see Ferran over by Caswal's stuff," Lagash said.

"But you weren't watching him the whole time either," Borros said.

Lagash shrugged.

Borros motioned at Caswal. "Check your pack. It's probably there."

Caswal checked, pulled everything out, but there was no pie.

"I tell you I didn't move from where I was sitting," Ferran said. "It wasn't me."

"Do we have any more?" Borros asked.

"No," Lagash said. "That's it. And the last of the raisins. There will be no more raisin pies until we get to Broniss."

Caswal's face set in anger.

"I won't abide thieves," Borros said looking at Ferran. "Nor will I countenance liars," he said and looked at Caswal. "But since it's impossible to know which is which here, we'll solve it with a slice. Ferran, give him half of what's left of yours."

Ferran's mouth hung open. "But—"

Borros cut him off with a look.

"Fine," Ferran said. This was intolerable. It was unjust. But he broke the rest of his pie in two, walked over to Caswal and held out a piece to the horrid toad.

"You broke it," Borros said. "Let him choose. That's how we keep things fair."

Caswal looked over the two pieces and took the one that was larger, his face as sour as vinegar.

Ferran gritted his teeth.

"There," Borros said. "And if we have any more incidents, someone's going to feel some fire."

Ferran was already feeling a bit of fire. Caswal must have eaten his pie as he was walking back out to fix his fencing mistakes. Gobbled it like an idiot, and then come back, regretting his lack of control, and wanted Ferran's.

Ferran walked back to where he'd been sitting and tried to put Caswal's lying theft out of his mind. He tried to go back to the sweet pieland he'd been in, but the pie, while delicious, just didn't taste the same in his mouth.

Borros took the last bite of his pie and said, "Nobody cooks them like our Master of the Pot." He made a small sound of satisfaction and licked a bit off his finger. "Delicious. Now, it's time for some work. I don't expect to find anything worrisome in the blight. But then I didn't expect a korrog. Or what appear to be the runes from a wolf mage. So we're going to continue your training. Up until now, you've been learning mostly how to fight on your own. And you need to continue improving those skills. But if you want to save your skins, you've got to go beyond that."

He motioned at them. "Go get your spears."

2

FIX AND FLANK

T HE BOYS RETRIEVED their spears and lined up.

Borros said, "So, tell me what you learned from our recent battle."

"That tails can pack a whollop," Krov said and stroked the side of his injured head.

"And the bone in the edge of wings can be like iron," Winwalom said. "It was like getting clobbered by a post."

"They're tough," Borros agreed. "What else?"

"We were caught out," Caswal said.

"What do you mean?"

"Nobody saw the third one until it was on those men."

Borros nodded.

"The big one surprised us too," Winwalom said. "And who would have guessed its wings would kick up enough dirt to blind us?"

"We underestimated it," Ferran said.

"Underestimated a korrog?" Borros asked.

"Well, we thought there was just the small one. We thought we had an easy kill and went after it, not knowing there were two more."

"So what's the lesson to be learned?" Lagash asked.

"Don't rush?" Ranoc offered.

"Sometimes you need to rush with all the speed you have," Borros said.

The boys fell silent, thinking.

They had acted blindly. Well, they'd seen the one, so they'd acted with partial blindness. But they hadn't known how the creatures would attack. And they hadn't known how many there were. Suddenly Ferran thought he had the answer. "Know your enemy," he said.

Borros nodded. "Put an extra bone in Dog Boy's soup."

Ferran tried not to beam too noticeably at the praise.

"You will never know everything you need to about your enemy. But the more you know, the better you can fight. This is why we post sentries and send in scouts and spies. You want to know as much as you can before you engage. Now, I had ordered all of you, as soon as the creature was spotted, to gather to the thicket. Why do you think I did that?"

"Because we didn't know enough," Winwalom said. "You wanted to give us time to gauge our enemy."

"Did you hear what Long Hair said?" Borros asked.

The boys nodded.

"Ranoc," Borros said. "You went after the smallest korrog first. You are a brave lad. It does you credit. But foolhardiness mixed with bravery is one of the quickest ways to find yourself on the end of a sword. Or in a korrog's jaws."

Ranoc nodded, a bit abashed.

"How many of the rest of you went after the smaller korrog?"

All of them raised their hands, except Caswal.

Borros pointed at him. "He's the only one that followed my order."

Caswal glanced at the other boys. His expression was quick and subtle, and to someone from outside, it wouldn't mean much, but Ferran knew that condescending, self-satisfied look. And he knew Caswal was going to be more insufferable than he already was.

"Battle is a hard thing to gauge," Borros said. "If there had only been one, and Ranoc had killed it, we'd all be celebrating his nerve. And we would have ignored the risk he took."

Krov raised his hand. "But running to the thicket and gauging risks —well, it feels cowardly."

"It was following orders," Caswal said.

"Running isn't good or bad," Borros said. "Running is running."

Krov looked confused at the answer.

"Sometimes you charge," Borros said. "Sometimes you run."

"Sometimes you skulk in the shadows," Lagash added.

"When the right action is to charge in, brave men charge in," Borros said. "It doesn't matter the risk or how fearsome the enemy. Fear might grip them, but they go nevertheless. Cowards, on the other hand, shrink from acting when the time for such action comes."

"But how do you know when to charge and when to run or skulk?" Ranoc said.

"That's a good question," Borros said. "I can't tell you when to act in every situation. It depends on a number of things. But I can tell you one thing—you're new to this. And that's why you follow orders."

Ferran could see he should have run to the thicket when the first korrog appeared above the field. But what about when Krov was out there, dazed and about to become korrog dinner? He couldn't imagine hanging back and letting him be struck down. It just didn't feel right.

"Something bothering you, Dog Boy?"

"No," Ferran said. "Nothing."

Borros lifted an eyebrow, but Ferran didn't dare share what was on his mind. Borros shrugged. "What else did we learn?"

The boys sat there silently. One thing might be that driving cattle wasn't the pie bake they had thought it would be.

Lagash spoke up. "How was the threat of the big one eliminated?"

"A sharp thrust with Borros's spear," Ranoc said.

"Yes, but what allowed that? It's clear the front side of a korrog is not the best one to approach. Claws as long as daggers, wings like iron posts, and those jaws. In fact, it's probably the worst approach." He gave Borros a look that showed how little he fancied the line of attack the big man had taken. "Our fearless leader went right up to the business end of the beast. How was he able to do that?"

"It was distracted," Winwalom said. "Ferran hit it in the eye with a stone. It reared back and left itself open."

Lagash nodded. "Fix and flank. Dog Boy unwittingly fixed the beast.

Fixed its attention." He motioned at Krov and Ranoc. "I want you two to face off against Caswal. Two spearmen against one."

The boys moved and faced each other.

"Hold your spears out like you mean it," Lagash said.

They pointed their spears at Caswal, two against one.

"Both of you slowly attack Caswal from the front. Caswal, do your best to defend yourself. Go slow."

Krov and Ranoc performed a slow lunge and stab, both of them going for Caswal's face. Caswal slowly stepped to the side, knocked Krov's spear shaft into Ranoc's, then lunged slowly at Krov.

"Good move," Lagash said. "Let's do it again. But this time, Krov, you come at him head on. Ranoc, take a step to the side and come at him from the flank."

Krov lunged in slow motion again at Caswal's face. Caswal moved equally slow to parry that attack, but as he did, Ranoc lunged forward, catching Caswal in the side.

"Good," Lagash said. "Try it again with some different lines of attack."

They did. This time Caswal tried to block Ranoc, but missed Krov's attack. They tried it twice more, and both times one of them succeeded in striking Caswal. They tried it once more, and this time Caswal simply backed away. That seemed to be the only thing that worked.

"What did you learn?" Lagash asked.

Ferran said, "When Krov and Ranoc were together, Caswal could deal with them almost as if they were one. But when they took slightly different lines of attack, they became separate threats."

"They became two," Lagash said. "Two attackers. Two spears. Two headaches. What did Caswal do on the last turn?"

"Backed away," said Winwalom.

"So what did you learn from that?"

Ferran wasn't sure what Lagash was getting at.

"You have to fix him," Winwalom said. "Fix his attention. Fix him in place. You have to give him so much trouble he cannot retreat. Or doesn't think to. And then the second man strikes from the side, the flank."

"Fix and flank," Lagash said. "This is why you always seek to strike a smaller force with a larger one. With a larger force some of your men can fix the enemy in place while the others flank. This is part of what maneuvering is about—getting into positions where you can fix and flank your enemy and avoiding positions where the enemy can do that to you. Even in the shield line, you want to fix and flank. You keep the enemy in front of you busy while your companion behind you or to the side strikes."

And Ferran suddenly saw that this was precisely how Lome and Caswal worked. Caswal would fix him, and then Lome, Caswal's meatheaded brute of a friend, would come in with his fist or foot.

Borros said, "Good lesson, Master Cook. Amazing what a man can learn from chopping vegetables."

Except Ferran knew Lagash hadn't learned that from slicing carrots.

Borros continued. "Do you see why battles aren't won with single men? Unless of course I'm there."

"If he's there," Lagash cut in, "they run from the fearsome smell."

"The smell of my prowess," Borros said. "It's very potent."

"Is that what it was?" Lagash asked. "I thought it was windy bowels."

"Mighty bowels," Borros said. "But if you lack that, then battles are won, not singly, but with armies. With hosts of men. Fighting together as units. Surprising, fixing, and flanking. Which means it's time you learn to fight together so you're ready the next time a murder of korrogs come around."

"Next time?" Krov asked.

"Hope for the best, prepare for the worst," said Borros. "If others come looking for an easy feed, we need to be ready."

"We need to be a beast ourselves," Lagash said. "One that fights with spears, stones, and arrows. Beast against beast. What we do not want to be is a single boy and his dog, a one-eyed woodsman, and a villager with an affection for cow pies."

The boys looked at Caswal and chuckled.

Caswal lifted his chin disdainfully, still miffed about the cow pies Ferran had secretly spread out for his sleeping enjoyment.

"We need an order of battle," Borros said. "And not just for the korrog."

Because there were other dangers they might face in the blight?

"What do you think needs to be in our battle order?" Borros asked.

"A watcher," Caswal said. "Someone whose attention isn't fixed. Who can scan for threats."

Borros nodded.

"We need fixers and flankers," Ranoc said.

Borros said, "It appears they were actually listening to you, Master Cook."

"Of course they were. I'm the smart, good-looking one who still has fabulous hair."

"Hair is nothing more than a louse nest." Borros said. "It's also a threat." He pointed at Winwalom's hair. "I once saw a man in a battle with long hair like that. It spilled out from underneath his helmet in glory. One of the enemy grabbed him by it, pulled him backward and off balance, and gutted him. You should cut it."

"If we go into battle, I'll tie it up on my head."

"What if you don't have time? What if it comes loose?"

Winwalom shrugged.

"Right," Borros said. "So we need a watcher, some pointy ends, and something to distract our target so the pointy ends can do their work. And a haircut."

Ferran thought about Itch biting the thing's leg. He also knew that he was quicker than all the rest of the other boys.

"Itch and I can distract," he said. "We can run around back and stab and bite."

"You're going to bite the next korrog, are you?" asked Borros.

"Not me. Itch will bark and bite. I'll stab. Or sling."

Borros nodded. "That sounds good." He motioned at Krov. "The lover there can work with our cook who is in no condition to span a crossbow. Krov will be his muscle. And watch our backs."

"But Krov is as strong as any two of us," Caswal said. "Shouldn't he fight in the battle line?"

"With one eye? You want to be the one next to the man that's limited in seeing what's happening next to him?"

"Put me on the end where there isn't a man," Krov said. "I'll do just fine."

Borros looked dubious.

Winwalom spoke up. "I'll work with Lagash."

"The crossbow needs strength," Borros said.

"I have enough. And I have something else."

Borros waited.

"Two eyes," Winwalom said simply. "You wanted a watcher, well you can scan better with two eyes than one. Besides, my bruised ribs are going to limit what I can do for the next little while."

Lagash said, "It appears Long Hair has some brains in his head. Surprising."

Winwalom glanced at Ferran, and Ferran knew that Winwalom's two eyes had more to offer than he was letting on to the others.

"Can you actually span the crossbow with your injuries?" Borros asked.

"I'm doing okay," Winwalom said.

"Fine," Borros said. "The lover gets the end of the line. Then Ranoc, me, and Caswal will take the other end. If a korrog comes again, Dog Boy will run around behind and bite it, drawing its attention. And as it turns, we charge in."

Ranoc said to Ferran, "Bite hard, Dog Boy."

Caswal laughed, but Ferran just gave him a look because the fact was that Ferran had been the one to strike the korrog's eye, not Caswal, who had been sniveling in the trees.

"Good," Borros said. "Now that we have our battle order, it's time to practice it."

And for the next two hours and a half, the boys practiced fighting with their spears as a cohesive unit, then fighting with slings, then with all of them in a line, including the bait, then with some of them missing or down. They practiced moving as a group forward, back, and side to side. They practiced wheeling round. Winwalom and Lagash struggled at first because, with their injuries, neither could span the crossbow on his own. But then they figured out a way to span it together and soon the whole group was moving and working as one.

When they finished, Borros said, "Well done. Go cool off in the stream, and while you're there, gather another twenty sling stones each."

The boys and Itch took their spears and headed for the stream. They passed the wagon upon which lay the huge carcass of the korrog they'd gutted and cut into pieces. It was beginning to smell and had attracted a good number of buzzing flies, which meant that in a few days it would be crawling with maggots. It had also attracted the attention of a small flock of crows that were in the branches of a few nearby trees, gauging how easily they could fly in and peck a few bites.

The boys walked past the wagon and began to cross the fenced field. And that's when Caswal began to pick a fight.

3

BRANCHES

"YOU OWE ME a pie," Caswal said to Ferran.

"I think it's you that owes me," Ferran replied.

"I'm sick of you and your lies. You touch anything else that's mine, and I will pound you."

"I didn't steal your hog-farting pie."

"You're going to pay up. One way or the other. I guarantee it."

"Whatever," Ferran said and glanced at Winwalom, who waved his hand low, indicating Ferran should just let the matter go.

Ferran said nothing more as they walked through the cattle to the other side of the field. He jumped the split-rail fence and walked down to the stream. It was late summer, and the water was low, only running up to his mid calf.

Ranoc pointed out that they should probably post a watch. They agreed, and so one of them held the spears over his shoulder and kept watch while the others worked. The boys waded out, looking for a stretch where the bed had exposed stones. They soon found a good spot and began to harvest the best ones they could find.

What they were looking for were stones about the size of a hen's egg but more elongated like the shape of a human eye. Of course, it was the rare river stone that was perfect. Some were too flat or too big or had odd bulges, and so the boys had to sift through quite a few stones to find ones that would fly straight and true enough to rely on them.

If they'd been back in the village, they could have taken their stones to the farmer Cal or borrowed his stone-working tools to carve, grind, and smooth the stones until they were just the right shape. But out here they had to rely on what the river gave them.

The stream snaked its way from the mountains, and every time Ferran stood to put a stone in his pouch, he'd look up at the slopes. The old road to Broniss ran along the backside of that range. And he couldn't quite believe he was so close to the blight.

Itch splashed across the stream, shook his fur, then padded up the other side, sniffing and following some scent. Ferran figured it would be good to let him scout the other side and act as a sentry, so he let him run.

"Here's a good go of stone," Winwalom said, and Ferran joined him, the cold water running round his bare legs and feet. This run of gravel was filled with black and gray stones with the odd red and white one tossed in between. He found two stones good for slinging, moved up stream, felt around again, and touched a likely candidate. He pulled it up and found it was decent and slid it into his pouch.

Ranoc pulled up a stone, discarded it, and paused to look at the mountain. "Nobody at home would believe we're headed that way."

Krov reached down into the rock bed. "Borros doesn't seem to be too worried about it."

"Oh?" Caswal said. "If he's not worried, then why all this practice with the spear? It's like he's preparing us for war."

"Better prepared than not," Winwalom said.

"Unless you're Dog Boy," Caswal said, "and are too stupid to follow orders."

"We all made that mistake," Ferran said.

"I'm not talking about the first time. I'm talking about the second time it happened."

"Second?"

"When you finally hauled your stupid hind end to the thicket. There we were, and you ran right back out again."

"I ran to save Krov."

"Lagash ordered you to stay. You totally ignored him. And put everyone else in danger."

Ferran was shocked at the idiot words coming out of Caswal's mouth. "I saved him."

"Did you? There we all were with our slings. And Lagash with his bow. We could have knocked the thing out of the sky, but you were too stupid to notice that. So you ran out. And dragged the others with you. If we'd stayed, nobody would have gotten injured. Including Lagash. He's lucky that thing only grabbed him to carry him away instead of clutching his head and ripping it off his shoulders. Why he hasn't pounded you into the ground I'll never know."

"And what would have happened if we had missed?" Ferran asked.

"We weren't going to miss," Caswal said. "You almost got all of us killed. You and your stupidity."

Anger rose in Ferran. Caswal was doing this to justify his own actions. "Well, at least I didn't cower in the trees like some scared rabbit."

Caswal narrowed his eyes. "What did you say?"

"You heard me. You didn't come out once to fight. Instead, you hid in the woods, wetting yourself like a coward."

Anger curled Caswal's face. "You'll take that back!"

"How will you ever stand in our battle line," Ferran said with disgust.

"Ferran," Winwalom cautioned.

"Oh, that's right," Ferran said. "You won't. You'll be too busy peeing your pants."

Caswal face turned livid, then he snarled and charged.

Ferran wasn't going to run. He was sick of Caswal's insults and slights. Years of them, all piled up.

Caswal splashed through the water at him. Ferran crouched, waited, and just as Caswal sprang at him, he dodged to the side. Caswal splashed and stumbled and fell into the water and went under.

Ferran laughed, and when Caswal rose, water streaming from his face, Ferran struck. A right hook straight to Caswal's face. It was a good solid blow and knocked Caswal's head to the side. It also hurt Ferran's knuckles, but he just grunted at the pain, packed his fists tighter, and stepped forward. He swung and nailed Caswal with a left to the jaw.

Caswal reeled back a step, splashing through the water.

Ferran cocked his right arm, stutter-stepped forward, but just before he released, Caswal lunged forward and took Ferran by the throat.

Ferran gasped and swung, but his blow lost its power and glanced off the side of Caswal's head.

Caswal drove Ferran backward. And then Ferran stepped on some sharp rock with his bare feet, stumbled, and went down. Before he could get up again, Caswal was on him. He struck him in the face, the side of the head, the side of the head again.

Ferran was dazed, and his head was suddenly shoved under the water against the rocks. He struggled, struck out and connected with something.

Caswal released him, hit him in the face again, then shoved him back under.

Ferran tried to gasp for air, but took in water instead. His lungs burned, and he knew he was going to drown. He surged with panic, freed himself, and pushed himself up out of the water, coughing and choking.

Somewhere close, Itch was barking.

"You're done," Caswal said. He was holding a large river stone in his hand.

Ferran gasped for air.

Caswal's face was a sneer of hate. He wound back his arm, then struck at Ferran with the large stone.

Ferran brought up his arm to protect himself, hoping the stone didn't crack his skull, but the blow never landed.

Krov had caught Caswal's hand mid-blow.

"What are you doing?" Caswal growled.

"Saving your hide," Krov said, and then he ripped the stone out of Caswal's grasp.

Caswal reached into the water to grab another stone. Ferran scrambled back and out of the way. Caswal came up with another stone and moved to followed Ferran, but Krov blocked his way.

"Get out of my road."

Krov shoved Caswal back. "Leave him alone," he growled.

And then Itch charged in and bit Caswal on the hand.

Caswal cried out and hurled his stone at Itch, but Itch dodged back and snarled.

Ferran's wits finally returned to him. He and Itch could take the coward. A nice bit of fix and flank. He reached into his stone pouch, but Winwalom was there and grabbed his arm.

"No," he said. "Do you want Borros to throw you out? You made an agreement."

"He started it," Ferran said through clenched teeth. Water ran down into his eyes, and he wiped it away.

"Yeah," Winwalom said. "And if Borros throws him out, he goes back to his father. Big hairy whoop. If you get kicked off the crew, you go back to be sold to the highest bidder. Use your brains!"

Ferran glowered and yanked his arm free, but he knew Winwalom was right.

Itch was still snarling at Caswal.

Caswal grabbed another stone from the river. A big one. And drew it back to throw at Itch. "Call him off. Now."

How nice it would be to turn those teeth loose, but now wasn't the time. "Itch," Ferran commanded.

Itch stayed where he was, snarling.

"Itch!" Ferran said with more force and pointed down at his side. Itch stopped snarling, turned, and came back to Ferran.

Ferran glared at Caswal. Had he simply been out of control, or had he actually wanted to brain and kill Ferran? Drown him.

Caswal glared back at Ferran, but then his eyes slid away. Was he ashamed because Ferran had landed those early blows? Or was he simply sullen because he hadn't been able to carry out his design?

Krov repositioned the patch over his eye. "How many stones have we found?"

"Certainly not the twenty we were tasked with," Winwalom said.

"Right. So you and Ferran work this side of the stream. We'll work the other." He looked at Caswal and Ferran. "The two of you are done with your nonsense. We're going to find our stones and get back and enjoy some dinner. The sun's about set, and I'm not going to be out here in the dark. Understand?"

Ferran nodded, but Caswal just glowered.

"Come on," Winwalom said to Ferran and motioned at a run of stones on the far side. "Let's go over there."

Krov pointed at a bend a good distance upstream and on the opposite site. "You search up there," he said to Caswal.

"I'll work where I please," Caswal said.

"You'll work up there," Krov ordered and pointed. "Now go."

Caswal rolled his eyes, but Krov was big, and knew how to fight. That's all he and his large brothers seemed to do. He was not someone you wanted to tangle with. Even someone as turd-brained as Caswal knew that, and so he went.

They worked and found their stones, leaving the stream just as the sun dipped behind the mountains.

As they were walking up the bank, Krov caught up to Winwalom and Ferran. "If they ask, nothing happened out here. Just some friendly horsing around, right?"

"Right," said Winwalom.

"Nothing?" Ferran asked. "He could have killed me. Tried to kill me."

"He wasn't going to kill you," Krov said.

"Usually that's what happens when you beat someone in the head with a rock," Ferran said.

"You insulted him," Krov said.

"He insulted me."

Krov sighed. "Look. Sometimes things get out of hand. It wasn't his intent."

"That's what he said?"

Krov shrugged.

Caswal was one of those people with a streak of cruel in their hearts, and Ferran knew exactly what his intent was.

"So nothing happened," Krov prompted. "Right?"

Plenty had happened, but he wouldn't say a thing. He couldn't risk being kicked off the job. "Sure," he said. "Nothing happened." Then he picked up his spear. They walked back, their trousers dripping water onto their bare feet.

When they entered the camp, Lagash directed them to dump their wet bags of rocks into a sturdy wooden box in the back of the wagon. As they did, he said, "Thanks for the lemons."

"Lemons?" Ferran asked.

"It's a tart yellow fruit that grows in the shape of a wide-open eye with fat points on each end. In Soros, our slingers shape their stones to match, some a bit longer, some shorter. When the captains want an attack, they tell them to send over some fruit."

"Lemons," Ferran said. "Are they any good to eat?"

"They'll pucker a post hole," Borros said.

"I think I've heard of them," Winwalom said.

"Oh, you have not," Ferran said.

"I remember my father telling me about them. They're used in a drink made with honey."

"That's right," Lagash said.

Ferran sighed. Winwalom's father had been many places as a soldier and had many good tales, but sometimes Ferran got tired of being the one who never knew anything. And then he thought about his father, and the old pang of loss struck him.

"We're going to keep a common store of stones in this box," Lagash said. "For anyone to use. So fill it up."

As Ferran, Winwalom, and Krov dumped their stones, Ranoc and Caswal joined them and dumped theirs. And then Lagash motioned for them all to pick up a bowl and line up for dinner. Caswal quickly moved to get ahead of Ferran, but Ferran didn't care. It wasn't like he was going to get any bigger a share being ahead of Ferran in the line.

Lagash served Ranoc then Krov. When Caswal held his bowl out, Lagash said, "So what was all that shouting down at the stream about?"

"Nothing," Krov answered innocently. "We were just messing around."

Borros tunic was open. He scratched his chest, revealing a portion of the mage rune there, then pointed at Caswal's face. "Where did you get that black eye?"

Caswal touched the puffy part around his eye. "Oh this," he said, a sour expression on his face. "I tripped and fell and hit a branch." He wasn't very convincing.

Lagash motioned at Ferran's face with his big spoon. "You hit the same branch?"

"Yeah," Ferran said. "That stream is lousy with branches."

Borros and Lagash exchanged at glance, and Ferran knew they hadn't fooled these two. Borros said, "I told you I didn't want any fighting."

Caswal and Ferran both looked down.

"We're about to head into the blight, boys. Did we not just talk about fighting as one beast? You can't do that if you don't trust the man next to you."

None of the boys said anything. But Ferran was praying to his ancestors Borros didn't kick him off the crew.

"You'll save your fighting for when it matters. You hear me?"

"Yes," Ferran said.

"Look at me."

Ferran and Caswal both looked up at him.

"Do you hear me?"

"Yes," they both said more loudly.

Borros nodded, then turned back to his food. "Did you put something new in this?"

"Found some huge mushrooms, " Lagash said. "The size of platters they were."

Borros took a bite. "Tasty."

The mushrooms were tasty, although Ferran couldn't enjoy it like he normally would because he realized one of his teeth was a bit loose from one of the blows he'd taken. Furthermore, his face in general throbbed with pain. His only solace was that Caswal's black eye seemed to be swelling nicely.

They all ate in silence, the fire popping in the fire hole, the sky purpling as the light began to dim. When they began to scrape their bowls clean, Caswal rose.

He held his hand out to Borros. "I'll take your bowl and clean it."

Borros handed him his bowl and spoon. And then Caswal went down the line, cheerfully taking each person's bowl. When he got to

Ferran, he held his hand out and repeated his offer. Itch tensed, but Ferran stroked him, and Itch relaxed. Then Ferran held their bowls up to Caswal.

Caswal took them, smiling. But Ferran wasn't fooled by his show. Caswal was a dribble from the hind end of a goat. He looked Caswal straight in the eye, and their gazes locked. There was no kindness in Caswal's eyes. There was a glee in them. And malice. Like Caswal had figured something out. Like he had a plan. Some sweet torture that he couldn't wait to carry out.

Ferran smiled perfunctorily. Plan away, he thought. I'm on to you. And I'm done with your nonsense.

Caswal smiled to himself, like his little secret was the baker's delight, then walked over to the barrel attached to the side of the wagon, dropped the dipper in for some water, and began to hum a jaunty tune.

A complete goat dribble, Ferran thought.

4

VISITOR

THAT NIGHT BORROS set a double watch. Each rotation would last three hours. They'd start with Krov and Caswal, then Ferran and Winwalom, and finish with Borros and Ranoc. Lagash was excluded so he could rest and let his wounds heal.

Ferran was going to protest about Winwalom, who probably needed rest as well, but Winwalom waved him off. "I'll do my share," he said.

And so the two of them made their beds and lay down and looked up at the night sky. Itch lay between them. Ferran's face ached where Caswal had beat him. But surely Caswal was feeling a bit of discomfort from at least one of Ferran's blows.

The sky turned dark. A shooting star streaked across the heaven and flashed out somewhere over the blight.

"I don't like this road we're taking," Ferran said.

"He's a former grimsman," Winwalom said.

"Which means he might make it out of the blight okay, but what about us? What if I get caught out on my own?"

"Ooh, now that's a thought."

"Yeah," Ferran said with disgust.

"I'm serious. It means that when whatever abomination that's out there goes after you, I can get away."

"Thanks," Ferran said. "You're such a fine companion."

Winwalom laughed.

Ferran laughed as well, but then realized, of the two of them, he was the one lying on the side of the camp closest to the road. If anything did come out of the blight and decide to travel down the road this night, it would find him first. He blew out a breath. "I hope our grimsman knows what he's doing."

"We all do," Winwalom said.

"What are you going to do with the money you earn?"

Winwalom shrugged. "Save it I guess."

"You're not going to buy anything? Not even a sausage?"

"Well, I might buy that."

"I'm going to count my coin out," Ferran said. "I'll set aside what my family needs, and then I'm going to go find a baker and buy me the biggest honey butter cake I can find."

"With a black current sauce?"

"Maybe. But it must be bathed in fresh, sweet cream." Ferran could almost taste it, and his mouth began to water. He sighed.

"That does sound good," Winwalom said.

"And afterwards a wedge of sharp cheese." It had been a while since he'd enjoyed his mother's cheese. "My mother says the cheeses in Broniss have a slightly nutty taste. And then it's the road home. Although I don't know who I'll travel with."

"You can't take the coast road."

"No."

"So you'll be coming back through the blight?"

"I can't imagine that. There's got to be some other way through the spur. I wish you were coming with me."

"So do I," Winwalom said, then stopped. "Mage rot," he cursed.

"What?"

He sat up. "Can't you see it?"

"See what?"

"There," he said and pointed at the sky.

Ferran scanned the starry night, and then he saw the dark shape. If you peered hard enough, you could make out the shape of wings, tail, and long neck with snout, wheeling high above the field.

"Korrog!" Winwalom shouted and scrambled out of his bed.

Ferran followed him, his heart pounding, and grabbed his spear. "It's here!" he shouted. "The korrog. Above the field!" He slipped his stone sack over his shoulder.

The others in the camp rolled out of their beds.

"To me!" Borros said. "Battle order!"

They all rushed to where he stood and lined up as they had practiced. Ferran set down his spear and readied a stone. But the korrog didn't dive. It just rode the winds high above, a black smudge against the stars.

"I can barely see it," Lagash said.

"It's right there," Winwalom said and pointed.

"You have some sharp eyes, Long Hair," Lagash said. "Uncommonly sharp in the darkness."

A heartbeat passed.

"Where did you say your father was from?" Lagash asked.

"Buckle Hill," Winwalom said.

"And your mother?"

"My Da met her on one of his campaigns. Rescued her."

"Really? And where was that?" Lagash asked.

"Selvan" Winwalom said. "A kingdom across the sea."

"And he brought her home?" Lagash asked, as if that were signficant.

Ferran didn't know what was so special about Selvan, but he could feel this conversation was going to put Winwalom in a tight spot, and so he spoke up and said, "Winwalom's eyesight is overrated. I can see it just fine. It's right there."

Lagash grunted.

Borros said, "You're getting old, Master Cook."

"Not as old as you," he said.

"Now, now," Borros said. "There's a korrog above. Let's keep up the team spirit. What's it doing, Long Hair?"

"Just flying, sir."

"Yeah," Ferran said. "Just flying."

Borros said, "Looking for its chance, I'd say."

It wheeled above for a good quarter of an hour, then disappeared behind the mountains.

"I think we were too alert and spiky with spears for its taste," Ranoc said.

"Maybe," Borros said. "Maybe not."

They continued to watch. An hour later, Ferran's neck ached from looking up all that time.

"I say it's gone," Ranoc said.

"I doubt it," Borros said. "It's seen the herd now. Why hunt elsewhere when there's food's right here?"

"Maybe," Lagash said. "Or maybe it's just following its mother. I bet it followed her scent."

"Well, it's welcome to come visit her any time," Borros said.

"We should catch it," Ranoc said. "Cage it."

"Well, you let us know how that goes," Borros said. "Do be careful of the claws and jaws. As for me, I'm wanting some sleep. If something noteworthy happens, let me know. The rest of you can go to bed as well. Now that we know it's following us, we can keep an eye out."

An eye out, Ferran thought. How could anyone sleep? What if there were more of them? What if that thing decided the cattle were too big to go after, but the boys sleeping by the campsite looked just right?

"We need to move our beds," Ferran said. "I don't want to be out in the open where that thing can pounce on me."

Winwalom nodded, and the two of them moved their beds into the trees. Ranoc joined them, and when the three boys were lying on their beds and Krov and Caswal had begun their rounds, Winwalom said, "We shouldn't cage it. We should see if we can tame it. Befriend it."

"Tame it?" Ranoc asked. "You can only do that with predators when they are babes, hatchlings."

"Maybe it's not too old," Winwalom said. "And how do you know it hatched from an egg? For all we know, that thing could be no more than a week old."

"It's got to be older than that," Ranoc said. "And even if you do want to tame it, you should probably cage it first."

"I'm wanting to sleep," Borros said loudly from the wagon. "Korrog are untamable, like crocodiles. The first chance it gets it will dine on your heads like so many eggs for breakfast. So pipe down and go to bed."

"What's a crocodile?" Ferran asked Winwalom.

"Quiet!" Borros ordered, and Ferran fell silent.

5

SECRETS

FERRAN WAS AWAKENED by Krov. It was time for the next watch. And so Ferran, Winwalom, and Itch rose and made their rounds of the field and stood guard with their spears in the cool night air. Ferran kept testing Winwalom's sight, trying to see just how much better it was than his.

It was a lot better. His sight seemed to be able to penetrate the blackest of shadows. For example, he was able to spot a moth that flew in the pitch black shadows and landed on the trunk of a tree. It was a huge thing, as big as Ferran's hand. Ferran hadn't seen it, but Winwalom had. He'd walked right over to it, captured it on the tree, and brought it back for Ferran to view in the moonlight.

"You haven't always had this keeness of eye," Ferran said.

"No."

"When did it start showing up?"

There was a pause. "A little more than a year ago."

"A growth spurt then?"

"Who gets growth spurts in vision?" Winwalom asked.

Ferran shrugged. Nobody got growth spurts in vision. Not that he knew of. It only went the other way and got worse.

A beat passed.

"Are there other things showing up?" he asked.

Winwalom blew out a big breath. "Maybe."

"Like what?"

"Like none of your business."

And suddenly Ferran knew why Winwalom was going to Broniss. "This is what your apprenticeship is about, isn't it?"

They walked a few steps in silence. And just when he thought Winwalom wasn't going to answer, he said, "I'm doing a piss poor job of it."

"Of your apprenticeship?" Ferran asked. "It hasn't even started."

Winwalom looked around to make sure nobody was around who could overhead. "You could get me killed, you know that?"

Ferran waited.

"I was put under strict command to keep my mouth shut. I'm not supposed to say anything to you. To anybody."

"You don't have to," Ferran said. And he meant it. He trusted Winwalom with his life. And if Winwal was in danger, then Ferran would do what ever it took to help him.

Winwalom looked around again and sighed. "I'm going to someone who can help me."

"Because something is wrong?"

"It depends on your definition of wrong."

Ferran began to feel apprehension. In the stories, the Old Blood were nightmares, shadow walkers that haunted the darkness and changed into raveing animals that slew men and stole children.

In an earlier time, a war had been fought between the Lords of the Wildwood on one side and the mages on the other. The Lords of the Wildwood had sent the Old Blood to hunt the mages down and kill them. They came at night. Terrors in the dark.

But the mages had eventually defeated the Lords of the Wildwood and their Old Blood allies. However, they didn't wipe them completely off the face of the earth. And so now and again, one of the shadow walkers would wander into a village at night and touch someone, give them powers, corrupt them, turn them against the mages. Turn them against the light.

Ferran looked at his friend. There were mages who could break anointings and other magics. "Are you sure you don't need to go see a mage?" Ferran asked. "A breaker?"

"You want to get me killed?" Winwalom asked.

"No."

"The last thing I need is the administration of mages and wizards. Things aren't always what they seem, Ferran."

"I know that better than most. I'm always being accused of stealing pies. And I can say truthfully that at least half of those accusations are false."

"So you did steal Caswal's pie."

"No, I did not."

"Huh, then it's a mystery."

"It's no mystery. He ate it."

Winwalom fell silent. And Ferran's curiosity began to build. He decided to nudge him. "So you're going to someone who helps people like you?"

"Yes."

"Can it be cured?"

"Why would I want to cure a blessing?"

That didn't sound like Old Blood. Maybe this was something else. "If it's a blessing, then why the secrecy?"

"Because not all see it that way."

"Including the mages."

"Especially the mages."

Ferran didn't know what to say, but dread lay in his heart. If Winwalom was touched by the Old Blood, it would only lead him down a path of ruin. Ferran had to know if that's what this was. To help save his friend. He didn't know how to frame the question delicately, so he just said it.

"So this isn't some shadow walker thing?"

Winwalom looked at him, the moonlight on his face. "What if it was? But what if what the mages tell us is lies?"

"What do you mean?"

"Anointings are said to be fragments of the ancient language of the creators, right?"

"Right," Ferran affirmed.

"None now know how to voice them. But they can write them. And when written with earthgrace they carry power. But do the mages know all of the words of that language? Is their language complete?"

"I don't know what the mages do and don't know."

"Think about it. The various mage houses in the different lands used many similar runes. But some have knowledge that others don't. That's why the various houses send their spies and thieves to steal from each other. So what if some other group knows some of that ancient tongue that our mages do not?"

Ferran said, "You're talking about another mage house with some special knowledge? Like how the house of Akken knows how to anoint with charm, but the filthy wizards in Gorland do not."

"Exactly like that."

That was not how Old Blood lore was described in the stories. The Old Bloods had different lore. A black lore that seethed in their veins. A lore that corrupts. That twists what is right and good.

Winwalom said, "Is vision that penetrates the darkness such a terrible thing? Is it any different, really, than the stamina given to the queen's warriors?"

"Maybe not vision, but turning into a ravening beast doesn't sound very holy."

"What if that's a lie? What if the Old Blood never turned into something else?"

How could that be? That's what they were.

"Think about it. They hunted at night. With animals."

"Not just animals. They didn't come with a bunch of rabbits. They came with wolves, bears, snakes."

Winwalom ignored the interruption. "The night is dark. You see or hear a man, and then see beasts. How easy would it be for those being awakened to the horror to become confused and think the humans had changed form?"

"You're saying they don't change into something abominable?"

"My mother..." He trailed off.

Ferran waited. And waited.

"Your mother what?"

Winwalom shook his head. "You cannot say a word."

"My lips will be like iron."

"I'm going to get into such trouble, but since whatever is in the blight will get you first, maybe I don't have to worry."

"Hey, now."

"You cannot say a word."

"I won't."

Winwalom paused. "Okay. Let me ask you. Do you think my mother was evil? You think she was corrupt?"

Ferran remembered nothing but kindness from her. She had always gone to the aid of the sick in the village. Sick people and sick animals. She also kept bees. And Ferran she'd always had honeyed treats for him.

Ferran said, "She was as kind a woman as I have ever known."

"She was," Winwalom said.

"And my father?"

"He's hard-working. Has dumb jokes. Loved your mother."

"Do you think he's an idiot?"

"No, he's smart. Brave."

"He is. And so I trust him. I trust her. And that is what she said." He paused then pitched his voice in a whisper that Ferran could barely hear. "It's lies, Ferran. Members of the Old Blood did not turn into ravening beasts. They were those with a different lore. And an ability that ran in their blood to do other things. They threaten the mages, and so the mages make up stories about them."

Ferran blinked. What Winwalom had just said would earn him a horrible death should others hear. It would earn him a cruel torture from the inquisitors.

Winwalom said, "Your eyes look like they're going to pop out of your head. I've told you too much. I did exactly what I was ordered not to."

"No," Ferran said. "It's just that, well, I don't know about these things, and it's not every day that your best friend spouts the talk of a shadow lover, which means my association with him will probably lead me to having my eyes gouged out and my tongue cut off by the inquisitors. Other than that, I'm fine."

Winwalom grinned wryly. "You'd only have your eyes gogued out if you didn't turn me in."

"Right," Ferran said. "And since that's not going to happen, we need to make sure I keep them in my head."

Winwalom said, "I know this puts you in danger. I wanted to keep my rotted mouth shut. I didn't want to do this to you."

"Death, maiming, torture—what else are friends for?"

Winwalom said, "It's not a game."

"I know that."

"I guess I expected you'd be more stressed out about it."

Oh, Ferran was stressed. He was stressed beyond belief. He was heading for the blight, and his friend had the blood of shadow walkers in him. What could go wrong?

"We're going to be fine," Ferran said. "Just fine."

"It's a load off, letting you know. But you can't talk."

"I'll do a better job of keeping my mouth shut than you have." And Ferran would even though he felt dread. And a bit of horror, and confusion, for everyone knew that Old Blood were the very incarnation of evil. And yet here Winwalom was, a goodly lad with goodly parents saying the Old Blood was a goodly thing. And that they didn't turn into ravening beasts. Next thing he knew, Winwalom would probably say they did nothing more than go about picking daisies. It was all a bit much.

"So," Ferran said. "Look at the stars. How they do twinkle in the night. And shine with goodness."

Winwalom laid a hand on Ferran's shoulder that made Ferran jump.

"Thank you," Winwalom said.

"Anytime."

They were both silent, watching the cattle in the night, but Ferran's mind was racing. Winwalom was going to a stranger in Broniss to learn about what was manifesting in him. How had Winwalom learned about that man? How had arrangements been made? It could have only happened if there was a network of some sort. And that meant Winwalom's mother and father were connected to it somehow.

Furthermore, his father had never been to Broniss. Not that Ferran knew of. So the members of that network must travel through the villages taking news and messages to each other.

The idea startled him. It meant they were out there, right now. A whole network of them.

And then another thought tumbled in. Winwalom's mother was from Selvan, a land across the sea. A few years back, stories had come flooding out of that place. Stories about trouble with the Old Blood there. And that meant this network surely stretched across the sea.

All this time, Ferran had lived happily in Buckle Hill, thinking things like this only happened in far away places. But it was here. A whole world he'd not known existed. And if people as normal as Winwalom's parents and some felter in Broniss were part of it, who else was? A whole network of people with wicked powers that, according to Winwalom, weren't wicked at all. It was shocking.

And Ferran wondered if all this meant he was now part of some dark cabal. Would the Old Blood of this network find out about Ferran and come have a chat. Join us or we'll rip your throat from your neck. And then they'd work some dark rite, and then Ferran and Winwalom would be two peas in a pod, traveling down the wicked path together.

Winwalom pointed at the wagon with the korrog corpse on it. "There's something over there."

Ferran's heart jumped with thoughts of shadow walkers.

"I think it's a skunk," Winwalom said.

Relief washed through Ferran, and they went to investigate. They found it wasn't one skunk, but three, all of them drawn to the smell of the carrion.

Winwalom said, "Tommorow, let's suggest we park the wagon farther away from camp."

"Agreed," Ferran said.

Then again, they had korrog stalking them and Old Blood on the crew. What were a few skunks?

They continued their rounds, talking about the korrog and Broniss and anything but the Old Blood. A few hours later they handed the watch off to Borros and Ranoc. Ferran checked his bedding for some petty prank, found none, and lay back.

He looked over at Winwalom. What his friend had shared tonight was a lot to take in. Winwalom had never shown any sign of having changed into a ravening beast. And maybe everything Winwalom had

41

said was true. What did Ferran know of such things? As far as Ferran could tell, Winwalom was still the same good old Winwalom he'd always been. Same long hair, same smarts, same loyalty, but now with a couple of secrets, and a couple of budding dark graces, and connections to dark lords.

Ferran looked up at the stars and wondered what it meant to have such a friend. And what that might mean for his future.

6

ACCUSATION

H E WAS AWAKENED by Lagash shouting. He assumed the korrog was back, and quickly rolled out of bed and fumbled for his spear and stones. The soft light of dawn had lit the sky, and he snatched his weapons and stood.

"Everyone here. Now!" Borros commanded in an angry tone.

Ferran scrambled over and took his battle order position. He glanced up at the sky, but couldn't see anything there. He looked over at the herd, expecting to see that some cattle had been slaughtered in the night, but the herd looked just fine.

All the other boys arrived. Itch was still lying back on the bed. Ferran called for him.

"Where is it?" Ranoc asked.

"Not an it," Borros said. "A who."

"A who?" Krov asked.

"Ossonites?" Ranoc asked, looking down the road.

Lagash walked out in front of the boys, glowering in anger. "We've got a problem."

Ferran was confused. He glanced up and down the road for trouble, looked up to the sky, but trouble wasn't anywhere to be seen.

"I woke up this morning to make you breakfast, and what do I find?

Someone's been in the food. I'm missing jerked meat, pickled eggs from a sealed crock, and a few onions."

"Someone got into the food?" Krov asked.

"In addition to that, I'm missing my purse and my knife. The one with the silver fox inlaid in the hilt."

Borros folded his arms and glared at the boys. "Did any of you see anything odd over by the wagon during your watch?"

They all shook their heads and said no.

Borros walked up to Krov and leaned in close. "Breathe in my face."

Krov blew out. Borros took in a big whiff. Then he moved to Caswal and all the rest of the boys, smelling their breath. When he was finished, he stepped back and shook his head. "None of them smell like primroses, but I can't smell onion, vinegar, or meat on them either."

The boys all looked at each other.

"I didn't steal anything," Caswal said.

"Neither did I," said Krov.

"I was with Borros during my watch," Ranoc said.

They all looked at Winwalom and Ferran.

"We didn't touch a thing," Winwalom said.

"Dog Boy?" Borros asked.

"It wasn't me."

"I don't care so much about the food," Lagash said, his lips tight. "Even the coin can be replaced. But that knife was given to me by my grandfather."

Ferran couldn't believe this. Which of the other boys would be stupid enough to steal his knife?

"Maybe it was someone else," Winwalom offered.

"Someone traveling in the dark of night?" Borros asked.

"Maybe somebody lives around here," Ranoc said.

"Have you seen any sign of anyone else?" Borros asked.

"No," Ranoc said.

"Seen any sign that anyone's been using this road?"

"I haven't seem much of the road," Ranoc said.

"Well, I have. And nobody's been on this road for a few days at least."

"We are close to the blight," Caswal offered. "Maybe it came from there."

"Right," Borros said. "A troop of tiny men in pointy hats came out on a midnight raid."

"I didn't say that."

"I've looked all around the camp for sign. I went out on the road. The theft happened before the dew appeared because there's no sign of the dew being distrubed."

That would have been sometime during the first two watches. One of which was Ferran's and Winwalom's watch. Ferran looked at Winwalom, who just shrugged.

Ferran said, "The only thing we saw was some skunks around the wagon with the carcass."

"Well, skunks didn't take the purse," Borros said. "No, the most likely explanation of this and yesterday's incident with the hand pie is standing right here."

"If it had been a thief from the outside," Lagash said. "They wouldn't have bothered with onions. They would have taken a cow or three from the far end of the field. Maybe the mules. Maybe Borros's spear. My spices have some value as well. If they were going to rob us, they would have robbed us. But whoever did this wanted it not to be noticed. Or wanted it to be small enough that we might conclude we miscounted or maybe lost the items. This is the type of thievery that goes on with those who have constant access to the goods. A little drip, drip, drip until you're dripped dry."

The boys just stood there in shock. All except Caswal.

He said, "I don't want to cast aspersions on anyone. We're trying to be a team, but..."

"But what?" Borros asked.

"Well, Ferran is known to have, on occasion, been guilty of stealing. I don't accuse him. But it's happened."

Krov and Ranoc nodded slowly.

Incredible. It was unfair. Unjust. Unfit.

Ferran looked at the three of them. The whoresons. And then Caswal let slip a little smirk, like he knew something. Like this had been planned all along.

And Ferran suddenly knew exactly what was happening.

Caswal had done it. To frame him.

Borros turned his gaze on Ferran. "Dog Boy?"

Ferran was livid. "It was not me." He looked at the other boys. Were they all in on it? Krov too, even after Ferran had saved his lumbering hide from the korrog?

"I bet the items are hidden away in his pack," Caswal said.

"They are not," Ferran said.

"Well, there's one way to find out," Borros said. "Let's go look."

Suddenly Ferran had a sinking feeling. It would have been beyond easy for Caswal to plant the items there. He cut a glance at Caswal, who smiled back eagerly.

"Well, what are you waiting for?" Borros asked.

Ferran couldn't refuse. Couldn't delay. That would only make him look guilty. He grimaced and trudged over to his pack, his mind racing, knowing the items would be there.

"Empty it," Borros said.

Ferran sighed, his mind failing to come up with any response for the moment when the purse and knife fell out. "If anything is here," he said. "It was not put here by me."

"Dump it," Borros said.

7

SEARCH

FERRAN TURNED THE pack upside down. The items dumped out onto the ground. Grief and rage and humiliation welled up in him, even though he'd done nothing wrong. He looked down to view his doom.

But there were no onions or jerked meat. No purse. No coins. No knife.

"Shake it good," Borros said.

Ferran did, but nothing else came out, and relief flooded him.

Borros squatted and separated out Ferran's fire bow and drill, cordage, and spare clothes. He searched the clothes, including the pockets.

"It could be in his browse bag," Krov said. "That's where I'd hide it."

Borros nodded and motioned at Ferran.

Ferran's dread rose again. Caswal had already put stones in there. Of course that's where he'd plant the items.

They were going to find the stolen goods, blame him, and Borros would send him packing. And he would go home, and if he didn't get eaten by the korrog, he'd be sold into bondage.

Caswal had outwitted him, and it made him furious.

"Come on. We haven't got all day."

Ferran undid the bindings on his browse bag. With every knot he loosened, his spirits sank further. When they were all undone, he turned it over and shook the grass and leaves out onto the ground.

Borros spread the debris out. He examined the bag. But nothing was there.

The noose that had been around Ferran's neck suddenly loosened.

Borros ran his hand over his bald head. "Did you stash it somewhere, hoping to retrieve it on the way back?"

"No," Ferran said. "I didn't stash it because I never had it."

"Don't believe him," Caswal said.

That maggot. Ferran said, "I say we have Caswal empty his pack and browse bag. Have him strip as well because maybe he's hidden it on his person."

"That's a tremendous idea," Borros said. "All of you strip and put your clothes on the ground."

There was some grumbling, but all the boys shucked their trousers and tunics and stood in nothing but their small clothes in the brisk morning air.

The boys watched as Borros and Lagash searched their clothes and came up with nothing. They watched as well as each boy emptied his pack and browse bag. Still nothing was found. Then they waited as Borros and Lagash made a search of the area for any sign of where the money and knife might have been hidden for later retrieval. But they found nothing and returned.

Borros ran his hand over his gray-streaked bear. "By my rights, I could beat each one of you until I got a confession. But I'm going to give you a chance to redeem yourself. I'm assuming you ate the food. That leaves the knife and purse. If these items are returned by tomorrow morning, I will simply deduct the stolen food from all of your pay, and we'll say no more about it. If they are not, then each of you is suspect. And because the last thing I need is to have to guard myself against my own men, I will send word back to Pencoy's, or some other village we passed along the way, and replace you with another crew."

The words hung in the air.

And Ferran realized he wouldn't just replace them. He'd make allegations, and if some magistrate got involved, who knows what would happen?

Caswal glared at Ferran in disgust. Ferran glared right back at him.

"You have until tomorrow morning to return the items," Borros said. "Now pack up. We're moving out."

Ranoc raised his hand. "What about breakfast?"

"Breakfast?" Borros asked. "Ask your thief. He has your breakfast."

"Right," Ranoc said and dropped his hand.

"Get moving," Borros ordered.

The boys turned and began to head back to their things. Ranoc's face soured, and he looked at Ferran. "This has got to be the dumbest thing you've ever done."

"Don't look at me," Ferran said. "I have more to lose than anyone here. Why would I screw that up?"

"Because you've got a turd for a brain," Caswal said.

"I've put in days of work," Ranoc said angrily, the wicked scar on his neck more livid in the early light. "You're not going to take that from me."

"It's not me," Ferran said. "You know exactly—" And then he caught himself.

"Know exactly what?" Caswal asked.

Ferran had been about to say Caswal knew exactly who had done it. But saying that that would only alert Caswal that Ferran was on to him. Far better to be cautious. Far better to let Caswal think he'd gotten away with his plot. To think nobody was watching.

"He knows he's guilty," Caswal said. "Look at him."

"I didn't do it," Ferran said. "I swear upon my father's name."

Caswal rolled his eyes and scoffed, then stormed over to pack his things up.

Ferran watched Caswal and the others go pack. The three of them were whispering to each other and glancing his way with angry looks. They were plotting something, that was for sure.

"Come on," Winwalom said.

"I won't be accused falsely," Ferran said, following him over to their bedding and packs. "I won't stand for it."

"Ferran," Winwalom said.

"What?"

Winwalom pitched his voice to a whisper. "Was it you?"

"What are you talking about?"

"Did you steal the items?"

Ferran was shocked. How could he even think that? "Are you kidding me?"

"Well?"

Last night he'd listened to Winwalom say treasonous things without batting an eye, and now Winwalom was questioning him? It was beyond belief. "I didn't steal anything. Not one grain of barley. Not a nibble of beef. Not one sniff of eggs or coins or a knife. Nothing." And then his indignation rose. "Maybe it was you."

"No," Winwalom said calmly, then looked up and stroked his jaw in thought. "I didn't take anything. Why would I? Why would you? And I can't see why anyone of them would steal any of those things either. It just doesn't make any sense. Why risk it? We'll get more coin from the job than what was in that purse."

"But the knife was nice. Did you not see the handle of that knife, all inlaid with silver. It was fine."

"Not that fine. And even if it were, why risk it now? Why not wait until after you've been paid?"

"I'm surprised you don't see the answer. It's right in front of you."

"You're right in front of me."

"Not literally in front of you."

"Who then?" Winwalom asked.

"You say it doesn't make sense for any of us to steal anything now. You're right. None of us would steal something and risk losing this job. But they weren't taking that risk."

"How can you say that? We are all about to lose our jobs."

"They stole it because they never intended to keep it," Ferran said.

"You're not making any sense."

"You're usually the brainy one," Ferran said. "But maybe my intelligence has gone through a growth spurt. Maybe I'm passing you by."

"Hardly."

Ferran smiled bitterly. "They stole it to frame me, Winwal. Caswal said as much."

"But he didn't have the items on his person or in his belongings. None of them did."

"I've been thinking about that. I think he stashed them on the wagon somewhere. You know how fussy Lagash is that everything be in its right place. So Caswal put it somewhere Lagash wouldn't think to look. At the bottom of some barrel. Or if it wasn't Caswal, it was Ranoc. Maybe even Krov, the ingrate. And they're waiting for the right moment to retrieve the stolen items and plant them in my bag."

The lights went on in Winwalom's eyes. "That makes some sense."

"Indeed it does."

"So it's easy then," Winwalom said. "Let's have Borros search the wagon."

"Are you kidding? If I suggest a search, and he actually does find the items on the wagon, they'll all conclude I knew to search there because that's where I put them after I stole them. Who else could have known they'd be there but the thief?"

Winwalom grunted. "You're right."

"Of course I'm right. So we're not going to suggest that. We're going to do something else. Caswal's a sneaking and slithering snake. And we're going to catch him out."

"And how are we going to do that?"

"I don't know yet. I'm working on it."

8

TRUST

THEY ALL FINISHED striking camp, and then Ferran fetched the harness for the mule that would pull the second wagon upon which the carcass of the korrog lay while Winwalom lead the mule over. A number of crows were already on the beast, trying to yank away bits of flesh. They cawed a warning and flapped up into the trees when the boys approached.

Ferran got the harness on, and then they began hitching up the mule. The carcass was smelling even stronger than it had yesterday. He groaned. "I'm glad I'm not driving this wagon."

"Yeah, tell me about it," Winwalom said. "It's going to smell grand during the heat of the day. If you look back and see the wagon driver-less, you'll know I passed out and fell off the seat from the fumes."

"And the smell hasn't even reached its peak yet. It's just going to grow over the next few days."

"Thanks for reminding me. I'm going to get some pestilence from the vapors. You wait and see."

Ferran laughed. "Maybe you can argue for a change of guard."

"I think my ribs will probably be completely healed by mid-day today," Winwalom said. "I will then inform Borros I'm fit as a fiddle and no longer need to ride."

"It takes at least a couple of weeks for ribs to heal."

"No," Winwalom said and gingerly moved his arms up and down. "See, I'm just fine." And then something caught and he winced.

"Have fun with the crows," Ferran said and tightened the last buckle.

Winwalom climbed up onto the wagon's seat and took the reins. He removed the yellow flag that had been attached to his cattle prod and made it into a bandanna, which he pulled up to cover his nose.

Ferran laughed, called Itch, and the two of them threaded their way to the back of the field behind the cattle and began to herd them out. And then the whole crew began to drive the cattle down the road.

Maybe two miles later, three steers at the back end of the herd headed up into the trees. Ferran and Itch ran and moved them back to the road. They finished the job close to Lagash and the supply wagon. A good distance behind Lagash, Winwalom drove the corpse wagon, batting at flies. A number of crows had found their courage and now stood on the creature, riding along. In the sky above, vultures circled.

Ferran walked alongside the wagon and said, "Looks like Winwalom is making lots of new friends."

Lagash removed his wide-brimmed hat, scratched his head, and looked back. "A few more days, and it's going to be like a king's parade. I wouldn't be surprised if it draws some characters we don't like. I'd say we're dragging two tons of bear bait behind us. I told Borros to just cut the runes out, that the cattle have already drawn enough predators, but he wants the whole prize. Wants to make an entrance for the queen."

"Bears? You really think we'll get bears?"

"Why wouldn't we? Bears, wolves, who knows what. It's a traveling buffet." He flicked something off one of the feathers in his hat band, then donned his hat again. "And if they don't come, I'm sure we'll draw bandits that want the carcass for show."

Ferran thought about Winwalom back there all by himself. "What do we do if something does come? How's he going to get the mule freed quickly enough?"

"Depending on what happens tomorrow morning, Winwalom may not have to worry about it," Lagash said.

Tomorrow morning? Ferran cocked his head, not understanding. And then he realized Lagash was talking about the theft back at camp.

Ferran said, "Winwalom didn't steal those things. He's as honest as the day is long." And then Ferran thought of Winwalom's secret and realized that wasn't totally accurate.

"Well, if that's true, that leaves four other culprits."

Three, Ferran thought. He looked up at Lagash on the wagon seat. "Master Lagash, I swear by all that is holy I did not take any of those items. Not the food, not the money, and especially not your knife. I know what it is to have something from someone who is gone."

Lagash looked down and considered him for a moment. The mule clopped forward. The wagon's wheel rotated. Itch trotted along at Ferran's side.

Lagash said, "I believe you're telling the truth."

Most adults hardly ever put any stock in what he had to say. He was a little surprised. "You do?"

"Should I not?"

"No, you should. Because it's true."

Lagash said, "But believing that doesn't change the situation. The items are still gone."

Ferran wanted to tell him of his suspicions of Caswal, but thought it would make him look petty. So he kept it to himself and said, "I have great faith that the thief will be revealed soon enough."

"Let's hope. Or none of you will have to worry about bears or cattle or the blight."

Ferran thought to lighten the mood with some humor. "Maybe there really was a troop of little men in pointy hats. A buggan raiding party."

Lagash smiled. "You ever see a buggan?"

"No."

"Nasty little things. They lace their weapons with poison. Did you know that?"

"I did not."

A big horsefly landed on the mule's rump, and Lagash flicked it off with the reins.

Ferran said, "You sound like you might have seen one."

"More than one. I once saw a hunting band. You're happy it wasn't one of them."

Ferran was intrigued and wanted to ask more, but the steers he'd just urged back to the herd had decided to try their luck again.

"You'd better get them," Lagash said.

Ferran nodded, then quickened his pace and shouted for Itch to head them off. He appreciated Lagash's trust. He was going to show him that it was not misplaced, and he figured he knew just how to do that.

9
———

TURN OFF

THEY TRAVELED A few more miles and came to a turnoff where a board had been erected on an eight-foot post. Borros and the others waited at the sign, letting the cattle mosey a little farther past the turnoff to get a drink at a ford that crossed the stream there.

Ferran walked up to the post and looked up at the board. It had been painted yellow. The paint was old and weathered and had flaked off in places. In the middle of the top half of the board, the symbol of the queen's mage had been carved and painted red. Below it was carved one word.

Ferran knew some basics of lettering and tried to sound it out. "Forb," he said, then recognized the word. "Forbidden."

"This is the old road to Broniss," Borros said.

The road was as wide as the one they'd been traveling. However, unlike their current path, small bushes and even some saplings had sprung up there; the limbs on the trees on the sides of the road were also crowding in, turning it into something of a tunnel, all of which was a clear sign the road hadn't been used for a number of years.

"The actual border of the blight is many miles ahead," Borros said. "They simply placed this sign here to save travelers the time of having to turn around."

The road led into a thick wood that lay in a vale between two mountains. In years past, there would have been a lot of traffic on this road. The travelers would have foraged, fished, and hunted along the way. There would have been multiple groups camping at various sites. There would have been traders and tinkers and minstrels and maybe even an ale-wife or two plying their trades to the travelers along the route. There would have been armed companies of rangers coming through now and again. It would have been a relatively tame place.

It was wild land now. Quiet and foreboding.

Borros said, "Krov and I will work ahead, clearing any bushes or saplings that would trouble the wagons. Cow Pie and Ranger Boy, you two are going to have to manage the sides of the herd by yourselves."

Ferran smiled to himself about Borros using Cow Pie as a nickname for Caswal. It was perfect.

Borros walked over to the wagon, removed two woodsman's axes from the back, and held one out to Krov.

Krov took it and eyed the old road nervously.

"Give us a good head start," Borros said to Lagash. "Keep the cattle back. The last thing we need is for you to crowd us and have the cattle get ahead." He motioned to Krov, and the two of them began to walk up the old road. When they came to a bush or sapling that was too big, they hacked it and tossed it to the side.

Winwalom arrived with his wagon and stopped, flies buzzing, crows and magpies riding on the beast like a bunch of travelers. The vultures still circled overhead. "What's going on?" he asked.

The stink was powerful. "Whew," Ferran said.

"Tell me about it." And then he raised a large fly swatter made of willow and struck at a fly.

"You make that?"

"I did." It was a willow branch, and it appeared Winwalom had tied one end of it into a wide circle. He'd then braiding flexible twigs into that circle to make a paddle the size of a man's head.

Winwalom watched a fly, then smacked it, sending it flying. "Ha!" he said.

Ferran motioned at the saucy crows riding on the wagon. "Look like you've attracted a lot of friends."

"You should have seen who came to visit about a mile and a half back. Hornets. A whole nest of them came out for a look-see. I was battling for my life."

Ferran laughed.

"We're definitely taking turns with this driver's job. I'll dance with my broken ribs all the way to Broniss if I have to."

"Let me know when the bears and wolves start to show up."

"That's all I need," he said.

"Just make a bigger fly swatter," Ferran suggested.

"Very funny."

At that moment a large shadow streaked across the road. Ferran looked up, expecting to see a vulture swooping low. But it wasn't a vulture. It was the small korrog, soaring overhead. It flapped a couple of times, then flew over to a spot high on the slope of the hill on this side of the vale. It landed on the trunk of a large dead tree that had fallen.

"I kind of feel bad for it," Winwalom said. "It's mother and brother dead."

"It brained Krov and would have eaten his liver," Ferran said. "I don't feel bad for it at all. It's a menace. Like some great snake or spider. You don't feel bad for them, do you?"

"Sometimes."

"No you don't."

Winwalom shrugged. "What if it could be tamed?"

Ferran thought about it. He imagined riding such a creature. He imagined hunting with it. It would be splendid. But it would also be splendid for Ferran to become a lord with servants, fancy clothing, and tables of food, and Ferran figured that it was just as likely.

And then he thought about their conversation the previous night. The Old Blood had hunted mages at night with their animals. He looked at the korrog in the distance and then back at Winwalom. Was this some Old Blood thing?

"You don't think it would be awesome?" Winwalom asked.

"Borros says they can't be tamed. Besides, if Ranoc has his way, it will be dead in a trap. Or a cage. Which might be the best thing."

"Sometimes wolf cubs are found and raised. Maybe this one is young enough to be like that. Why not try to win it over?"

"I think the fumes of this corpse have truly gone to your brain," Ferran said.

"No, think about it."

"How would you feed it? Nobody in the village would stand for it. It would regularly tear into their pigs and sheep and goats. It might eat one of the children. And if you let it hunt the lord's lands, you'd have him after you."

"I don't know," Winwalom said. "People have kept korrogs before."

"Legends," Ferran said.

"You don't believe the stories?"

He did, but he just couldn't imagine it. "You don't have the wealth to keep such a thing fed."

"If it's trained, maybe I could hire my services out. Maybe the queen would keep me as her korrog-man. Did you think of that?"

He hadn't thought of that. And neither should Winwalom because that would bring him close to the mages. But he could see Winwalom was serious. "You've got some plan, don't you?"

"Maybe."

"How are we going to trap it?"

"Who said we were going to trap it? I think what I need to do is earn its trust."

"You're going to ply it with fine words, are you?"

"I'm thinking we feed it," Winwalom said.

"You're going to get yourself killed."

"And you're going to help me."

"Oh, sweet ancestors. Another one of your schemes."

Lagash whistled at Ferran and motioned at the cattle which were crossing the stream.

"I need to head some cattle," Ferran said. "We'll see if your good sense returns when the vapors have cleared from your brain."

Ferran and Itch ran into the water and headed the cattle, and pushed them back to the bank. And when all had drunk their fill of water, he helped herd them to a spot in the shade of the trees along the edge of the wood because Lagash wanted to keep them together so they'd be easier to defend should the korrog decide to attack. Fortunately, the cattle were more than happy to lie down in the shade and chew their cuds.

When they'd all been moved to the wood's edge, Ferran looked around for Winwalom. He found him building a rock fish wier in a narrow backwater of the stream. The backwater was about knee-deep and in the shape of a finger.

"What are you doing?" Ferran asked.

"I'm hungry, you're hungry, Fufu is probably hungry, and this stream is chock full of fish."

"Fufu?"

"The korrog."

Ferran groaned. "Those vapors truly have gone to your brains."

"Come help me."

Ferran sighed, but he was hungry. So he stepped into the water and helped him build the rock wall that would seal off the mouth of this little inlet. Ferran did most of the work because Winwalom's injuries didn't allow him to move very fast. And also because one of them needed to watch the korrog. But it didn't take long before they had a wall with a V shaped mouth in the middle it that would help funnel the fish in.

"I'll stand upstream," Winwalom said. "You go downstream and walk up." And so, as they waited for Lagash to give them the signal to follow Borros and Krov, they herded almost a dozen fish into the trap and then closed the mouth with rock. Some of the fish were very large indeed, which suggested that not many people came this way.

The two boys walked back to the others.

"How's our friend up there?" Ferran asked.

"He's hardly moved," Ranoc said.

"I don't think he wants to try us again," Lagash said.

"That's good," Ferran said. "Unless maybe he wants to do it at night."

"Maybe," Lagash agreed.

"Do you have a net?" Winwalom asked.

"Not big enough for him."

"For fish. We caught some beauties in a weir."

"That's what you've been doing? Why didn't you tell me. I could have had Ranoc help." Then he opened a box in the wagon and pulled out a decent-sized net and handed it to Winwalom.

The two boys went back and caught the fish with it and set them on the bank, their sides flashing with a silver sheen in the sun. Three of them were almost two-feet long. These Winwalom set aside.

"What are you doing with those?"

"Earning Fufu's trust," he said.

"If you want to earn its trust, you should give it a proper name. Slasher, Iron Claw, Ripper, Night Death."

"Fufu was the name of a killer dog my mother befriended when she was a girl. It's a Selvan word. It means wild."

"No it doesn't."

"That's straight from her lips."

Ferran grunted.

"Are you going to gut, or you just going to stand there?"

Ferran squatted at the side of the water and pulled out his knife for the first fish. "Fufu," he muttered under his breath.

"Mighty Fufu," Winwalom said.

"It will never grow up right," Ferran said and sliced the belly of the first fish. They gutted all the fish expect those Winwalom was saving for the korrog. Then they strung them on a cord and took them back to Lagash.

Winwalom took the three big ones out into the field in view of the korrog. Then he shouted and whistled and waved one of the fish around. After his performance, he shoved three long stakes into the ground and hung the fish on top of the stakes. One fish was too heavy for its stake and toppled over, and so he had to replant it in the ground.

"What's he doing?" Lagash asked.

"Winning Fufu's trust," Ferran said.

Lagash chuckled, then laughed out loud. Then laughed again. A big belly laugh full of mirth. When his mirth subsided, he said, "I figure we've given our fearless leader about an hour. It's time to move out."

The boys got the cattle up, then began to herd them onto the old road to Broniss. The road that led right into the blight.

10

THE OLD ROAD

THE HERD OF two-hundred and fifty cattle moved up the road, treading down much of the grass and weaving around the other small brush that had grown up. Every thirty to forty feet was the stump of a bush or sapling that Borros and Krov had hacked away. This left a good path for the mules and wagons which were tall enough to pass over what remained.

Lagash came first. Winwalom lingered behind, watching his fish on sticks. At the first bend in the road, Ferran glanced back. It was a good distance back to the turnoff. Winwalom was still back there, sitting atop the wagon seat, his yellow bandana around his nose and mouth.

The korrog hadn't moved from its perch on the slope, but seemed to be looking intently at Winwalom, and Ferran began to wonder if it was wise for Winwalom to lag so far behind. What if the korrog attacked? It could easily swoop down and strike him in the head with the hard club part of its tail. What if something else came out of the woods? After all, they were getting close to the blight.

Ferran waited at the bend until Lagash caught up and said, "Winwalom's a bit exposed back there, isn't he?"

Lagash looked back. "He's not going to tame a beast such as that."

"That's what I told him."

Lagash whistled twice loudly. Winwalom turned, and Lagash waved for him to catch up. Winwalom turned in the seat and flicked the reins to get his mule moving, but kept glancing back to the korrog.

"He's got the crossbow," Lagash said. "I suspect he'll be just fine."

"You don't think it's going to attack?"

"I don't know. But it's not the huge beast its mother was. And we did wound it. I think if it had wanted to attack, it would have already done so. Of course, I could be wrong."

Back down the road, Winwalom flicked the reins to urge the mule on.

"I'll wait for him," Lagash said. "You keep the cattle moving."

And so Ferran did. He and Itch worked their zig-zag route behind the cattle, which meant they walked more than anyone else.

The woods here were thick and dark, encroaching on the road. Some branches hung down almost to the ground. The road passed a couple of open, weathered structures that were no more than walls on two sides and a roof above, and Ferran supposed the area had been a place for travelers to stop at night.

Farther along, there was an old outhouse and a couple of huts. The roof of one of the huts had a large hole in it, and a sapling was growing through it.

After that, they passed a little waterfall that tumbled down the slope of the mountain and joined the stream running down the side of this valley. Ferran thought the pool at the bottom of the waterfall would be a great spot to fish, but he supposed the source of the stream itself was in the blight. If it was, would any of the fish be safe to eat? And then he realized this stream joined the stream at the turnoff where they'd created the fish wier. Which meant they'd be eating blight-tainted fish this evening.

They continued up the old road for a number of miles and at last came to a spot with an open field next to a little fold in the slope of the mountain. There was some fencing, but much of it had fallen over. Borros put all the boys to work finding the pieces that were still good, chopping others, and erecting a fence.

Krov, Ranoc, and Caswal worked together. And every so often, Ferran would catch one or more of them looking his way. He knew they were talking about him, plotting something.

When the fence was done, Borros ordered them to practice their battle order again. And it was during practice that Ferran found out what they'd all planned.

As they moved through wheeling, turning, and fixing and flanking, Ferran would suddenly get jabbed in the side with the butt of a spear or knocked in the head or elbow. He'd just been hit again and was going to give Ranoc a piece of his mind when Lagash said, "Our friend is back."

They all looked where he pointed and saw the korrog wheeling high overhead.

"Do you think it's spying on us?" Ranoc asked.

"Yes," Borros said. "It's up there scribbling away, getting ready to report our position back to its master."

"Well," Ranoc said. "You never know. I'm betting it has the runes of that wolf mage on it as well. And you never know what one of them will do."

"You never do," Borros said.

That gave Ferran a pause. Was Borros pulling Ranoc's leg, or would the wolf mage actually be interested in them? This herd was a nice bit of money on the hoof. If you could steal it, you'd stand to make quite a bit. And what better place to steal it than along some deserted road nobody was supposed to be on.

Furthermore, the other two korrog had been his property. Surely, they were valuable to him. So maybe he wanted revenge for their deaths. And recompense.

Ferran suddenly did not like their position. "Do you think the wolf mage is coming after us?" he asked.

Borros said, "Number one. These are korrog, not men. It's not like the wolf mage would be able to read their minds or communicate with them."

"I thought there were runes for that," Krov said.

"That's Old Blood nonsense," Lagash said.

"Well, maybe this wolf mage is Old Blood," Ranoc said.

"A more likely story," Borros said. "Is that these creatures escaped their master's grasp and fled. Wolf mages are reckless in their hunger for the secrets of power. Half the time they kill themselves trying to learn the lore. My money says the wolf mage injured or killed himself, and the korrog escaped."

"But what if he didn't die?" Caswal asked.

"All the better reason to quickly get this herd to Broniss. And all the more reason why I need to be able to trust those working for me."

Caswal and the others glared icily at Ferran. Ferran looked right back at them and said, "I agree completely."

"Good," Borros said. "If we're all agreed, then that matter surely will be resolved shortly."

"Oh, it will be," Caswal said.

"I'm so happy to hear such positive responses," Borros said. "And I think we're done practicing, which means dinner."

Ranoc said, "I can't wait."

"Neither can I," Borros said and turned to Lagash. "Master Cook, what are we having?"

"Fish, porridge with a little something special in it, and nut and honey pie."

Ferran, Ranoc, and Krov all made little exclamations of delight.

"Excellent," Borros said. "Please prepare dinner for two."

"Two?" Ranoc asked.

"Yes, two," Borros said. "Me and our illustrious cook."

"But—" Ranoc said.

Borros said, "I don't feed thieves and liars. And since our little matter has yet to be resolved, you're all suspect. Remember? So if you want to eat, you'll have to go find something out in the woods. I'm sure there's plenty of game. Don't you agree, Master Cook?"

"I agree completely."

Ferran's spirits sank. He was hungry, dead tired, and loved Lagash's porridges. Every morning he looked forward to breakfast. Every evening he looked forward to dinner and another one of Lagash's delights. Today, having missed breakfast, he'd been especially looking forward to it. And if this nut pie was anything like the raisin pie, it was bound to be magical.

"Dinner for two coming up," Lagash said.

The other boys' faces filled with disappointment. And anger.

"Come on, lads," Caswal said meaningfully. "Let's go find some food."

Krov shook his head in frustration. Ranoc gave Ferran another icy look. And then the two of them followed Caswal.

When the trio was well into the woods, Ferran pointed the exact opposite direction and said, "Winwal, I say we go that way."

He nodded.

Ferran said to Borros, "If I bring back something good, would you consider letting me trade it for a bowl of porridge or some pie?"

"That depends on what it is," Borros said.

"Fair enough. Can we borrow the cords and fishing hooks?"

"Do we lend our stuff to suspected thieves?" Borros asked Lagash.

"Probably not," Lagash said.

"Sorry," Borros said. "I truly am."

"You know that Winwalom and I caught the fish you'll be eating."

"Caught them on my time. So technically they're mine."

Ferran nodded. He could understand Borros's anger. It was totally justified.

"We'll get something with our slings," Ferran said and slung his stone satchel over his shoulder. Winwalom did the same, and then they strode out of the camp and across the road.

Both boys stopped at the edge of the wood and peered into the shadows beneath the trees. The woods looked dark and forbidding. And both knew these woods were close to the blight.

"It's pretty thick in there," Ferran said.

"Easy to get lost."

Or run into some nasty piece of work. "I say we just walk along the road," Ferran said.

"Excellent idea," Winwalom said. "I'm sure we'll see plenty of game."

11

_____

INTO THE WOODS

T HEY WALKED A few paces up the road, and then a squirrel chittered somewhere in the woods close by. Another ran along a branch not too far in and stopped. A third ran along a branch beyond that.

"Looks like the squirrels have done well," Ferran said.

Another squirrel stopped on a branch maybe only twenty yards in. It had a reddish coat and tufted ears.

"Have you got a clear shot?" Winwalom asked.

"I think I do," Ferran said, laying his spear on the ground and unlooping his sling. The red squirrel ran a few feet along the branch and stopped again. Ferran loaded his sling pouch with a smaller stone, set himself, whirled the sling once, and released.

The stone sailed through the trees, a good, clean shot. The squirrel saw it, tried to dart away, but it was too late, and the stone struck the animal and knocked it off the branch. It fell to the ground below and lay there, unmoving.

Ferran looked at Winwalom. "I hit it. You fetch it."

"It's your squirrel."

'I fetch it, I eat it."

"What about him?" Winwalom said and pointed at Itch.

"Get it," Ferran said to Itch and pointed, but Itch hadn't been watching and only darted a few steps into the wood and back again.

"Looks like it's you," Ferran said.

"How about we both fetch it," Winwalom said.

"Freeloader," Ferran said, but he picked up his spear, and the three of them entered the wood. They found the squirrel clean and healthy. A nice specimen, but it wasn't very large.

"If they're all this small, we're going to need five or six just to make a meal for one of us," Winwalom said.

"Well, there's a second," Ferran said and pointed farther into the wood.

"What about the road?" Winwalom asked.

"A bird in the hand is worth two in the bush," Ferran said.

"Or squirrel," Winwalom said.

"And there's another," Ferran said. "It's like a squirrel village in here."

"Fine," Winwalom said. "We'll get them and get out. I don't want to be in this wood when the sun goes down."

Winwalom hit the second squirrel. They both missed a third that ran straight up the tree into a bunch of branches that ruined any clean shot, but there were more squirrels farther in the wood, some of them larger, and the boys went after them.

They soon lost sight of the road, but the hunting was good, and it didn't take long before they were carrying seven dead squirrels by their tails. And then Winwalom spotted a slash of light through the trunks of the trees ahead indicating a small clearing along with some thick brush.

"I bet there are some rabbits there," Winwalom said.

Some rabbit would be nice to have along with all this squirrel. And because rabbits were bigger game, Ferran figured they might be able to get what they needed and get out of this wood quicker. And so they slowly moved forward. When they were maybe thirty feet away from the clearing, they stopped. Winwalom set the squirrels he carried by the tail on the ground. He then wet the inside of his index finger with some spit, then sucked hard, making a sound like that of a young, distressed rabbit. Ferran readied his sling.

Winwalom called again, and a few moments later, a fine-sized rabbit poked its head out of the base of the thick briar. Winwalom called again, and the rabbit took one hop out, then rose up to see better.

Ferran whirled his sling and let the stone fly, but the rabbit saw him, spooked, and ran back into the briar.

"Should we send Itch to flush a few out?" Winwalom asked.

"That briar is pretty thick," Ferran said. "They'll just hide in there. Why don't I move over a bit? You call them and draw their attention again. I'll get them from the side."

"Fix and flank," Winwalom said.

"Exactly."

So Ferran put about thirty feet between him and Winwalom, then signaled.

Winwalom started up again with the cry of distress. Soon another rabbit showed itself. Winwalom kept up the finger-sucking squeak. And then the rabbit ventured out a few hops from the briar giving Ferran the perfect shot. He slung. The stone flew true and stuck the rabbit in the head, felling it.

Winwalom started up again, and another rabbit showed itself a little farther on, but Ferran didn't have the best line. He cautiously moved a few yards forward to spot with a cleaner shot, then slung. And now there were two rabbits for them to pick up.

Itch had seen the rabbits and keened with excitement.

"Get 'em," Ferran said and motioned at the rabbits. Itch raced over to the briar, picked the first rabbit up and brought it back and dropped it at Ferran's feet.

"Good boy," Ferran said and gave Itch a scratch on the neck. "Get the other now," he said and motioned at the second.

Itch took off, grabbed the rabbit, and brought it back. Ferran bent to examine the animals to make sure they were clean. Both were good-sized. They had healthy coats. And then he heard the sound of something large walking through the dry leaves of the forest floor. Something walking toward him.

He turned and looked in the direction of the sound, peering through the trunks of the trees at the shadows of the wood. But nothing was there.

Behind him the sound of another set of footsteps rose.

Itch began to growl.

Ferran took the rabbits by the hind legs and moved toward Winwalom, who was now moving toward him, scanning the trees.

The sound of footsteps rose again, and Ferran caught a glimpse of something moving through the trunks. His heart raced. And then the figure appeared again.

It was a man. Ferran imagined some crazed abomination twisted by feral magic.

"Ranoc?" Winwalom said.

Ferran realized it was Ranoc, and he relaxed.

"What are you doing?" Ferran asked. "This is our area."

Ranoc didn't reply. He walked toward Ferran and Winwalom, then stopped about twenty yards away.

Behind Ferran came the sound of an additional set of footsteps. Ferran turned around. Krov stood there about twenty yards away. There was the sound of a third set of footsteps, and Caswal appeared halfway between the arc that ran from Ranoc to Krov. The three boys were in a semi-circle, blocking the path back to the road.

"This ends now, Dog Boy," Caswal said.

"You're going to tell us where you stashed the knife and purse," Ranoc said. "We're not losing our jobs over your stupid greed."

"Excellent," Ferran said. "Except I didn't do it."

"Spare us," Caswal said and motioned at the other two boys, and the three of them began to advance.

Itch barked in a friendly way, then realized it wasn't that kind of a meeting, and his bark changed tone.

"I didn't take anything," Ferran said and backed up a step.

"Watch him," Ranoc said.

"You're making a mistake," Winwalom said.

"You stay out of this," Caswal said.

Ferran backed up another step.

Ranoc put a stone in his sling. "Run, and I'll knock you silly."

"And if I stand, you'll knock me silly," Ferran said. "What a lovely choice."

"It's up to you," Caswal said. "Just tell us where the items are, and there doesn't need to be any knocking."

Except Caswal knew Ferran couldn't tell them anything. He knew Ferran was innocent. And so the three of them would beat Ferran and learn nothing. And then Caswal would frame Ferran with the stolen items and get to enjoy both Ferran's beating and his dismissal.

But Ferran wasn't going to let him enjoy either. The clearing with its thick briar stretched fifty or sixty yards farther into the wood. It was maybe thirty across. And that gave him an idea. He backed up another step and lowered his voice. "We lead them on a chase around this briar," he said. "Then high-tail it back to camp."

"Good idea," Winwalom said. "We need to separate a little. Make it harder to target both of us at the same time."

"Don't be planning anything," Ranoc said and trailed his arm back, readying his sling. "All we need from you is the truth, and we'll leave you alone."

"Now!" Ferran said, and the two boys turned and ran, squirrel and rabbits still in their hands. Ferran cut left a bit and ran a couple of yards wide of Winwalom. Itch barked then joined them.

"Get him!" Caswal cried.

Ranoc's sling whistled round. Ferran darted to the side. A moment later a stone whistled past, then smacked into the trunk of a tree up ahead. It surprised Ferran. That had been a full force shot. If it had hit him, it could have broken a rib. If it had hit his head, it might have killed him! Anger surged through him, and he poured on the speed.

"Cut them off!" Caswal shouted, and the three boys began to chase after them.

Ferran ran full out for a number of paces, then realized that if he put too much distance between him and the other boys, they'd see his plan, and one or two of them would turn back and try to go the other way around the briar and cut him and Winwalom off. And so he slowed his pace just enough to stay ahead of Caswal and crew, tempting them to follow.

They took the bait. Ranoc stopped to try his sling again. This time the stone sailed just a foot past Ferran, raising goose pimples along his arm.

The far end of the clearing neared. Ferran figured he needed to lead them around the end, and then he and Winwalom could pour on the speed as they raced back to camp. They turned the corner, jumped a fallen tree, landing in some on the other side with their bare feet, and continued on. There were wet parts here, and their feet squelched in the mud.

Winwalom jumped a log and dropped one of the squirrels, but he let it lie and continued to run. And then they moved out of the muddy area, across a patch of fallen leaves and through some light undergrowth, then past the skeleton of a horse lying along the ground. There were still patches of dried skin clinging to it, sunken in between the bones. And hair. It was odd seeing that there.

They sped on, and Ferran had to avoid another set of bones of something smaller, a badger maybe. And then there were the bones of a mouse, white against the dark of the old fallen leaves.

They ran a few more steps, came around a bush, and suddenly found themselves facing three six-foot tall Xs made from two thick pieces of wood being planted in the ground. A human skeleton had been tied to each of the Xs in a spread eagle. The skulls of two of the people were still attached, jaws hanging down. The skull of the third had fallen off its neck and lay on the ground.

Ferran and Winwalom came to an abrupt halt, eyes wide.

Around them lay the skeletons of more animals. Deer, birds, rabbits, snakes. They stretched out in all directions.

"The king's eyes," Winwalom cursed in shock.

They looked around. And then, through the trees, Ferran spotted a slope. There was an outcropping of rock there and a couple of large boulders. And in the middle of that cluster of rock was a gash, a dark opening, that looked like the entrance to some cave.

Fear coursed through him.

And then Caswal and Krov came racing round the bush. "We've got you now, maggot!" Caswal said, and then he saw the Xs and skeletons. His face fell, and he stopped in his tracks.

Whatever was here was welcome to have Caswal, Ferran thought. He yanked on Winwalom's shoulder. "Run!" he said, then dashed between a little litering of toad bones and ran for the far side of the briar thicket.

Itch and Winwalom chased after him. Caswal and Krov fled as well.

Up ahead, Ranoc, who had obviously gone wide to prevent Ferran escaping, set himself to tackle Ferran. It was clear he hadn't seen the bone yard. But then he must have noticed the expressions on Caswal's and Krov's faces, and the fact that they weren't really chasing Ferran anymore.

His eyes went wide. "What's going on?" he said.

"Run!" Krov cried.

It was enough, and Ranoc turned and ran. The four other boys and Itch followed him, cutting through undergrowth, leaping downed branches and rotted logs, ignoring the rocks that poked and stabbed their bare feet. Ranoc burst out of the woods first onto the old road, followed by Ferran and Itch. Winwalom and Caswal were next. Krov came a few seconds later. And they all ran back to the camp.

As the wagon came into view, Caswal begin shouting in panicked alarm. "There's something out there!"

Borros stood. "What's going on?"

"There were bones! Everywhere!"

"What bones?" Lagash said. "Calm down. What did you see?"

The boys raced up to the wagon where the two men and camp fire were.

"Three crosses," Winwalom said. "Three bodies spread eagled. Nothing but bones. And all around the crosses were the bones of dozens of animals."

Lagash and Borros glanced at each other, some communication passing between them.

"Battle order," Borros said. "Right over there." And then he walked over to the wagon and fetched his spear.

Lagash grabbed his crossbow. The boys formed up, and Ferran realized he'd left his spear on the ground out by where he'd been hunting the rabbits. He gulped and went over to the wagon to grab his practice spear.

Borros took his position in the line, then said, "Now tell me again what you saw. Tell it slowly. Give me every detail."

Ferran told him the tale from hunting rabbits, the chase, then seeing the bones and the cave. Winwalom and the others added details.

When they finished, Borros asked, "Just bones. No flesh?"

"Bones," Winwalom said. "Parched skin, some fur."

"But no stink?"

"No."

"Sounds old," Lagash said.

"Now that you say that, yes," Winwalom said. "I didn't see a corpse anywhere. Only bones."

And then Ferran remembered that thin plants had been growing up between the ribs of many of the animals. In fact, now that he thought of it, the skull on the ground not only had a greenish tint to it, but a pale, woodland flower had been growing out of one eye socket. Lagash was right. It *was* old. It would have taken at least a year for the flesh to be eaten by maggots and birds and other carrion eaters. Another year or two for what remained to decay.

"What are we going to do?" Caswal asked.

Borros put on his drover's cap, its scarlet badge blazing in the sunlight. "How far in did you say this was?"

"Three or four hundred yards," Winwalom said. "Maybe a little more."

Borros looked up at the sky. The sun was just about to set. Evening would soon be upon them.

"I want to see it before dark falls. Dog Boy, lead the way."

12

INVESTIGATION

F ERRAN MOST DEFINITELY did not want to lead the way, but he followed orders and led the group up the road and to the point where Ferran and Winwalom had entered the woods.

The boys and Borros carried their spears at the ready. Lagash had his crossbow and short sword. They moved through the trees steadily, but with caution, all of them alert and scanning the woods.

The chittering of the squirrels became ominous. A hare bounded away from them in fright. Itch was alert, his ears perked forward.

When the boys had first stumbled upon the place, whatever lived in that cave might not have heard them arrive. But surely it had heard them yell and leave and was now alerted to their presence. Ferran's anxiety rose.

He swallowed, crunched a branch, and continued forward. They advanced around the briar, across the muddy stretch, and when Ferran cleared it, he pointed ahead and said, "You can just see it up there. The edge of one of the great Xs. The cave is beyond it."

"What does our watcher see behind us?" Borros asked.

"The trunks of a great many trees," Winwalom replied.

"Lead on, Dog Boy," Borros said.

And Ferran moved forward, his ears straining to hear the slightest sound, his eyes wide and scanning the woods. A slight breeze gusted in the trees. It dislodged a dead branch, and it cracked a couple of times against other branches as it fell to the earth.

Ferran thought he saw something shadowy move in the distance and stopped. But after scanning, he decided it was nothing.

They continued forward until the Xs were clearly visible. Beside them was the skeleton of a small fawn.

What would do this?

They walked another twenty paces and approached the Xs. Borros ordered them to form a circle and stand watch. Then he walked up to the human skeletons and examined them. "These first two were men," he proclaimed. "This one was definitely a woman."

"How can you tell?" Krov asked, his good eye scanning thhe woods.

"The hips."

He then examined the wooden posts and the ground around them, scuffing the fallen leaves to see if they were hiding anything. He and Lagash then examined a number of the other skeletons lying about the wider area.

As Lagash walked over to the bones of a snake, he spotted the rabbits and squirrels Ferran and Winwalom had dropped in their shock at seeing the Xs. He looked at Ferran. "These yours?"

"Yes," Ferran said.

"Good haul."

But Ferran didn't move to retrieve them.

"You're not hungry?"

"Not for cursed meat."

Lagash motioned at the area. "They're just bones."

"I've never seen a collection of bones like this," Ferran said. "Something's wrong here."

Lagash shrugged.

Ferran let the animals lie. None of the other boys wanted to touch them either.

The skeletons lay scattered in a wide circle maybe twenty or thirty yards in diameter. Lagash and Borros counted thirty-seven of them— snakes, deer, squirrels, birds, the horse Ferran had seen, rabbits, and others. When they finished, Borros told them to form up into loose battle order because they were going to investigate the cave.

Ferran's mouth went dry, but he took his place at the far end of the battle line with Itch. It was his and Itch's job to detach from the line, if needed, and distract the enemy, to fix the attention of whatever enemy they faced so the others could kill it. Ferran decided he didn't much like being a distractor. It seems the others should be the ones fixing while he attacked from the flank, but he brought his spear down to the ready position with the others, and then Borros motioned them forward to thread their way through the sparse trunks of trees.

"If something comes out of that cave," Borros said, "stay in your line."

Ferran's tension rose. It was probably some awful monster, some creature blight-twisted with speed and malice.

Lagash said, "Ranoc will probably fart."

Ferran startled, then laughed.

"That will fix 'em," Borros said. "And after that?"

"We'll swing the ends of our line up onto the flanks," Winwalom replied.

"Exactly. Now prepare yourselves. When the mouse comes out, you need to be ready."

Mouse, indeed, Ferran thought.

"So you don't need me to distract?" he asked.

"Hum," Borros said. "That's a good question. Master Cook, should we send him in as bait?"

Bait? Ferran thought in alarm.

"It's an excellent idea," he said. "Dog Boy might be just the tasty morsel to draw whatever's in there out."

Ferran blinked.

"Yes," Borros said. "But don't go just yet. Maintain your position in the line, Dog Boy, until I give the order."

The next time, Ferran told himself, he would keep his mouth shut.

Borros motioned them forward, and they approached the gash in the rocks. When they were a few yards below the outcropping, Borros motioned for them to stop. Lagash stood next to him, crossbow braced against his good shoulder.

They all watched the gap in the rocks, which was just a few paces farther up the slope.

"All right, Dog Boy," Borros said. "You ready?"

"What if I said no?" he asked.

"Count of three," Borros said. "Into the cave and right back out. If you want to yell a bit when you get in there, feel free."

Ferran gripped his spear tighter, blew out a big breath. Then another. He wasn't ready. This was madness.

"One, two, three, go!" Borros said.

Ferran swallowed, but what could he do? Refusing would only make him a coward in all of their eyes. So he blew out another breath, then charged up the hill. He covered the distance in two steps, then saw the gash between the rocks was not the entrance to any cave at all. It was just a gap between some large rocks that was no more than three-feet deep. He stood there confused, and looked around for a cave entrance, but there was none.

"What's wrong, Dog Boy?" Borros asked.

Ferran turned around. Borros had a wry smile on his face. Somehow he'd known nothing was there. And now Ferran knew it as well, and he got an idea.

Ferran turned back to the rocks. "Come out you foul beast!" he shouted. "Come meet your match. He did a jig, then shouted in alarm and acted like something had grabbed his leg. He flung himself to the ground. "Help!"

The other boys all startled, their eyes wide as saucers.

And then Ferran began to laugh.

Krov narrowed his eye, then strode up the slope and saw the mighty cave. "Ah," he said. "Good one." He gave Ferran an appreciative nod.

The other boys looked at each other in curiosity, then drew closer.

"There's no cave," Winwalom said, seeing the joke, then smiled.

"I thought Ranoc was going to crap his pants," Caswal said, grinning.

"I think I did," Ranoc said.

They all laughed. And then Borros looked up through the branches and leaves of the trees at the sky. Twilight was setting in.

"The light's going to fade fast," Borros said. "We could do a wider sweep of the area, but not tonight. Let's head back. Stay in loose order. Long Hair, keep an eye on our backs."

Ferran looked down the slope and surrounding ground and saw no trail leading to the rocks. No sign that anything came or went that way. In fact, there was hardly any sign of anything traveling through this area at all, just one animal trail that crossed the the side of all the bones. If he hadn't been so scared, he would have seen that. But both Borros and Lagash must have noticed as they approached. Which meant the whole thing about him charging into the cave had been a practical joke.

Ha, ha, he thought. One of these days, he'd get them back.

The group began to stride back the way they'd come, but just as they entered the circle of bones, Borros suddenly halted them. "Hang on, now," he said, then bent down and drew something from the leaves on the forest floor. "What's this?" he said and brushed it off.

It was a knife in a scabbard.

He looked it over, then kicked the leaves around the spot to see what else might be there, but he didn't find anything. "Spread out a bit," he said. "As we walk through, scan the ground for any other sign."

Ferran had his wits about himself now and searched the forest floor diligently. He saw lots of bones, plants, fallen branches, and leaves. He saw some mushrooms. He even saw a millipede, but nothing else that shouldn't be on a forest floor. Nobody else found anything either.

When they reached the far size of the circle of bones, Borros had them form up again, then pick up their pace, for the light was now truly beginning to fade.

They reached the camp as the first stars began to appear, still maintaining their battle order. Borros told them to be at ease, then went over to the fire to examine the knife. It was a long knife, almost a dagger. He wiped the scabbard clean and looked at it as best he could in the light.

The knife itself had a leather-wrapped handle. He pulled it out and examined the blade, which had something etched in it.

"Where's it from?" Lagash asked.

"No idea," Borros said and handed both blade and scabbard to him. "Any of that look familiar to you?"

Lagash looked them over and shook his head, then he ran his thumb across the knife's blade. "It's a good blade though. Taken some rust, but the edge is still sharp."

"I'm sure someone in Broniss will be able to identify those marks," Borros said.

"So what was that back there?" Ranoc asked.

Borros said, "That's the question. If it had just been the human bones on the Xs, I would have said it was murder, pure and simple. But all the other bones tell me something else was going on."

"It's the blight," Krov said.

"The blight is still a number of miles away," Borros said.

"Maybe it's extended its borders."

"That site is years old," Borros said. "The queen's mages have been through here. And that is not so far off the road. If there was anything dark there, they would have sniffed it out."

"How you can be sure?" Caswal asked.

"They bring hounds."

Ranoc said, "When you were a grimsman did the mages always find every abomination that grew from the wild magic and destroy it?"

"We thought so," Borros said.

Ranoc groaned. "That's what I'm talking about."

Lagash said, "That circle might be the work of the mages."

Borros frowned.

"You don't think so?" Lagash asked.

"I don't know. Abominations are usually burned."

"So we don't know what it is," Winwalom said.

Ranoc motioned at Borros. "Our dark slayer just said it's possible they missed something."

Borros nodded. "It's possible something slipped through their sweep of the area the first time. But the second, third, fourth, and fifth?" He shrugged. "Whatever it was, it was years ago."

Lagash said, "We'll inform the mages, and they'll send their hunters. Meanwhile, someone at Broniss will recognize the markings on this knife. The answers will come."

"Unless whatever did that comes for us," Krov said.

"You leave the bones to me," Borros said. "Right now, your job is to watch the cattle. We'll make three watches tonight." He assigned them out. Krov and Caswal would take the first watch, followed by Winwalom and Ferran, and then finally Borros and Ranoc.

When he finished, he said, "I will also point out that the time for returning the items that were stolen is running out. If they're not here by tomorrow morning, you won't have to worry about the blight or cattle or anything else, because you'll be going home. Without pay. Now, I suggest you eat whatever you caught and get what sleep you can, because, one way or another, tomorrow's going to be a long day."

Ranoc scowled and shot Ferran a look.

Ferran ignored him and turned to Winwalom. "Did you keep hold of anything?"

"One squirrel," Winwalom said. "I'd looped its tail in my belt."

Ferran sighed. It looked like his fast was going to continue. "Give my portion to Itch."

Lagash motioned at the other boys. "Didn't you get anything?"

"No," Ranoc said.

No, Ferran thought, they were too busy sneaking around the woods with the intent of beating him to a pulp. It served them right.

"Tomorrow morning," Borros prompted.

"The items will be there," Caswal said. "Won't they, Dog Boy."

"Only you would know," Ferran said.

13

WATCH

B ECAUSE ALL OF their bags had been dumped, the boys split up to gather more dry grass and leaves before the last light completely faded.

Ferran and Winwalom spotted a good patch of dried grass and weeds. Ferran made sure to grab his pack, and then he joined Winwalom there.

He cut a big swath of dried grass with his knife and stuffed it in his bag. "Did you hear him back there?"

"Who?"

"Caswal." 'They'll be there, won't they, Dog Boy.' Well, he'll be eating those words tomorrow."

"What's your plan?"

"He's got to plant them on me. So I'm going to give him the perfect opportunity. And when he's in the middle of the act, we'll raise the alarm. We'll catch him red-handed. Me and you. Our two witnesses against his."

Winwalom cut some grass and stuffed it in his sack. "You know, Ranoc was talking earlier today, wondering if maybe Borros was trying to cheat us."

"Cheat us?"

"It would be a clever way for him to get out of having to pay us."

"If they were wanting to wiggle out of paying us our wages, wouldn't they'd wait for us to drive the cattle almost all the way to Broniss and only then claim we'd stolen something. That way they'd get all of our labor for free."

"True. But what if he's a shaver, someone content to make lots of small winnings? What if he contracted with a group at Pencoy's? He could dispose of us, then pay them for the remainder of the journey. That would cut his costs in half, and he wouldn't have us in Broniss complaining to the magistrate about stolen wages. Think about it. They already showed up once without a crew, claiming theft and poison. Maybe they've been doing this all along."

It was possible. They could be greedy shavers. But there was a snag in the theory. "You're overthinking it. You're forgetting his dogs. They were poisoned. We saw them. Nobody would do that to his own dogs. No, it's Caswal. You heard him all smug and self-satisfied. He's been wanting me gone right from the start."

Winwalom nodded. "You're probably right."

"You know I'm right. And tonight, all his schemes will turn on his own head. And it's going to be Caswal making the long walk home."

They finished stuffing their bags, then carried them to the spot Ferran had selected, which was at the edge of a nice, flat clearing. Of course with the korrog above, they didn't want to sleep in the clearing. So they moved them back a bit into the trees.

Ferran kept his voice low and said, "So he's got to get the things into my pack, right?"

"Or your browse bag."

"Oh, he's not going to get anywhere near my browse bag because I'm not sleeping tonight. If he tries to slip it in, I'll just ask him what he's doing."

"So how are you going to catch him?"

"We don't want to leave our packs on the ground for something nasty to crawl into, do we? And wouldn't you know it, but that dead tree over there in the clearing looks like a great place to hang them. So we're going to hang our packs over there. Nice and high. And we're going to tie them with one of Old Harm's impossible knots."

Winwalom nodded.

"Caswal will have the items with him. The moment he touches the bag, we grab him and raise the alarm. Two of us against one of him."

"You're going to wake me then?"

"Shush," Ferran said. "Keep your voice low. You won't be going to sleep. We need two witnesses."

Winwalom groaned.

"I'm as tired as you are," Ferran said. "Besides, it's only one night."

"What's in it for me?"

"I'll buy you a dinner at some tavern when we get to Broniss."

Winwalom pointed at him. "I'm going to hold you to that."

"Besides, who can sleep with those bones over there and the korrog in the sky?"

"It didn't come," Winwalom said dejectedly.

"What didn't?"

"The korrog. At least not while I was watching. I gave it plenty of space."

"Did it even see your fish on sticks?"

"Oh yes, I made sure to capture its attention. It looked right at me."

"Maybe it prefers red meat."

"Maybe. Tomorrow, we'll get squirrel and hares and see if that doesn't tempt it."

Ferran shook his head. "And if that doesn't work, you'll use one of Borros's cows?"

"Maybe we can get a deer."

"Maybe," Ferran said.

"Do you think they're telling us everything? He's had us practicing like soldiers since we left Buckle Hill. Even when we were only supposed to be herding cattle to Pencoy's. It's like he's expecting something. Like something else is going on."

Ferran shrugged. "He is a military man. Maybe that's his way of keeping us busy."

Winwalom nodded. "Perhaps."

"Well, whatever it is, we can deal with that after we deal with Caswal."

"The things we get ourselves into," Winwalom said.

"We'll be fine," Ferran said.

Except the more Ferran thought about it, the more the bones began to spook him. But then he told himself that Borros was an ex-grimsman and knew about these things. And Lagash had probably been part of the Raven Guard. These were men with experience. And there was nothing Ferran could do about it anyway. Besides, if Ferran didn't catch Caswal, he wouldn't have to worry about korrog, bones, or blight.

So Ferran took his pack, tied the flap over the mouth of it tight, then tossed a cord over a branch on the dead tree, hauled the pack up, and tied it off with one of Old Harm's knots. He then did the same with Winwalom's and walked back to their beds and lay down. But he found a bush blocked his view of the tree, so he and Winwalom slid their bags over until they had a perfect view.

Krov and Caswal began making their rounds. Lagash slid into his hammock and began to snore. Ranoc and the others had made their beds in the shelter of a big boulder in the dark shadows under some trees by the wagon. It was a perfect place to sleep if you wanted to skulk about in the shadows. But the shadows wouldn't help Ranoc or the others because the pack was in the small clearing, illuminated by the moonlight. Whoever was coming would have to show himself to plant the stolen items.

So Ferran stretched out and propped himself up with his elbows. But then he realized they could probably see he was awake, so he lay down. But then his fatigue immediately began to overcome him, and his eyes began to droop. He forced his eyes open, but they drooped again. He slapped his face, but it did no good.

He rolled over and poked Winwalom.

"I wasn't sleeping," Winwalom said, his eyes still closed.

"This isn't going to work," Ferran said.

"Let's take turns," Winwalom said. "You don't need my eyeballs the whole night. Just when he's there. So let's split our vigil. As soon as he shows up, whoever's on watch kicks the other person awake."

"Fine," Ferran said. "I'll start."

"Lovely," Winwalom said and lay back.

But Ferran knew he couldn't stay on his bed. The thick soft grass in his bag was simply too inviting. So he brought Itch up onto the bed and covered him with his cloak so it looked like someone was there. Then Ferran quietly crept to a tree with a clear line of sight to the clearing and packs.

He was too far away to kick Winwalom awake, so he tried to reach him with his spear, but even that wasn't long enough. He carefully searched around in the dark until he found a fallen branch that was about nine feet long. Ferran decided he needed to test it, so he reached out with the stick and poked Winwalom.

Winwalom didn't move. Ferran poked him again.

"Stop that," Winwalom said and batted the stick away.

Ferran poked him again.

Winwalom rolled over. "What are you doing?" he said to Itch, not realizing Ferran had moved.

Ferran poked him again.

Winwalom saw the branch, then spied Ferran in the shadows.

Ferran leaned forward and whispered, "Just testing."

Winwalom sighed, then rolled over again and lay back down.

Ferran smiled to himself. This was going to work.

Krov and Caswal made their first round. As they finished, they veered close to the packs hanging in the dead tree in the small clearing, and Ferran readied himself.

Caswal silently punched his palm with his fist, as if indicating he wanted to pound Ferran, but Krov pulled him back, and they moved on. They made another round, and a third. Ferran fought his sleepiness and watched, but Caswal didn't make any move, and when the first watch was half over and Krov and Caswal were at the far end of the field with the cattle, Ferran woke Winwalom and told him what to do.

Winwalom groaned, but he took position in the shadows with the stick.

It seemed like Ferran had just fallen asleep when Winwalom was standing over him, nudging him awake with his foot.

"They're done. It's our watch," he said.

Ferran was so tired, but he forced himself up. "Did you stay awake?"

"Of course I did," Winwalom said.

"See anything?"

"Deer, bats, moths."

Ferran nodded and was a little perplexed that Caswal hadn't made his move. And then he realized why. It would be easier to plant the items when Ferran and Winwalom were on watch on the far side of the cattle field. Caswal didn't plant the items because he was waiting for Ferran and Winwalom to go on watch.

Well, that plot was easy enough to foil. "You get the browse bags," he said. "I'll get the packs."

"Why?"

"We're going to hide them so nobody can't plant anything in them during our watch."

Winwalom nodded, and so Ferran let the packs down, and the two of them started their watch by carrying their packs and bags with them. They stashed them behind some bushes in the darkest shadows at the other end of the cattle field.

As they did, Ferran realized having Winwalom on watch with him was probably even better than having Itch because not only could Winwalom penetrate the darkness, he could actually name what was or wasn't there. Of course, Winwalom didn't bite like Itch. At least not yet.

They made their rounds, keeping their eyes on the sky and woods, and with every turn, Ferran sent Winwalom over to where the other boys lay to make sure they were all there. Every time Winwalom returned to say he'd seen them sleeping away in their beds.

Halfway through the watch, Winwalom got the bright idea to climb partway up the side of the valley closest to the camp to a little outcropping that would give them a good view of the cattle field and the skies.

It took them only a few minutes to reach the outcropping of rock, which was well above the moonlit tops of the trees on the valley floor. In the day time, it would give them an excellent view of the valley and surrounding slopes. But right now the woods and slopes were dark masses illuminated by the moonlight.

"What are we doing up here?" Ferran asked.

"I'm looking for the korrog."

Ferran sighed and felt a bit envious that Winwalom could see clearly in the night. Ferran himself observed the dark shapes of the cattle, the moonlit field, and then the dark woods on the other side of the road. He could see the gash in the woods where the clearing was. The circle of bones lay in the trees just beyond it. He hoped Lagash was right and it was all the result of some mage work.

They stayed on the outcropping for another quarter hour, Winwalom scanning for monsters above, Ferran scanning for monsters below, but none showed themselves. And so they hiked back down and continued their rounds about the field.

At the end of their three-hour watch, they retrieved their packs and bags and checked them to make sure nothing had been added to them. They found they hadn't been disturbed, and so they made their way back. They couldn't stop yawning, but Ferran was anxious and excited because it was clear Caswal was waiting for this last watch to make his move. And that meant his demise was not far away. They woke Ranoc and Borros, then walked back to their beds.

"I'll stay up first," Ferran said.

"Lovely," Winwalom said and promptly crawled onto his bag and pulled his cloak up over him.

Borros and Ranoc rose and stretched. Ranoc walked a number of paces away from his bed and emptied his bladder on some bushes, and then they began to make their rounds

Ferran ordered Itch back onto the bag and covered him with the cloak. Itch was more than happy to oblige, obviously enjoying the master's spot. Ferran sneaked over to the tree in the deep shadows and settled back with his stick.

Above them the stars and a partial moon shone down on the camp. Lagash snored in his hammock. Every once in a while out in the field some cow moved, its hooves thudding softly. A small breeze picked up, rustling the leaves in the trees.

Borros and Ranoc made their rounds. And every time they went to the far side of the cattle field, Ferran prepared himself, execting Caswal to creep toward the packs. But after four or five disappointments, Ferran began to wonder if Caswal could see that Ferran was awake. But that was impossible—Ferran was sitting in the black moon shadow of a tree.

The minutes passed, Borros and Ranoc slowly making their rounds, stopping at the quarter points. A spider crawled onto Ferran's neck, and he flicked it off.

An hour passed, and Ferran told himself that surely Caswal must make his move now because in another hour the sky would begin to lighten. But Caswal didn't move.

The breeze blew stronger, increasing the sound of the rustling leaves. And Ferran's weariness began to catch up with him, making his eyes heavier and heavier. And then they closed.

He woke with a start, his heart racing. He looked at the packs, then looked at Borros and Ranoc, but they were only a few yards farther around the field than when Ferran had seen them last. He sat up straighter and began pinching the skin on the back of his wrist hard enough that the pain kept him awake.

And he began to wonder if maybe he'd missed something. Maybe Caswal wasn't going to plant the stolen items. Maybe he had just tossed them in the clearing close to Ferran's bed during Ferran's watch. Maybe his plan was to simply walk by and point them out with a raised voice.

Ferran was just about to begin searching the area around their beds when something moved in the shadows of the trees in the corner of his eye.

He turned and peered over by where Lagash slept. And then it moved again. Something dark by the wagon.

14

THIEF

F ERRAN'S PULSE QUICKENED, and he peered closer.

It was not an animal, but someone in a dark cloak, hunched over by the trees a number of paces away from the wagon. Someone Caswal's height.

How had he gotten over there?

And then Ferran realized that he'd assumed Caswal had figured out a way to hide the items that had been stolen. But what if he hadn't? What if he hadn't found a good time to retrieve them with Borros and everyone else watching, and had been forced to leave them behind?

That meant, if Caswal wanted to frame Ferran, he'd have to steal something new and plant it. And the best time to steal something from the wagon was when Borros wasn't sleeping in it!

Ferran was now fully awake. This was perfect. He could catch Caswal, not just holding stolen items, but in the very act of stealing them.

He reached out with his stick to poke Winwalom, but he moved too quickly, and in his haste, he didn't lift the tip of the branch high enough. The tip caught on the ground, the branch bent, and then it broke with a small snap, leaving Ferran holding only a third of its length.

The dark shadow by the wagon looked in Ferran's direction.

Ferran froze.

Caswal waited, watched, then quietly edged closer to the wagon. He was moving slowly, making sure not to make one peep.

Ferran couldn't reach Winwalom with his stick. And the moon had moved so that the ground around their beds was illuminated. If Ferran walked over and woke him, Caswal would see him.

Ferran felt around for something to throw at Winwalom, but all he found was grass and small twigs.

The shadow was now at the wagon, and Ferran knew he didn't have much time. He couldn't just call the alarm, because then Caswal would run out into the darkness and back to his bed and pretend he'd just been awoken.

What Ferran needed to do was get close enough to see when Caswal had whatever he was going to steal, and only then raise the alarm. He would shout loud enough to wake the whole woods. He would shout when Borros and Ranoc were close. And they'd catch Caswal red-handed.

Ferran began to creep toward the wagon on all fours. He kept himself low and reached out with his bare foot to make sure he wasn't going to step on anything that would snap, and slowly moved forward. He took another low, quiet, probing step, and another. He moved like a giant, four-legged spider.

The breeze gusted through the trees, masking any sounds Ferran made.

The dark figure that was Caswal popped open the lid to a small barrel, then looked over at Lagash and paused.

Ferran froze in the dark. Waited. Watched the deceitful snake.

Caswal turned back to the wagon and reached in the barrel, and Ferran began to move again, another low-crouching step, and another. He paused behind a tiny pine just a few paces from the wagon, then crept around a small patch of moonlight shining down through a break in the leaves above and stole to the back corner of the wagon.

Caswal slowly stuffed something from the wagon into a pocket in his cloak.

Ferran grinned. This was going to be better than one of Lagash's pies.

The hooded figure looked out at the field where Borros and Ranoc made their rounds. He glanced over at Lagash in his hammock and then reached back into the wagon bed for something else, his back toward Ferran. And then Ferran realized Caswal wasn't stuffing things into the pockets of his cloak but into a sack. And then he drew the mouth of the sack shut tight. He was finished stealing.

Ferran looked out at the pasture. Borros and Ranoc were making their way back to the campsite. They weren't as close as he'd like, but now was the time to shout the alarm. The breeze gusted again and sighed through the trees.

Ferran rose. At that same time, Caswal turned to make a quick escape and walked right into him.

"Thief!" Ferran shouted into Caswal's face and grabbed his arm.

Caswal startled, then ripped his arm free and fled, but Ferran tackled him from behind. They went down in a tumble of limbs a few paces away from the wagon.

Caswal twisted and kicked, freeing himself. He surged up and tried to scramble away.

"Thief!" Ferran shouted louder and lunged for Caswal, grabbing him round the waist and pulling him down.

Caswal swung his elbow back, nailing Ferran in the forehead and knocking him onto his butt. Ferran grabbed the edge of Caswal's cloak. Caswal back-handed Ferran with a fist to the side of his head. It was a hard blow. It jarred Ferran, but not enough to prevent him from yanking Caswal's hood back to reveal his face for all the others to see.

Except it wasn't Caswal's face. It wasn't the face of anyone Ferran had ever seen.

The thief was in shadow. A dark scarf covered the lower half of his face, but there was enough moonlight filtering through the leaves to see that his face was thinner than Caswal's. His hair was cut in short clumps like someone had taken a knife to it. His features were angular.

"Who the—"

But the thief rose and stomped at Ferran's face.

Ferran ducked, but wasn't quick enough, and the blow hit him in the shoulder. It was a full force wallop and slammed Ferran flat on his back, banging his head on the ground.

He lay there for a moment, dazed and a bit disoriented.

It wasn't Caswal! He needed to raise the alarm!

Ferran rolled over and pushed himself up. He looked around. Scanned the dark shadows under the moonlit trees around him. Scanned the field out to the road. But there was nobody there. Only the breeze as it moved the branches and leaves.

Ferran spotted the thief's sack and the small round of cheese lying on the ground. He grabbed the sack and the cheese and stood, his head still feeling a bit wooden from the blows he'd taken. But it wasn't so wooden he couldn't feel a bit of righteous indignation.

Even if he hadn't sent Caswal packing, at least he'd solved the mystery. And they would all know it wasn't him that had pilfered the items. They would all have to eat their accusations.

"Thief!" Caswal shouted. "Thief! Thief by the wagon!"

Ferran turned.

Caswal was out of his bed, spear in one hand, pointing at Ferran with the other.

Running footfalls approached from behind. Ferran turned to see Borros and Krov rushing toward the wagon, spears at the ready.

"Stop where you are!" Borros commanded.

"I caught him," Ferran said, but the breeze was up.

Borros rounded the corner of the wagon, his spear ready for battle. "Show yourself!"

Ferran realized he was in a dark shadow, and that they must not have recognized him. They might not have even heard him clearly.

He raised his voice. "It's me," he said and raised his arms. He stepped forward into the moonlight, the sack in one hand, the cheese in the other.

They recognized him and relaxed their spears. And then Borros's eyes went to the sack and cheese in Ferran's hands. "What's that?"

"There was a thief," Ferran said. He held the sack and cheese out. "I caught him stealing this."

Caswal came running in. "I saw him! I saw him! It was Ferran."

"It wasn't me," Ferran said. "There was a thief here. I caught him. Didn't you hear me shouting?"

Borros said, "I don't see that you've caught anybody." He turned to Krov. "Did you see a second person here?"

"No," Krov said.

"He's got one eye," Ferran said.

"There wasn't anyone else here," Caswal said.

"There was a thief," Ferran said. "He ran off."

"Which way did he go?"

"I," Ferran stammered. "We fought. I was on my back. I don't know. Somewhere in that direction."

Borros looked out into the darkness, then looked back at Ferran, his face hard.

"He was here," Ferran said. "I swear it."

Lagash walked over from his hammock. "What's going on?"

"Did you see anyone?" Borros asked.

"No."

"Hear a scuffle?"

Lagash rubbed his eyes. "I heard Caswal sequealing like a pig."

Borros turned back to Ferran and gave him a look.

"What's going on?" Lagash asked.

"The Lover and I heard Caswal shout. We spotted something moving in the shadows by the wagon and came to investigate. We found Ferran with a cheese and sack in hand." Something on the ground drew Borros's attention. "And what's that?"

Ferran looked down. Two onions lay there. They must have fallen out of the sack.

The others were now gathering around, and a knot of dread began to form in Ferran's gut.

"There was a thief here," Ferran said. "They must have dropped out of the sack."

"I told you," Caswal said and pointed. "I told you he was the worm all along."

Itch came up with Winwalom and sniffed around on the ground. "Itch will smell him out," Ferran said.

But Itch didn't seem to notice a smell worth barking for.

Ferran said, "Winwalom and I have been watching all night, haven't we?"

Winwalom nodded, bleary eyed.

"I thought for sure it was Caswal who'd stolen the other tiems. I was sure he was wanting to plant them in my things. I wanted to catch him and prove my innocence."

Borros motioned at Itch. "If you wanted to catch the thief, why didn't you let your dog loose on him?"

"Because I didn't know it was someone else. I thought it was Caswal."

"Why didn't he bark?" asked Krov.

"I don't know," Ferran said, his panic rising. "He was upwind of the wagon. He wouldn't have smelled the thief."

"He wasn't barking," Caswal said, "because there wasn't any mystery thief. The proof is right in front of us. He's still holding the cheese and sack in his hand."

Ferran dropped the items like they were hot coals. "I wasn't stealing. Mark me, when the sun comes up, you'll see other foot prints."

But when the sun rose, it only revealed the grass of the field and campsite. And scouring the area field for subtle signs like bent grass didn't help because the grass everywhere was bent and trampled from when they'd driven the cattle in. Ferran examined the dew, but either the dew hadn't fallen by the time the thief came, or he'd run through the woods.

Ferran said, "I'm sure if we search inside the tree line, we'll find his trail."

Borros folded his arms across his chest and glared at Ferran.

"Give him a chance," Lagash said. "If there is someone out there, we should know it."

And so they spread out and carefully searched. But nobody found any sign, and as they walked back to the camp, Borros said, "I wanted to believe you. But I can't abide liars."

"Sir," Ferran said.

"I can't abide thieves. Food would have been one thing. But you stole money and personal things."

"I promise you," Ferran said.

"You've got ten seconds to get your gear and go."

"Sir," Ferran said. He could not go home empty-handed. It would mean more than slavery. It would mean shame on his mother. His father.

"Ten seconds," Borros said. "And then I will use the horse whip to drive you out."

Ferran looked at Lagash, hoping to find some support, but Lagash only shook his head with disappointment.

Ferran turned to Winwalom who looked dismayed, as if he couldn't believe Ferran had stolen the items.

"One," Borros said.

"I didn't do it!" Ferran said.

"We all saw you," Ranoc said.

"He struck me in the head," Ferran said. "Right here. It's tender. Probably bruised. Can't you see it?"

"The spot where Caswal hit you?" Krov asked.

Ferran's anger rose. "Why would I do this? Think about it. It makes no sense!"

"Two," Borros said. "Caswal, get me the whip."

"With pleasure," Caswal said in smug satisfaction and ran to the wagon.

And Ferran knew there was no way to convince them.

"Three," Borros said, and Ferran ran.

By the time Borros counted five, Ferran had his pack, bag, and cloak.

Borros counted to six.

Ferran fled the camp, away from Caswal who had the horse whip in hand and was flicking it eagerly up and down. Away from Krov and Ranoc and their accusatory glares. Away from the job that promised to make his future so bright. He ran with all the speed he could muster, flying over the ground, his bare feet wet with the morning dew on the weeds and grass, Itch galloping at his side.

A stone zipped past him.

Ferran glanced back. Caswal had his sling out and looked like he'd just slung a stone. Ranoc was placing a stone in his sling's pouch.

They were hurling stones!

He dodged left toward the trees.

15

NEITHER HOG NOR THUNDER

F ERRAN COULD NOT believe this was happening. It was impossible!

He raced for the cover of the trees, and then, out of the corner of his eye, saw movement. He glanced back. Caswal and Ranoc were running after him, Krov not far behind.

Caswal's face radiated with cruelty and anticipation, an expression Ferran had seen before. He knew that if Caswal caught him, he'd be beaten to within an inch of his life, maybe farther. And Itch wouldn't be able to save him because they would whack him with sticks and strike him with stones thrown from their slings until he fled whimpering or fell dead.

Itch barked.

"Run!" Ferran said. "Run!"

And they ran into the trees, over rocks, past brambles and fallen branches. The shouts of the boys diminished, but not because they were falling behind. They were simply saving their breath, focusing on the chase. Ferran knew this because every now and again he heard a "there!" or "that way!"

And they were gaining on him. A branch snagged his browse bag and ripped it out of his hands. He stopped to pick it up, but saw a flash of the boys through the trees and decided to let it lie. It was slowing him down anyway. He shoved his cloak in the space between his back and the pack to free his arms and poured on the speed.

With the consistent meals these last days, his strength and stamina had improved. He figured he might be able to outlast them. That was if he wasn't stupid and didn't run himself into a dead end or twist his ankle or poke his eye out on some hard-to-see finger branch.

He took two strides down a gully, jumped the ferns and small brooklet at the bottom, and scrambled up the other side.

"Dog Boy!" Caswal growled from somewhere in the trees behind.

A chill ran up Ferran's back.

And then he heard a thud some distance off to the right, followed by Ranoc shouting. Ferran angled away from Ranoc.

And then he wondered. Was Ranoc so stupid he'd shout and reveal his position, or was he doing it on purpose, trying to drive Ferran like some deer?

He angled back in the original direction and sprinted past a rotting trunk of a tree that had fallen years ago. He continued along an animal trail where the small branches and leaves whipped him in the face.

His breath was coming hard, and he knew he would have to soon slow his pace and run at a rate he could maintain for longer distances.

And then he broke out into a clearing. On the far side, a cluster of spruce towered toward the sky. And Ferran got an idea. He raced for the spruce.

When he was a few paces away, he glanced back, but none of the boys had reached the clearing yet. In front of him, the spruce trees stood tall and massive. Their lowest boughs covered the ground. He ran past the first tree, and the second, then went around to the back of the third.

"Itch," he called and motioned for him with both arms to come. Itch stopped and ran at him and jumped up in his arms.

"Be a good boy. Be quiet," Ferran said. Then he hitched Itch over one shoulder, pushed his way into the spruce, and began to climb. The branches were like the spokes of a great wagon wheel. And he quickly climbed them like a crazy set of stairs, holding Itch steady on his shoulder with one arm. He rose until he was thirty feet in the air and could see the clearing through the gaps in the branches.

Below him the boys broke out into the clearing, and Ferran froze.

"Which direction?" Krov said.

Itch wiggled a bit and whined.

"Shush," Ferran said softly and moved his left foot to another branch for a wider and more secure stance.

Itch held still.

"Good boy," Ferran whispered into his ear and nuzzled him with his cheek.

"There," Caswal said, pointing at the ground. "Is that his trail through the grass?"

"Clear as day," Krov said.

Ferran leaned a bit to see through one of the gaps in the boughs. His trail would be clear as day through the dew-wet grass. He swallowed.

"Ranoc!" Caswal shouted.

"Ferran's too fast," Krov said. "We're not going to catch him."

"Ranoc!" Caswal shouted again.

"Here!" Ranoc shouted to the left of the field. And then he crashed through some bushes and appeared at the far end of the clearing. "Where is he?"

"That way," Caswal said. "And look at this." He held up a cloak. "He dropped it."

Ferran's heart sank. That couldn't be. He steadied himself and felt for his cloak which he'd stuffed between himself and his pack. But the cloak was gone, and he cursed under his breath.

"Is it filled with fleas?" Ranoc asked and walked over to join the others.

"We should burn it," Caswal said.

"It's perfectly good," Krov said. "You don't want it, I'll take it. I can wash that and sell it in Broniss."

"Maybe I'll sell it," Caswal said.

Krov shrugged.

Ferran looked at Krov with his patch and massive hands and shook his head. Ferran had saved him, and look at how quickly he'd turned. That was gratitude for you.

"I knew it was that sneaking turd," Caswal said. "He lied right to our faces."

"I thought Borros was going to take him apart," Ranoc said. "Did you see his face?"

"He should have cut his hand off," said Caswal. "That would have taught him a lesson he wouldn't soon forget."

"Do you suppose he'll go back to Buckle Hill?" Krov asked.

"You mean if he doesn't get killed or eaten along the way?" Ranoc asked.

"He's not going home," Caswal said. "What's he got back there besides that whore of a mother and sister to take care of? If he goes, he'll be going into bondage. Unless he sends his sister. And that will leave him looking for work. And he might get some, but not for long because then we'll be back. And we'll tell the tale of his thieving. And how he almost lost us our wages and ruined the reputation of all those that vouched for us. And who will employ him then?"

Ferran's spirits sank. Caswal was a pus-filled sore, but he was right. There was nothing back in Buckle Hill but slavery or extreme poverty. He'd be an outcast.

Winwalom appeared at the edge of the clearing behind the other boys. "He's been whistling. He wants us back."

"What do you say about your friend now?" Caswal demanded. "Or were you in on it with him?"

"I wasn't in on nothing," Winwalom said.

"Right," Caswal said, clearly not convinced.

"Ferran won't go back," Ranoc said. "He'll do just like his father did."

Krov scanned the area, including the spruce where Ferran hid. In fact, it seemed like Krov looked directly at him, but then he looked away.

"You three can sit here and jaw," Winwalom said. "But Borros is waiting on us to move the cattle. And now our number's one fewer. Two if you count Itch. We need to get back."

He turned and disappeared back into the woods.

Ranoc brought his hands up to shout. "Run, Dog Boy!" he bellowed, then turned and followed Winwalom.

Krov loaded his sling. Ferran became alarmed. But then Krov simply slung the stone far over the tops of the trees in the general direction

Ferran had run. The stone sailed over the spruce trees. A few moments later it crashed through some distant branches.

"Dog Boy, next time I see you," Caswal shouted, "you're pig's meat. Do you hear me? Dead pig's meat!"

His shout echoed and fell away. And then he and Krov turned and disappeared into the trees where the other boys had gone.

Pig's meat, Ferran thought. And not only that, but dead pig's meat. Well, that was something to look forward to.

Itch wriggled a bit, causing the ache in Ferran's shoulder from his weight to blossom into a full-blown throb, but Ferran didn't move. He quietly shushed Itch and waited.

A bird called. The breeze blew. He suddenly noticed the rough bark of the branch he clung to was digging into his palm. Sap gummed his hand.

Ferran waited. And then something moved in the thick greenery at the edge of the clearing. It was Caswal. He had not followed the other boys, but hidden himself, hoping Ferran would show himself. He stood and scanned the clearing and the trees, including the spruce. But he didn't see Ferran and turned back into the woods.

Ferran still did not move. The throb in his shoulder had grown into true pain, but he waited, counting slowly to three hundred. And when he'd satisfied himself that nobody was there, he shifted Itch to his other shoulder and blew out a huge sigh of relief.

Itch licked his face.

"You were a good boy," Ferran said. "A very good boy. And now we need to get out of this tree."

He found that going down with Itch on his shoulder was harder than climbing up, but he soon neared the bottom. When he was six feet from the ground, he tossed Itch out to land on his feet, then he made his own way down. His hands were sticky with sap, and so he rubbed them in the dirt until most of the stickiness was gone.

He decided it wouldn't be smart to go back for his browse bag just yet. In fact, he didn't know what the smart thing to do would be. And so he sat down, stroking Itch's head and neck and thought about his options.

It angered him that they hadn't listened to him. And the more he thought about it, the angrier he got. Ferran had actually seen the thief. He was an eyewitness. An eyewitness that had almost lost an eye to the brigand when he'd tried to stomp Ferran's face!

But Borros had ignored his report and accepted Caswal's fairy story instead.

Caswal had dripped poison into their ears, and instead of taking it with a grain of salt, they had simply turned their ears up so he could pour in more.

They were dolts. If Ferran had wanted to steal something, he wouldn't have bumbled about in the dark. If he was the big thief they all claimed him to be, he wouldn't have stolen so anyone would notice. Not until the very end.

It rankled him. And then an idea popped into his head. If they wanted a thief, he could show them what real thieving was. He could demonstrate it all the way to Broniss.

By the king's eyes, he could follow them and steal a couple of cows!

If he was going to be accused of theft, he might as well have something to show for it. He could sell the cows on the sly to someone in the surrounding towns outside of Broniss and go home with coin! Maybe enough coin to pay the debt. Or at least get the lord to give them more time.

The idea grew in him.

He'd have to keep his distance. Which meant it would be just him and Itch on their own in the blight. But he figured whatever might be out there would be more interested in a couple hundred cattle than it would be in him.

Or it could be the exact reverse. Wolves like to cut a single animal from the herd. They liked the stragglers. And that's exactly what he'd be —a straggler. An easy picking for all the predators that would be drawn to the scent of so much meat on the hoof.

But there was still a good chance he might make it through anyway. He was canny and sharp. All he'd need to do is keep his wits about him.

Ferran thought about trying to sell the stolen cattle in the area around Broniss. He didn't know the villages or people. If he went from place to place trying to hawk cattle, it would draw the attention of the headmen. Or a true thief. Or a gang that had far more venom in them than he did. They'd beat him and take the cattle for themselves. And it didn't necessarily need to be outlaws. Because if a buyer was willing to purchase stolen cattle, he might be willing to simply take them and tell Ferran to scat or he'd send for the authorities.

What then?

He'd be worse off.

And what if he were caught stealing the cows?

Borros would hang him.

Ferran shrugged. Those were the risks. And showing those fools they were wrong just might be worth it.

But then he thought of his mother and sister. If he was eaten by some abomination in the blight, one of them would go into bondage. If he was hung, it would be the same.

If he only had himself to worry about, he might try to make his own way in the world. He could offer his services to someone in Broniss or some headman of some village somewhere. He could volunteer for ship duty, not that he knew anything about sailing or ships.

But he wasn't on his own. And doing anything like that would leave his mother and sister with the debt and the shame and the pain of knowing their son and brother would rather run than pay the piper. It was cowardly. Craven. And it would only confirm what people said about his father. Like father, like son, they'd say.

What kind of man could live, knowing he'd done that?

Not any Ferran aspired to be.

He thought of his father. A strong man who was always joking. A man who liked to work and tease Ferran's mother. Ferran remembered a time when he was very young and his father had taken him along to fish the river. It had been on a day the lord had granted his tenants leave to take two fish per person. It had been summer. Ferran remembered the shimmering water and the large copper dragonflies that glinted in the afternoon sun as they buzzed about the reeds along the riverbank.

His father had a black eye, and Ferran had asked his father to tell the story of how he'd gotten it again.

The black eye had not come from a fist fight. It had come from a feral hog. A man from Lathan, a village a number of miles away, had helped

Ferran's father with their roof. Father had promised to pay him a barrel of wheat for his services.

The man was poor and needed to make a payment himself, or he'd lose his horse. And so Father had assured him he would deliver the wheat on a certain date. That day had arrived with rain, and Ferran's father had waited, hoping the weather would clear. But instead of clearing, the clouds turned dark as bruises, the wind began to howl and thrash the trees, and then lightning cracked, thunder boomed, and the rain came in sheets.

He waited for the storm to clear until he could wait no longer, and then he set out with the barrel under a hemp tarp on his two-wheeled handcart. Father pushed his way through the mud and thunderbolts. And it had gone well enough, but in the woods between the two villages, he startled a large feral hog that blundered onto the road.

The hog turned on him and tried to make him into mincemeat. His father dodged and yelled. The cart tipped. The barrel fell, and when it struck the ground, the lid popped off. The grain surely would have been eaten by the hog, but his father battled the animal with stick and stone, and the hog finally ran off.

But it was during that battle, on one of the occasions when the hog had charged him, that he'd dodged aside and ran face first into the handle of the cart which stuck up into the sky. It just about knocked him out. That's how he'd gotten his black eye.

On the bank of the river, after his father finished his retelling of the epic tale, Ferran had declared that if it were him, he shouldn't have gone into the woods with lightning and murderous hogs, but waited.

But his father had said that a man was measured by only a few things. And among those things were his courage, his willingness to work hard, and whether he could be relied on. He had given the thatcher his word. And come thunder or hogs, he would keep it.

Ferran smiled ruefully at the memory. He missed his father. And despite what Caswal and others said, Ferran's father had not just run off. There wasn't a bone of unreliability in his body. His disappearance was a mystery and a tragedy. And Ferran wouldn't be shaming his memory.

He sighed. Oh, how he wished he could steal a couple of cattle.

Itch must have sensed his mood, for he looked at Ferran.

But Ferran would not leave his mother and sister to the mercy of the likes of Hellum and the new lord.

"We're going back home, boy," Ferran said. "The whole world will paint me with dishonor. But you and I will know the truth. The little comfort that brings."

Itch wagged his tail.

Ferran sighed again. He had given his word to his mother and sister. And come thunder or korrog, he was going to keep it. Even if it meant bondage.

He stood, then quietly made his way across the clearing. He entered the trees on the other side, scanning and watching the woods as he went. He found his browse bag and thanked his ancestors for that. And then Itch raised his head and looked off into the trees.

"What is it?"

Itch looked a bit longer, then lost interest and began to snuff something at his feet. But Ferran peered through the gaps between the trunks of the trees around him. A bird chirped, and then the wood fell silent.

The blight was just up the road. The circle of bones was even closer.

Ferran suddenly felt as if he were being watched.

"Come on, boy," Ferran said. "Let's get back to the road."

16

CAMPFIRE

THEY FOLLOWED THE road back toward the mouth of the canyon. The hooves of the cattle had churned the turf and broken saplings, leaving a light scar on the land that showed their trail for anyone with eyes.

The woods on either side of the road were dark and deep. And as he walked, he felt more and more alone. More and more exposed out here on this silent road with no company for the two of them but the occasional cow splat buzzing with flies.

He began to imagine what he'd do if a bear popped out of the woods in front of him. Or a pack of wolves. What would he do if the korrog swooped down at him from the sky. Or something else came out of these woods? Something unnatural.

The hairs on the back of his neck prickled. He looked around and saw nothing, but that didn't mean something wasn't there.

"Itch," he said. "You see anything?"

Itch looked at him but continued to pad along as if nothing were there.

Ferran blew a breath out. This was not good. Not good at all. He cursed himself for failing to grab his spear or stone bag, but it had been all he could do to grab his browse bag and pack. Still, he wanted more than his knife and Itch's teeth for protection. He had his sling. And a stone from a sling could send all manner of things packing. And so he scanned the ground for stones as he walked.

He found six passable stones as they walked the miles back to the turnoff. Going by himself on foot allowed him to travel faster than they'd been able to walk with cattle, and he was surprised he made it back to the turnoff by midday.

There was the post with the yellow-painted board with red lettering. And there were the sticks Winwalom had put his fish on, but the fish were gone, and one of the sticks had fallen over. Ferran scanned the sky for the korrog, then went over to investigate. He imagined some animal had eaten the fish, but when he examined the ground about the sticks he found two prints like the ones they'd seen around the cattle the korrog had eaten.

So the korrog had eaten Winwalom's offering afterall. Of course that didn't mean the beast could be tamed, only that it was willing to eat free food.

With the thought of food, Ferran's stomach rumbled. He was hungry. Very hungry.

He scanned the skies again. There was no korrog to be seen. There wasn't anything here but birds in the trees and some butterflies flitting across the meadow. Ferran decided he had time enough to make a stop and find some food.

Despite the fear that the stream might be tainted with some evil from the blight, he walked over to the stone fish weir he and Winwalom had made. It was still there, but there were no fish in it. He'd expected he'd have a rough time driving them in all by himself. But he was willing to try. However, after an hour and almost a dozen fruitless attempts, he sighed and wondered if he needed to try a different method. And then he looked to the west.

Dark storm clouds had been brewing in the distance. They were now blacker and larger, much larger. The storm was growing. "That's not good," he said to Itch.

The rain would swell the stream and render the fish weir useless. In fact, the water was already higher than when he had started.

Ferran sighed again and decided fish were not going to be on the

JOHN D. BROWN

menu. He climbed out of the stream and looked around for something else to eat.

A stand of cattails grew a little farther downstream. His spirits rose. Cattails weren't buttercream, but they were better than nothing. In the spring, you could peel and eat the white bottoms of the plants. In early summer, the shoots that grew into the brown heads were still green and tender and could be eaten raw. Later, when the pollen appeared, you could take it and add it to a pottage. The roots were good too. More than once, Ferran's mother had pounded them to flour and made ash cakes.

He rushed over to the plants. It was late summer, but it was sometimes possible to find a straggler that had just begun to grow. He stepped out into the water and searched through the stalks, but there were no young plants. No tender green heads. And so he began to pull up plants. He could harvest the bottoms and roots.

He tossed a number up onto the bank. Itch recognized the plants and began to gnaw on a root. And then Ferran noticed a dead and decaying fawn hidden in the stalks. Half its body was out of the water, half of it in. It was still covered in patches of fur although something had eaten the skin around the head and had exposed the teeth alongside one jaw.

Ferran dropped the cattail he held in his hand. Cattails were good for food, but not when they'd been polluted with rot and disease. He stepped out of the stalks.

Ferran's stomach growled. "The king's stinking feet!" he cursed.

He looked at the storm heading his way. What Ferran needed to do was make a proper camp while it was still light, then look for food, but he didn't feel safe here. He wanted to put as many miles between him and the blight as he could. And so he decided he'd look for animals and birds he might hit with his sling as he traveled the road. In fact, if he was quick, he might be able to keep ahead of the storm all the way back to Pencoy's lands.

He set out. He killed one hare and fed it to Itch. He tried to hit a few birds for himself, but the stones he'd found weren't the best shape, and they flew off the mark. However, by that time a dark wall of rain was approaching.

He looked around to find some shelter and thought he could make a patch of trees about a mile ahead. He ran, but the wind and rain blew in with a gust and the rain caught him as he reached the trees. By the time he and Itch took cover under a fat oak, he was drenched. And then the clouds blotted out the sun, and the temperature dropped. Now was when he needed his cloak, but he made do with his browse bag.

The storm thundered. Lighting cracked. The rain turned into a flood. And Ferran sat on the fat exposed root of the oak with Itch at his side, the two of them wrapped with the thick browse bag that became more and more sodden with each passing minute. They squatted there for a few hours as the dark heavens turned the earth to mud. And then the rain lessened until it stopped, and all that dripped was the water running off the leaves of the trees and plopping about him.

The sun hadn't set yet, but everything was soaked. And night was coming. The temperature would drop even further. He needed a fire. He also needed food.

Thunder boomed in the direction the storm had gone, and he knew that he also needed a better shelter. One that was out of the wind. So he got up and scouted around and found a spot behind a large boulder that was shielded from the wind, and he and Itch huddled there, tired, thirsty, hungry, and cold.

At some point he nodded off. He woke freezing to a sky full of stars and a slip of moon. The clouds still covered the sky far to the west, but here it was clear and cold. In fact, it was the cold that had awakened him. He tried to get comfortable, but he was still damp. Itch whined, then licked his face.

"I'm sorry boy," he said. "I've got nothing."

But he couldn't just sit there. He'd freeze to death. They needed some fire. So he opened his browse bag and, here and there, found bits and pieces of the grass that were still dry. So he had tinder. But tinder wouldn't last more than a few seconds. He needed kindling and larger sticks.

He stood and looked about. Down the gentle slope below this thicket of trees lay the road, a gray ribbon in the weak moonlight. He walked toward it, looking for branches on the leeward side of the trees that might still be dry. He didn't expect to find any dry spots after such a flood, but then he spotted a big pine standing tall and dark against the sky a hundred yards or so up the road. If it was thick enough, the outer branches would have shed the water, leaving dry needles at the base. Maybe smaller twigs.

So he walked up the road, Itch at his side, the cold, squishy earth clinging to his bare feet and smushing between his toes. When he came to the pine, he pushed into the leeward side and did indeed find bark and twigs and needles that seemed to be dry enough and brought them out and put them in a pile on a rock. And then he saw in the moonlight the naked trunk and limbs of a large tree that must have fallen months before the storm had come through.

Ferran's spirits rose for there was a whole tree's worth of seasoned wood. He turned his attentions there and found a number of branches that were small enough for him to break, yet thick enough to have dry wood inside. He broke one off with a loud pop and crack. Then broke another. He laid the first at an angle against the trunk and broke it. Sure enough, the wood inside was dry. So he searched about for a hard stick to use as a baton so he could begin splitting the branches to get the dry parts inside, but then he caught a faint whiff of wood smoke.

He stopped. Sniffed again. It was definitely wood smoke, which meant there were other travelers up the road who had been caught in the storm. Other travelers with a fire.

His hopes rose. He could offer work for food and fire. He began to salivate at the thought of stew or porridge or squirrels sizzling over a fire. But then he felt a warning.

They might be friendly. But they just as easily might not be, in which case he did not want to attract their attention with the sound that would carry as he split wood with a baton and knife in the night. Nor did he want to accidentally give away his presence with the light of a fire.

But he and Itch were wet and freezing. Were they supposed to simply shiver themselves to death?

He needed to know if he was in danger. And that meant he'd have to get closer.

17

TRAVELERS

F ERRAN FOLLOWED THE smell of the wood smoke, carefully picking his way forward with his bare feet, staying to the darkness under the trees. He kept the soft, moonlit ribbon of road in view to his left. The scent of the fire at first came and went with the wind, but soon it was constant. And he smelled food.

Itch knew they were sneaking. They'd done it often enough, but Ferran softly reminded him to keep quiet. They continued to move forward, and not long after that, a glimmer of a camp fire appeared through the trees. Itch saw it as well and stood alert, but Ferran gave him a pet and shushed him. Itch was a smart dog and well trained, and as they moved forward he kept quiet. And so they continued to creep forward until Ferran was close enough to see the camp.

There were three men by the fire. A big bearded one, a bald one, and another older one with curly, but graying hair. Beyond the fire was a makeshift tent set up under a the limbs of a big tree on what looked like a bit of dry ground. Under another large tree stood five horses that had been hobbled. Five saddles and blankets had been stacked close to the trunk of that tree to keep them dry.

Ferran carefully picked his way forward a few more steps in the darkness so he could see better and squatted in the deep shadow of a large rock.

The fire crackled. The light of the flames danced on the faces of the three men. The older one with graying hair tended a black frying pan sitting on some rocks at the edge of the fire. Meat was sizzling there, and Ferran's hunger flared. It had been almost two days since he'd eaten.

The bearded man and the bald man were each holding wooden cups, drinking something warm.

"When are those going to be done?" the bald one asked. He had an accent from the coast.

"Aren't you supposed to be on watch?" the gray hair said.

"In this kind of weather?"

"Make sure mine is good and crispy," the one with the big beard said. He sounded like he was from way up north.

The fire popped. The smell of frying sausage wafted over to Ferran, and his mouth began to water.

Ferran longed for just a bite. Itch must have smelled them as well, for he keened just a bit and looked up at Ferran, but Ferran quietly shushed him. Five saddles meant five men. Although, maybe they were cycling through the mounts for speed, so it could be three men with two extra horses, but then he caught the snoring of someone in the tent. So it was at least four.

He scanned the camp again. Standing up against another tree trunk were spears. And two shields. So these weren't simple travelers, but someone's men. They didn't wear the colors of Osson, but they weren't wearing the livery of any lord either. Of course, only a lord's personal men would wear that.

And then a thought popped into his head—they could be Pencoy's men, come to fetch Borros back to take the coast road. If so, that meant they were friendly. And if that were the case, then Ferran could surely earn some of that sausage for him and Itch. He began to think of how to approach them.

"Here you go," Gray Hair said and skewered two links of sausage with a knife. He held them out to the bald one who slid them off the knife and quickly set them in his cup because of the heat.

The bald one took a bite, then said, "Tomorrow's going to be our day.

And then it won't be old sausage, but fresh beef liver, and onions, and beer, and a lass upon my lap."

"Unless he gets you first," the big bearded one said. "Like the last time."

"You're one to talk," Baldy said.

"Let's just pray the storms stay away," Gray Hair said. "I've had my fill of freezing my loaf off."

Ferran paused. These did not sound like men going to fetch Borros. It sounded like men going after someone. There weren't any official badges, hats, armbands, or markings of any kind in sight, and Ferran began to get a bad feeling.

Baldy took another bite of hot sausage. "I'm going to gut him," he said.

And that decided it for Ferran. Whatever business these men were up to, it was not anything he wanted to be involved with. He'd gone hungry before. He'd gone six days once. And he didn't recommend it to anyone, but he could do it again if he had to.

He turned quietly to Itch, put his finger to his lips. "Shush," he said in the softest of whispers, then pointed back the way they'd come. Itch looked at him, looked at the fire.

Ferran pointed again, and Itch relented.

And at that moment, a tickling irritation formed in Ferran's left nostril. It built suddenly and he felt a sneeze coming on. He closed off his traitor nostril with one finger, but the compulsion was building, and before he could pinch his nose shut, he sneezed. It was a big one. Followed by a quick second.

The men all looked over in his direction.

"That should move things along," Gray Hair said.

The others laughed.

"How long are you going to be squatting out there?" the bald one asked.

Ferran froze. Had they somehow seen him?

Behind Ferran a man spoke out. "I've been finished for a while. Been enjoying watching the three of you being spied upon."

"Spied upon?" the big one said.

"Oh yes, indeed," the man said.

Ferran turned. Behind him a few paces was the silhouette of a man. Itch growled.

But the man said, "Come on, boy. No use standing out in the cold. There's place by the fire."

Ferran's pulse quickened. If he was going to run, now was the moment.

The man approached. "Come on," he said all friendly. "Tonight's not a night to be wandering around. Share the fire with us."

And then Gray Hair picked up a loaded crossbow, and Ferran knew his moment had passed. If he ran, Gray Hair might shoot. There was a good chance he'd miss. But there was also the possibility he wouldn't. Ferran stood.

"Have we got an extra link for a boy and his dog?" the man asked.

"Maybe," Gray Hair said.

"Put it on," the man said and walked up to Ferran. He held a drawn sword in his hand. He wasn't holding it in any menacing way, but Ferran knew that could change in the blink of an eye.

"We're not going to bite. Come on," the man said and motioned for Ferran to move to the camp fire. And then he stepped out of the shadows and into the firelight. He had a big friendly grin on his face. His eyes were outlined in the Southern style with kohl. "You know it's not polite to spy."

"I didn't want to intrude."

"That was very considerate. So let us repay you with a cup of hot broth and some sausage. You're wet and look like you're nearly frozen to death."

There was such warmth in the man's voice that Ferran's alarm backed off a little. Ferran was freezing. And hungry.

"We don't need to stay long," Ferran said. "Just enough to warm up a bit maybe."

"Of course," the man said. "The rule of the road: be nice to fellow travelers, and your courtesy will come back tenfold." He motioned with an open arm at the camp.

Ferran could warm up and then go. He didn't have to stay long. "Thank you," he said and turned toward the camp. He threaded his way between the bushes and out to the fire.

"A little broth for our friend," the man said generously. "And a little sausage." He walked over to the pan and poked one with his knife, then held it out for Ferran to take.

The big bearded man scowled. There had only been two sausages in the pan. This one must have been his.

"That's okay," Ferran said. "The broth will be more than enough."

"You don't like our food?" the kohl-eyed man asked.

It was rude to refuse food freely offered. "I," Ferran said. "Well, thank you." And he took the nice crispy sausage off the knife. It was hot, and he danced it a bit in his hands, then broke off half and set it on the ground for Itch. Itch gulped it down in two bites.

Big Beard's scowl deepened.

Gray Hair spooned some broth from a pot sitting on the ground into a wooden cup and handed it to Ferran. It smelled delicious. Ferran took it and had a sip. It was a fine bone broth. And the heat from the fire was lovely. He stretched his cold, wet, legs toward the ring of rocks round the fire and felt the warmth seep into his feet like a blessing.

"So," Kohl-eye said. "What brings you out on a stormy night?"

Ferran took another sip of broth and felt a warning about telling the truth. So he said, "I'm going to visit a cousin to help with the harvest."

Gray Hair nodded. "Many hands make light work."

"Aye," Kohl-eye said. "We ourselves are going to visit some old friends." He looked at his companions. "Good friends, wouldn't you say?"

The bald one smiled. "The best of chums from way back."

Ferran nodded and smiled politely, knowing they'd been talking about gutting the person they were going to visit tomorrow. Something was off here. He didn't know what it was. But it was off, and he knew he'd made a mistake in not running.

"And where is this cousin?" Gray Hair asked.

"Pencoy's," Ferran said.

"Pencoy's," Kohl-eye said warmly and looked over at Baldy. They grinned at each other, and some communication passed between them that made Ferran think he'd said something wrong.

"What were you going to harvest at Pencoy's?" Kohl-eye asked.

"Barley," he said.

"Of course," he said. "I'm sure the fields are white with it."

"Probably," Ferran said.

Baldy grinned as if Ferran had made some joke. Something was wrong.

"I know you from somewhere," Big Beard said. "Have we met?"

Ferran had never seen the man. "I don't think so." And he decided the best way out of this was to eat the sausage, drink the broth, and then take his leave.

"No, I never forget a face. We've met."

"I couldn't say where," Ferran replied.

Big Beard looked down, thinking. And then Kohl-eye removed his gloves to warm his hands by the fire. In the bit of flesh between his thumb and forefinger was a tattoo. A little loop and two dots. It jarred Ferran. He had seen that only one time before.

It had been on the road to Cor's Village earlier this year. Him and his wheelbarrow and barrel with barley in the bottom of it. He'd been going with all the money his family had to buy used cheese vessels from a kindly widow. Four men had robbed him. Ferran hadn't been able to see their faces because they had worn grain sacks with slits cut for eyes. But he had seen the leader's hand. And seen it up close. He'd seen that exact tattoo, right in the flesh between this thumb and forefinger.

"What is that tattoo?" Ferran asked.

Kohl-eyes looked down at it. "The mark of a society of do-gooders."

Baldy snorted a laugh.

An alarm began to sound in Ferran's mind.

"I've got it," Big Beard said and looked up with satisfaction. "I knew I'd remember." He pointed at Ferran. "Boy and dog."

"Your mind's blazing tonight," Gray Hair said. "That is indeed a boy and dog we have as guests. Well done." He rolled his eyes at Big Beard.

Robbers, Ferran decided. He'd just landed amidst robbers. Surely they were fellows to the whoresons that had robbed him. But he knew he couldn't let them know that. He had to play the role he'd taken. And so he leaned in conspiratorially and said, "Been at the grog, has he?"

Gray Hair grinned. "Not grog." He mimicked grabbing at flies in front of his face. "He was hit in the head a couple of weeks ago. Hasn't been right since."

Big Beard ignored them and looked over at Kohl-eye. "That farmer. It's the boy."

Kohl-eye appraised Ferran again, then broke out into a wide smile. "Well, I'll be smoked. Where did you say you were from again?"

Ferran took a big sip of the broth, trying to calm his fear. "I'm from Green Hollow. A good jog up the road, and then into some hilly country."

"Smooth," Kohl-eye said. "Isn't he boys? Didn't miss a beat."

Ferran had no idea what he was referring to, but he knew that now was the time to leave. He casually plopped the rest of the sausage into his mouth and stood. "All this warmth has finally got the body working. Where are the jacks?"

Kohl-eye said, "Stay a bit."

Ferran said, "I'll be right back."

Kohl-eye raised his sword and pointed it at Ferran. "Please stay. We're having such a fine conversation."

Itch began to growl.

"And quiet that dog," Big Beard said.

"I'll be just a moment," Ferran said and took a step back.

"Bootstrap," Kohl-eye said.

It appeared that was Gray Hair's nickname, for he picked up his crossbow.

"The king's feet," Ferran said. "I just need to use the jacks."

"You can stop the act," Kohl-eye said and stood, his sword tip still pointing at Ferran.

"I'm not lying."

"Pencoy's barley has already been harvested," Kohl-eye said. "And you're not from any Green Hollow. You're that snot-nosed kid from Buckle Hill. And you're out here with the drover. Or were." He waved the sword tip at Ferran. "Did he send you to spy on us?"

Ferran looked at the crossbow. It was loaded, and if the man was any good at all with it, he'd send and arrow straight through Ferran before he could run four steps. "The drover didn't send me." Ferran said.

"He's lying," Big Beard said.

Ferran knew he couldn't show any weakness. He needed to bluff them. Act brave. He rolled his eyes. "The drover cut me loose," he explained. "Sent the others to chase me off."

"Another good story," Big Beard said.

"But true," Ferran said.

"Well," Kohl-eye said. "We'll soon find out." He motioned at the others. "Grab him."

18

PRISONER

GRAY HAIR RAISED his crossbow and pointed it at Ferran, his finger on the trigger.

Ferran had a bow drawn on him only once before, and it was not a good feeling. He held both hands up. "Put that down."

Big Beard approached with a rope, but Itch barked, then snapped at him, making him jump back. "Rotted dog," he said. "Shoot that thing."

Gray Hair turned the crossbow on Itch.

"No!" Ferran cried and stepped between Itch and the crossbow. "Good grief, has one scrawny boy got you all so worried? You'd think I was Karnock the Bloody. Just calm down."

"Then get your dog under control," Kohl-eye said.

"Itch," Ferran commanded. "Sit!"

Itch barked again.

"Sit!"

Itch sat.

"Give me a cord," Ferran said, "and I'll tie him up."

Big Beard tossed him a rope. Ferran caught it, then looped one end around Itch's neck and tied a bowline knot. Then he grabbed the leash by the neck and said, "I'll tie him up to that tree. Everyone just keep calm."

"Watch him," Kohl-eye said, and Gray Hair and Big Beard followed Ferran to the tree. There had to be a way to make a break for the trees, but the crossbow was pointed right at his back. He couldn't see any way to run without getting shot.

Ferran tied Itch to the tree, his mind racing.

"Okay, now back to the fire," Gray Hair said.

Itch began to bark again.

"Shush," Ferran ordered. He had to get out of here. His whole body was screaming for him to run, but now was not the time to run. Now was the time to set them at their ease. Win a little trust. And so he returned to the fire.

"Put this around your neck," Kohl-eye said and tossed Ferran the end of another rope that had a loop tied with a slip knot on it. Ferran did not like the choice of the slip knot, and said, "Let me fix this."

"Put it on," Kohl-eye ordered.

Ferran sighed and pulled the loop over his head. "I hope you all feel safer now."

"Don't get smart," Big Beard threatened.

Kohl-eye tossed the other end of the rope to Baldy, then walked up to Ferran. "Why were you spying on us?"

"Because he fired me. And I lost my cloak when they chased me. And I was wet and freezing. And I was hoping for some friendly warmth, but you can't always be sure who is on the road."

Kohl-eye slapped him hard.

The blow almost knocked Ferran to his knees. Tears sprang to his eyes, but he stood straight again. "It's the truth."

Kohl-eye struck Ferran in the gut. It was a hard blow, like someone had rammed him with a post. He oofed and doubled over. This time Ferran did lose his balance and fell to one knee. A sharp pain cut him where he'd been hit, and he sucked in his breath.

"He send you back for Pencoy's men?" Kohl-eye asked.

"No," Ferran gasped.

Kohl-eye grabbed a handful of Ferran's hair and yanked him toward the fire.

Ferran stumbled forward on his hands and knees.

"I think a little heat will illuminate the situation."

"No!" Ferran cried and tried to struggle free, but Baldy gave a tug on the rope tightening the noose around Ferran's neck. Ferran began to choke and grasped the noose with both hands and succeeded in loosening it just enough to breathe.

But Kohl-eye still had a hold of Ferran's hair and forced his face closer to the flames.

Ferran dug the palms of his hands in the earth and resisted. "Please," he said.

Kohl-eye pulled Ferran back, then took him in a one-armed headlock, and pulled a burning stick out of the fire. "I don't have to poke your eye out to blind you. All I need to do is hold the hot end right in front of the eye. The heat will cook it. Now tell me the truth."

Fear coursed through Ferran. Kohl-eye had Ferran in an iron grip. Ferran could go for the man's eyes. Dig them out. He was close enough. But as soon as Kohl-eye released him, Baldy would yank the rope and choke him. And Ferran might then fly at Baldy, but the other two would be on him.

Ferran decided fighting wasn't an option. If he told them what they thought was true, they'd beat him. Probably kill him. If he defied them, they'd beat him more.

"Have it your way," Kohl-eye said and brought the white-hot end of the stick toward Ferran's eye.

"No," Ferran said and realized exactly what he needed to do. "No. He fired me!" Ferran cried and began to blubber. "For stealing a cheese and knife and food."

Kohl-eye brought the hot end closer and closer.

Ferran shrieked, putting as much terror in his voice as he could. "Please! He said he can't abide thieves and liars."

Kohl-eye continued. Back by the tree, Itch was lunging at the end of his rope and barking.

"I stole from him!" Ferran wailed. "I stole! Please!"

"Gaw," Big Beard exclaimed. "He's going to wake half the district."

Tears were rolling down Ferran's face. And some of them were real.

Kohl-eye halted a few inches from Ferran's eye, and then he drove the burning end of the stick into Ferran's forehead, sizzling Ferran's skin.

Ferran wrenched back and cried out in pain.

"What did you steal?" Kohl-eye asked.

"There was a cheese and the cook's knife with the silver inlaid fox and three onions and some barley and a few of the sweet things. And I shouldn't have done it. But the temptation was overpowering. I'd been so long without food."

Kohl-eye looked at the other men for their assessment.

Gray Hair nodded. Baldy shrugged.

Kohl-eye released Ferran and tossed the stick back into the fire. And then he smiled like nothing had just happened. "So that whoreson caught you stealing, did he?"

Ferran sat back from the fire, the burned spot on his forehead throbbing with pain. He licked his fingers and put the spit to the burn in his forehead trying to cool it. "He caught me holding the king's cursed cheese," he said.

"Doesn't sound like you're a very good thief," Big Beard said.

Ferran shrugged.

A plotting grin broke over Kohl-eye's face. "You want to get back at him?"

"I'd prefer to steer clear," Ferran said.

"Come on, now," Kohl-eye said. "That's no way to talk. You could join us. What do you think about that? Fellow thieves."

Baldy cracked a smile.

"What are you talking about?" Ferran asked.

"He stole from us. We're going to take his cattle as recompense."

"The four of you?"

Kohl-eye grinned. "Four, plus Wilty Bottom there sleeping in the tent, plus twenty or so others. When the time comes, we'll have a right proper band of men. More than enough to deal with that whoreson and his cook."

Ferran suspected something about these four and said, "He sure has a lot of enemies."

"Oh?"

"You're not the only ones wanting to making things square. He came to our village without a crew. Said his had run out on him. Said they poisoned his dogs."

Kohl-eye and Baldy shared an amused glance.

"Poisoned his dogs?" Kohl-eye asked. "Who would do such a thing?"

Ferran shrugged.

"I think I heard about that crew," Kohl-eye said. He turned to Baldy. "Weren't they the ones taken to prison by the magistrate?"

"Marched right in by a bunch of angry fools," Baldy said.

"And then they were broken out," Kohl-eye said. "I hear the people of Mossby paid dearly for their part in it."

Ferran nodded. He was almost certain these were those men, and he decided to play up his woes. "He should have fed us more. I was only trying to get the food that was my due."

"Of course you were," said Kohl-eye. "If a man hires you, he's got to feed you. How can he expect you to run about all day chasing his cattle without the proper nourishment? He did you wrong. Then robbed you of your pay. So join us. You can't let people get away with such things."

Ferran nodded his head, acting like his indignation was rising. "Would I get a share?"

"A share? Of what?"

Ferran shrugged, then wiped his nose. "If I helped. Would I get a share of the take?"

Kohl-eye barked a laugh. "Oh, spoken like a true blackheart. You want justice and a little more, do you?" He looked at the other men. "What do you say, boys? Should we bring him in?"

Big Beard rolled his eyes, but Baldy and Gray Hair seemed game.

"There you go," Kohl-eye said. "You're now a part of the band."

"What would my share be?"

"Oh, you'll get a fair percentage. All that's due to you , plus more. Have no doubt."

These were the men who had tried to kill Borros. The men who had poisoned his dogs. Ferran knew they had no intention of bringing him in. They would kill him with all the others. But they'd probably want some sport before that, so they'd order him to do something dangerous and stupid for their amusement, and if he died, they'd laugh, and if he survived it, they'd kill him. Or set him another similar task. Ferran's throat went dry, but he smiled and acted hopeful.

"I can't wait," he said.

Kohl-eye grinned even wider, enjoying his own joke.

"Can I take this noose off?" Ferran asked.

"Sure, tomorrow. Tonight, you'll earn our trust by staying tied up and not trying to escape."

Ferran put on as willing a face as he could. "Okay," he said.

They bound his hands behind his back, then tied him and Itch up to a tree at the far end of the camp away from the road. Every now and again, the breeze would shift and carry some of the warmth of the fire his way, but most of the time it did not, and the cold air on his wet clothes chilled him. He began to wonder if the bit about another twenty men was a lie, but then a sixth man rode up the muddy, moonlit road and turned into the camp.

He wore a thick cloak with fur trimmed edges and rode a well-cut roan mare. He dismounted and tied the reins to a low branch so she could get at the grass. "He wants to know how close the drover is."

Ferran figured whoever had sent the rider must be the leader of this band of outlaws.

"Here have something warm," Gray Hair said and held a cup out to the man.

The rider took the cup and noticed Ferran and Itch. "Who's that?"

"A recruit," Kohl-eye said with a grin. "Says the drover cut him loose for stealing food that was his due."

The rider grunted and blew on his drink. "Where is he?"

Kohl-eye said, "The idiot whoreson has gone up the old road to Broniss."

The rider's eyes widened in disblief. "Toward the blight?"

Kohl-eye nodded. "I told you he was a fool."

"How far ahead?"

"Oh, about three or four hours at a good trot. If we set out early we can reach him before he actually enters the forbidden land."

Ferran figured that was about right. He'd traveled himself about ten to twelve miles yesterday coming back from their camp. Borros and the others would have traveled another ten along the trail in the opposite direction, which meant they were a good twenty miles ahead.

"Is he watching his back?"

Kohl-eye said, "Not that we've seen. He scouts ahead. The rest just follow. They've got nothing more than a wagon with a korrog on it bringing up the rear."

"That beast is something I want to see," the rider said. "They said it was bigger than the creature back at Pencoy's."

"It's bound to be a spectacle."

The rider nodded, blew on his drink again to cool it, and took a sip.

"How many?" the rider asked.

Kohl-eye turned to Ferran. "How many men with the drover?"

Ferran couldn't believe he was here, chatting with a bunch of killers. "One man and four boys," he said.

Kohl-eye turned back to the rider. "See? Easy pickings."

"Plus," Gray Hair said, "the fool's provided the perfect coverup. Everyone will simply think the blight took them."

Up to this point, Ferran had held out a small glimmer of hope that these men weren't as bad as they seemed, but that last comment snuffed the glimmer out. These men were going to slaughter the whole crew.

Winwalom and Lagash did not deserve that. And while the others were idiots and couldn't see beyond their own noses, they didn't deserve to be murdered either. Not even Caswal.

The rider blew on his drink and nursed a few more sips, then drained his cup and stood. "I'd best be going," he said and handed the cup back to Gray Hair. "He wants to start early. So be up and ready."

"We wouldn't miss it for the world," Kohl-eye said.

They would if Ferran could help it. There was no way Ferran was going to let Winwalom be murdered in cold blood. But he couldn't stop this crew, much less another of twenty men. However, he could warn the others.

Which meant Ferran wasn't going to sit here with this lot of murderous goat dribbles. He was going to have to make the trek back tonight. Alone. Just him and Itch. In the dark.

Of course that would only happen if he could free himself and Itch from their knots. And that had to happen quickly, or he wouldn't have the time to get to the others before these puss-eating maggots did.

19

———

SHADOWS

A S SOON AS the rider left, Kohl-eye went over to some saddle bags he'd hung from a branch and pulled out a wine skin.

"We're going to be rich men," he said, removing the stopper and taking a drink.

"Let's have some of that here," Big Beard said.

Kohl-eye wiped his mouth and handed it over. They passed the skin around a couple of times, and Ferran's hopes began to rise. Maybe they'd all get so drunk he could simply walk out. But these killers were more prudent than that, for after the third round, Kohl-eye said, "We'll save the rest for when we actually have the cattle in hand."

Big Beard stretched and yawned, which set all of the rest of them yawning. And then he rose and went to the tent. Baldy followed him. And that left Gray Hair and Kohl-eye who sat by the fire talking about the merits of the grogs from different towns around the kingdom.

Ferran tried to wriggle out of the knots around his wrists, but they were too tight. And they were too tight to pick apart as well. And then he saw the sharp nub of a branch on the tree. He had been squatting on a log. He now stood so he could stand in front of that nub, his bound wrists behind his back.

Gray Hair noticed the movement and looked over at him.

"How long have I got to stay tied up?" Ferran asked.

"Oh, a good while yet," Kohl-eye said with a smile. "You aren't anywhere close."

Ferran said, "And you promise I'll get my fair share?"

"Fair and square," Kohl-eye said. "Now shut up. People are trying to sleep."

Ferran hung his head a bit as if chastened and began to force the sharp point of the branch into the knot. At first the knot resisted, but then he found a weakness and the point slipped in. Ferran carefully pulled and worked at it, watching the two men at the fire.

He imagined these killers sticking Caswal with a spear, not a mortal wound, but a nice stab. It would be a nice little bit of justice. But then he imagined Winwalom receiving the same fate. And Ranoc. And Lagash. And suddenly it didn't seem like such a good idea.

As he worked, he realized that he was indeed a thief. He had stolen many things in his life. He'd stolen eggs just a few weeks ago. He'd stolen mushrooms and game from the lord's land, and Krov only hated Ferran because it was Krov's family's job to protect those lands.

If he were in the other boys' position, it would be easy to believe Ferran had stolen the items. Even though it made not one lick of sense.

Plus, he thought indignantly, every one of those boys had stolen things as well. Except maybe Winwalom, so they weren't pure little babes. It was just that he seemed to steal more often.

He sighed. And the knot suddenly loosened enough for him to remove his hands. His ice cold hands.

There was a strong breeze blowing. It had chilled him in his wet clothes. His bare feet were hurting from the cold as well, but he figured now was the time. Every minute he delayed put the others closer to danger.

The breeze shifted a bit, blowing the smoke of the fire into the face of the men. They moved out of the smoke and sat down on the logs Big Beard and Baldy had been sitting on. The ones that faced Ferran.

Kohl-eye looked at Ferran and muttered something to Gray Hair. The two men laughed and looked at Ferran.

Ferran had to loosen the noose around his neck, get it off his head, pull the end of the bowline he'd tied for Itch, and then run. And he had to do all of that before Gray Hair could get off a shot with his crossbow. Ferran didn't think he could do it. Not with them looking this way. And not standing up. And so he sat back down on a rock and waited for the smoke to change directions.

He waited, but it didn't change, and so he prayed to his ancestors. But they must not have been listening because the breeze continued to blow in the same direction. And so he mumbled a quiet prayer to whatever god or demon might rule this neck of the woods, promising he'd return with a gift in exchange for some help.

A few moments later the breeze changed directions and blew in the men's faces. They moved. Not so their backs were completely to Ferran, but at least they weren't looking directly at him. Kohl-eye reached into his trousers and began scratching his leg. Gray Hair took out a knife and began whittling at a stick.

Ferran thanked the forest god, figuring now was the time.

He didn't want to attract their attention, and sharp moves would do that, so he slowly brought his hands up to his neck. He grabbed the noose and began to pull.

And it was then that Gray Hair glanced over at him. He looked down at Ferran's hands, then back at his face.

Ferran yanked the noose wide and ripped it off his head.

"King's rot!" Gray Hair cursed and went for his bow.

Ferran's heart was racing. He grabbed the knot around Itch's neck, fumbled with the end, then finally yanked it loose.

"Stop!" Kohl-eye commanded.

But Ferran bolted for the dark night-shadows of the trees, and he wasn't going to stop. Not for all the puddings and pastries in the king's high court. Except he couldn't bolt because standing there in the cold had made his legs and feet as stiff as boards, and so he executed a fast lurch instead, Itch trailing behind.

Kohl-eye rose. "You little snot."

Ferran sped up his lurch, awkwardly leapt a branch and figured if the shot was going to come, it was going to come now, and so he reeled to the right.

The bow thwacked. The bolt sped past Ferran, and he slipped into the dark shadows.

"Bloody rot!" Kohl-eye said. "Get up!" he shouted to the others. "The little whoreson is loose! Get up!"

Ferran's limbs began to warm up and loosen, and he ran farther into the darkness of the woods, picking up speed. Behind him, the men were shouting and coming after him, crashing through the brush. If they caught him, they'd beat him, probably kill him. And so he ran with abandon, getting whipped by branches, and having to hold his hand up in front of himself so he didn't poke an eye out.

What a day I'm having, he thought. Running twice to save his skin.

When he'd sprinted for as far as he could, he realized he was running toward the mountain, away from the road. That was good. But he knew the noise he was making only gave them a target to run after, and so he began to pick his way more carefully and listen.

He could hear the men behind him. One was close. Ferran figured he was only maybe thirty feet away, nothing but the darkness and a few tree trunks between them.

"Can you smell that?" the man whispered and sniffed. "Wet dog."

Another man sniffed.

Ferran looked down at Itch.

Itch barked.

Well-trained, but not perfectly-trained. Ferran cursed.

"There!" the man shouted and surged through the brush toward them.

Ferran took off again, running for his life, the men charging after him. But now he had a plan. He ran eastward, in the direction of Pencoy's and the coast, away from the old road to Broniss. He ran until he came to something of a clearing, which was perfect. He streaked right across the middle of it, the moonlight shining down on him, wanting the men to see him. He ran right to the other side and slipped back into the dark shadows of the trees. A few paces father into the trees, he ducked down, turned off the line he'd been running, and crept through the bushes in a circle back to the dark edge of the clearing.

By the time he was set, Kohl-eye and Baldy were already halfway across the moonlit clearing. Ferran felt around on the ground, but there wasn't a stone or branch to throw. Instead, his hand wrapped around tall weed grass. He quietly grasped a number of the stalks and tugged. The root ball came free with a good quantity of wet earth, a rough ball the size of a small cheese. Ferran cocked his arm and tossed the root ball and weed in the direction he'd been running.

The weed ball flew for a bit, broke a branch with a good crack, and landed with a rustle in some brush.

There was a pause.

"That way!" Baldy cried, and they stormed into the trees. They ran past Ferran and Itch. A moment later a man Ferran didn't recognize broke into the clearing. That must have been the one sleeping in the tent. He heard the others, but walked for a bit, listening. And then ran at an angle to where the other two had run, obviously hoping the other two would chase Ferran into him. He disappeared into the trees at the far end of the clearing.

Ferran could hear the other men. They didn't run through the clearing, but moved through the trees. When they'd moved a little west of his position, Ferran reminded Itch to keep quiet and began to carefully pick his way through the dark shadows in the opposite direction, back toward the old road.

20

NIGHT WALK

I T TOOK FERRAN the better part of an hour to get past the camp site, but even then he wasn't in the clear, for while he was sneaking his way back, the men returned, angry and grumbling. Ferran had made sure to skirt the camp site, but he was close enough that if he made one sound, they'd hear it and be back in the woods after him.

"Idiot," Big Beard said. "We should have just killed him straight off. But you had to play your games."

"He might have had useful information," Kohl-eye said.

"Offa's going to rip your guts out," another said. "If that boy brings Pencoy—"

"Pencoy's down the coast," Kohl-eye said. "And that boy isn't going to say a word because he knows we know where he's from. We know his mum." He raised his voice and shouted at the dark forest. "We know your village, boy! You betray us, and we'll come for you! Come for your mother!"

The shout echoed through the woods.

"I'm telling you, we're fine," Kohl-eye said.

"He's not going to like it," Big Beard said.

"Well, it was your knots that he slipped out of, wasn't it."

"Don't go laying this on me."

"Stop it," Gray Hair said. "Just tell Offa you slit the boy's throat and threw him in the river. He's not going to go looking for the body."

"Ah, wisdom speaks," Kohl-eye said. "We'll tell him the boy started yelling and wouldn't shut up."

"If that greasy, little fart turns up—"

"He's not going to turn up," Kohl-eye said. "He stole from the drover. He's a thief. Disgraced. So stick to the story."

Ferran realized that him floating face down in the river probably would have been a true story had he stayed.

"This rain," Big Beard said with a growl. "We should have struck yesterday. All we've done is add a day to delivering those cattle."

"Relax. Enjoy the fire," Gray Hair said. "Tomorrow will come soon enough. We'll kill the drover, his dark cook, and those boys. Easy as pie. Everyone will think it was the blight. Everyone will say he was a fool for going that way."

Ferran had to make it back to Winwalom and the others. In the dark. Through territory right next to the blight. With these killers coming behind. Dread rose in him, and he closed his eyes.

Nobody could fault Ferran if he didn't go back. He could race to Pencoy's instead, or to some other lord or headman. He could tell the story in such a way he kept his reputation intact. But those were the thoughts of a cowardly, little piss.

Itch nudged him with his nose. And Ferran gave him a stroke on the top of the head. Dread or no, he had to move. He opened his eyes, put his fingers to his lips and quietly shushed Itch. And then they carefully picked their way through the dark wood.

Except the wind was turning him to ice, and there'd be no warning if Ferran got the cold delerium. And so when he figured he was a quarter mile past the camp site, he made his way down the gentle slope until he saw the moonlit road, and then he used it to find the spot where he'd left his browse bag. It wasn't a cloak, but some covering was better than nothing.

Itch whined, and Ferran gave him a pet.

He figured he'd walked ten to twelve miles yesterday. Maybe more. So he'd have to walk that again. In the dark. Which would mean it would take a lot longer. But that would only get him to the previous night's camp. He'd then have to hike another ten miles or so to catch them at their next camp.

Borros could go farther than ten miles a day with the cattle. They'd done it on the way to Pencoy's, but that had been on decent roads. The old road had patches that were overgrown and required a lot of chopping. So Ferran figured they probably made another ten miles today. Which meant Ferran had a night walk of a good twenty or so miles at the least.

He wondered if they'd already crossed into the blight. The thought gave him pause. But it didn't change the situation. If he didn't make it, Winwalom and the others were done for.

He looked down at Itch. "We've got a long road," he whispered. "And no food. And a band of murderers at our backs. And very little time. But I'll be hanged if those louts get their way."

Itch whined.

"I know. We'll get you some food. I'll get you a feast, I promise."

And then he pulled the wet grass out of the browse bag and tossed it onto the ground. He then tied two corners of the sack around his neck like a poor-man's cloak, pulled the pack over his shoulders, then headed for the road because right now the most important thing was speed.

He doubted any of the robbers had come this far, but he still paused at the wood's edge to make sure the road was clear. When he'd satisfied himself, he stepped out onto its edge, but he kept away from the main body of the road and its mud. He wanted to stay to the grassier parts. The grass would pad his bare, cold feet from the rocks. More importantly, it would hide his tracks. He didn't want the men to know he'd come this way. Right now, they thought he was running back home. If they learned he was running to the others, they would assume he was going to warn them, and they would surely hurry their trot. And that was the last thing he wanted. He needed all the time he could get.

He also knew this march might not reward him with any benefit, for the men might catch and kill them all anyway. But that was tomorrow's fate. Tonight, his destiny was this road.

He began, making sure Itch stayed off the road as well. Every few paces he glanced up into the clear, cold, night sky, expecting to see the korrog glide between him and the stars. But the korrog wasn't there. A hundred or so paces later, Ferran approached a bend in the road. The woods there were as black as the inside of a sock. It was the perfect spot for something with an appetite for lone boys and dogs to wait for its prey.

He gulped and moved forward. As he passed the spot, something moved in the darkness. Ferran spooked and ran across the road and down the other side with fright. He knew he shouldn't run. Knew that would only trigger the blood lust in whatever was there, but he couldn't help it. A hundred yards later, he was panting and out of breath and looked back, but nothing had followed. Relief flooded him, and he shook his head. It must have been a bat or simply his own eyes playing tricks on him.

And then he realized he and Itch had left prints back there, right across the road. He cursed, but knew he had to fix it. So he truged back, his fear rising, waiting for something to come out of the darkness at him. He found a bushy branch and scuttled the prints, then tossed the branch into the trees and began to hurry down the side of the road. He could afford no more such delays. A horse could trot anywhere from eight to twelve miles per hour on a good road, which meant if he and Itch didn't move quickly, the killers would catch him.

The breeze gusted, but with his sack cloak and pack on, it didn't chill him as before, and he lengthened his stride in the moonlight.

Itch ranged ahead, and despite Ferran's best attempts, the dog kept veering into the road. Eventually, Ferran decided it didn't matter. Just as long as the men didn't seen his footprints, they might assume it was just a stray dog.

Owls hunted that night. He saw three of them at different times, winging silent as ghosts between the trees. He ran from something that rustled in the leaves of the woods along one stretch. Sometime later he almost stepped on what had to be a snake, moving slowly in the cold. But he knew that owls and snakes weren't the only things that hunted in the night.

Shadow spawn like the gelangun hunted at night. Shadow spawn were malevolent creatures that walked the earth only in darkness, looking to steal the souls of careless men. He had no doubt they walked this night in this part of the land, and he wondered that none had taken notice of him. He wondered if that circle of bones in the woods across from the camp site was where just such a monster had stolen the souls of its victims.

He pressed on, eyes wide, despite his fears and the dark woods around him. But then he came to a stretch of road that ran down into a pitch-black hollow, and he figured that's precisely where a shadow spawn would be. Fear washed over him, and he could not bring himself to walk forward out of the dim moonlight of the road and into that blackness, which he knew surely held his death. He stood there for what must have been fifteen minutes, listening, watching, and imagining a gelangun with its long and wicked hands.

But then he thought of Winwalom being gutted by that bald robber, his innards spooling onto the ground. He imagined someone else bashing Ranoc's head in. They'd die because he couldn't face the dark, and so he mustered his courage and ran with a yell.

Down he went into the darkness, his fright rising and taking his wits, and then he was fleeing up and out of the hollow onto the other side. He continued to run for a good distance, and then realized that if there were indeed any gelangun out there, yelling like an idiot was an excellent way to attract their attention. And so he piped down, took a breath, and asked Itch what he saw.

But Itch only panted with weariness and looked at him with long-suffering patience.

Ferran tried to keep his footprints off the road but wondered if he'd been able to. He stepped in two cow pies, the mush squishing between his toes. He drank from a night-dark creek that babbled over rocks and wished he was farther along the trail. He prayed for morning. And, at long last, the thin, gray wolf-light of morning began to appear. He continued on, and in the half-light of dawn he found himself still a few miles from the camp where he'd caught the real thief, then been chased out instead of rewarded. He was weary. His feet ached. Spittle had dried at the corners of his mouth. Itch didn't look much better.

Ferran was dismayed he'd only come this far. The men, if they started out now at a good trot, could be here in less than two hours. In that same amount of time, if he hurried, he would be able to move another four to six miles down the road. But Ferran was weary, and the road was difficult, which meant he might get less. That meant the men would catch him in the next hour.

"We're not going to make it at this pace," he said to Itch.

Itch had lain down in the dirt and just looked up at him.

"We're going to have to run." But in the last twenty-four hours he'd walked twelve miles one way, ten back, been soaked and frozen and chased by two groups intent on doing him damage. He was weary. And hungry. He thought about sitting and knew that if he sat, he was not likely to get back up again.

"They treated me poorly," he said. "Even Winwalom, standing there silent as a post, refusing to defend me."

Itch just looked at him.

"I could say I tried. That I walked in the dark where most men feared to tread during the daylight. I could say the blight was only a few miles away. And the woods were full of menace. And I did it to save a bunch of goat-brained idiots who had willfully misjudged me."

Itch did not respond.

Ferran sighed.

He could indeed say all of that. And more.

"Catch up when you're ready," he said. Then he took a few tired steps farther up the road, increased his pace, then began a deadman's jog.

Two hours later the sun was up, and he was well past the camp site where the thief had appeared. Itch was with him. But they were no longer jogging. They were walking, then jogging, then Ferran would curse and jog again. And the whole time he kept looking over his shoulder, expecting the murdering outlaws to appear.

He drank from the creek when he was thirsty. And he imagined how nice it would be if a wedge of cheese had fallen off of Lagash's wagon and lay in the grass, just waiting for him to pick it up. Shanks, he'd even have settled for a nice, firm onion. But there were no cheese wedges or onions. There were only cow pies, cow splats, and flies.

And so he continued, imagining food, then sleep, then facing a horde of men with his sling and Itch snapping at the legs of the horses. And then he'd think about food again.

By mid-morning, he came upon the remnants of the new camp Borros and the others had made. He saw the footprints they'd made in the damp earth and the ruts of the wagon wheels. He quickly searched for scraps of food, but found none. He did find his sling bag lying in the grass and picked it up. It still held its stones, and he put it over his shoulder.

This camp was maybe only six miles from the other, and he supposed the thunder and lightning had started earlier up here, crashing about the canyon walls like shouts from an angry god. He susptected it had forced Borros to corral the cattle earlier. Ferran's hopes lifted a bit. He just might have a chance, although he knew that the band of killers must be getting close.

He looked back down the canyon, and suddenly a herd of deer ran up the slope as if startled. The deer reached a height and looked back down at the road.

Ferran knew what had spooked them. It was the men on their horses. He knew it. They were coming, and the thought sent a jolt of alarm through him. He set off again in a tired jog, his bare feet muddy, beaten, and stabbed.

He found his ungrateful accusers maybe another two miles down the road. And then, as he got closer, he discovered that he'd actually only found Lagash, the wagon, and Carrots the mule. The rest of the valley was empty save for the dark trail of earth that had been churned up by the passing of hundreds of cattle hooves heading farther up the overgrown road.

21

REPORT

T HE WAGON HAD a broken wheel, and Lagash was working on
it. He did not notice Ferran approaching, but the mule did. He
turned his head and eyed Ferran.

Itch barked, probably because he knew Lagash was the source of
delicious porridge, and Lagash turned and saw Ferran. He frowned.
Then shook his head and turned back to his work, pounding at something on the wheel with a wooden mallet.

Ferran ran up, panting. "There are men coming."

Lagash pounded a wheel brace with the mallet. "Do you want a beating?" he asked.

"There are men coming," Ferran said again more forcefully.

Lagash took another swing, then stopped. "What kind of men?"

"The rough kind," Ferran said. "Twenty to twenty-five of them. On
horses." And then he poured out the story of his journey, the deluge of
rain, looking for tinder, discovering the men, his capture, escape, and
then his march back in the perilous dark. He made sure to emphasize the
perilous part.

When he finished, Lagash narrowed his eyes. "You're telling the
truth?"

Indignation welled up in Ferran. He was not going to stand for this another minute. He squared himself and faced Lagash. "I haven't told one lie on this trip," he spat. "It is true that I have had filched things in my past. In fact, I once stole a dress from the blacksmith's wife, and that was no easy thing. But I touched nothing of yours. Or Borros's. Why would I steal food from you when you were filling my belly every morning and night with more food than my family has seen in weeks? And what do I care for your great grandmother's knife? My father's knife is more than its peer."

"Grandfather's," Lagash corrected.

"It could have been your great aunt's for all I care. The fact of the matter is that someone else stole those items. I discovered the thief. And all of you, like great turnips, accused me instead of looking for the real villain. And I'm telling the truth again now. This very moment there's a band of killers on their way to steal the cattle. I risked life and limb running through the night to save your hides. And if you're too stupid to believe me, then I will go up on that hill and watch them gut you and take your cattle, and then I will go home and tell everyone that the idiot drover and his cook led the boys, instead of the cattle, to the slaughter."

He glared at Lagash, feeling that had been a surprisingly good oration and expecting an immediate apology, but Lagash just stood there with a single cocked eyebrow.

Ferran waited for a response, but when it didn't come, he broke the silence. "Fine," he said. "I've delivered the message. My duty here is done." And then he turned and attempted to storm off, but he was too weary and too pained in his joints, and so he proudly hobbled away instead.

There was no gratitude in any of them. Or sense. Or brains. Or—

"Wait," Lagash said.

Ferran ignored him.

Lagash raised his voice. "I said wait."

Ferran sighed and turned around.

"Describe the men in exact detail."

Ferran did, including the tattoo on Kohl-eye's hand. Lagash listened intently, nodding as the words rolled out of Ferran's mouth. When Ferran finished, Lagash said, "The bald one, did he look like a hawk?"

Ferran thought about it. "You could say that. He had a strong blade of a nose."

Lagash blew out a breath. "This is not good."

That was an understatement.

Lagash rubbed his jaw, then looked Ferran up and down. "You walked twenty miles in the dark, eh?"

"Twenty-five at least," Ferran said, still indignant. "I found the men all the way back by that stretch where the cow chased Krov around the bush. So it was there and back again, on an empty stomach to boot, no thanks to you."

Lagash nodded. "Then we don't have much time."

"No."

Lagash's appeared to come to some decision, then took command. "Release Carrots from the wagon shafts, but do not remove his harness. Be quick."

Ferran hurried to the front of the wagon. In the meantime, Lagash removed four of the practice spears from the back of the wagon and began to lash them to make two shafts at least sixteen feet long. Ferran unhitched Carrots, took hold of his bridle, and led him to where Lagash was working.

"We're making a drag sled," Lagash said. "Slip a pole into the shaft loops on either side of the harness."

"A drag sled?"

"I can't ride him. Not with my wounds. And I'm not staying here. We'll need the crossbow and spear. And a few other things. Now hurry. Lash the points together so it makes a cross with the point behind Carrot's head."

Ferran slipped the poles though the tugs, tightened them and the breeching straps. He found some rope, raised the ends of the poles closest to the mule's head, and lashed them together. By this time, Lagash had used the axe to chop another two practice spears in half so he had four smaller sections of increasing length. "Help me lash these across the poles trailing behind him."

They wrapped and tugged the lengths of rope furiously until they had a drag sled with four cross posts that trailed the mule by a good ten feet.

Then they went to the wagon and grabbed Lagash's crossbow and quiver of bolts, Borros's real spear, and a barrel of sling stones and secured them to the sled.

When they finished, Ferran said, "We're starved. Have you got anything?"

One corner of Lagash's mouth curled up in a grin. "A horde of killers are riding to meet us, and you're thinking about food. I'll get you something, but I want you to turn around."

Ferran's annoyance rose again. "Because you don't trust me to see where you keep it? Like I don't already know where all the food in that dumb wagon is?"

"Turn around," Lagash ordered.

Ferran turned, angry. However, he sneaked a quick glance back, and saw Lagash remove one end of a hog's head barrel and then pop open a false bottom. There was something wrapped inside. It didn't look like food.

Lagash looked up, and Ferran quickly turned back.

"I told you to turn around!" Lagash said.

"I'm turned," Ferran said.

"I told you not to look!"

"What is that, some secret cheese you've got hidden there?"

"You blasted boy," he said. "Look straight ahead until I say so."

Ferran rolled his eyes, but looked away.

Lagash banged about, fiddled with something, and then said, "Here's something for the two of you."

Ferran turned, and Lagash tossed him a thick slice of grease cake and two squares of hard tack. Ferran caught them. He broke a bit off the grease cake and gave it to Itch. Then broke a piece for himself. It was waxy, meaty, and delicious. He made a small sigh of extreme satisfaction.

"Get up on Carrots. Quickly."

Ferran broke another piece off for Itch, then stuffed the rest of the food in a pocket and clambered up onto the mule's back. He wasn't much of a rider, but he'd seen it done many times, and he grabbed the reins. But these were wagon reins and much too long for riding, so he looped them up and tied off the extra length. Behind him, Lagash put on his dark hat with the bright feathers and clambered onto the sled and settled himself. He called to Itch and patted his lap. Itch clambered up onto him.

"Go," Lagash said.

Ferran gave Carrots a hup and slapped him gently with the reins. The mule started forward.

"Faster," Lagash said.

Ferran gave him another hup and slap, and Carrots kicked into a slow trot.

"Good boy," Ferran said and gave him a pat on the neck.

"He's a lazy whoreson," Lagash said. "So make sure he keeps the pace, or we're both dead men."

They trotted for a number of paces, the sled bouncing over the ground. Lagash pulled some greasecake out of his pocket, broke off a piece, and fed it to Itch.

And then Lagash cursed.

Ferran turned in his seat. About a mile back a huge flock of startled blackbirds rose above the trees by the road.

"That's them," Ferran said.

"Go!" Lagash said. "Go!"

22

RIDERS

F ERRAN HAD RIDDEN a horse twice in his life. And never bareback. And he was finding it difficult to squeeze with his knees and time his bounces so Carrots didn't bounce him completely off.

But he wasn't the only one having a problem. This was a rough stretch of road, and behind him Lagash grunted and groaned in pain each time the sled bounced and banged across the uneven ground. And then the drag sled lurched, Lagash cursed, and Ferran glanced back to see him holding onto the stuff they'd tied to the sled.

"Do you want me to slow down?" Ferran called back, fearing he himself was going to fall at any moment and be run over.

"No! Speed up!"

Ferran gulped. "Hup," he said and gave Carrots another slap with the reins, but not a very vigorous one. Lords, it all looked so easy when you were standing on the ground. But once you were in the seat it was a different thing entirely. And Ferran couldn't imagine what kind of madman would want to sit up so high off the ground and move at speed with nothing to keep you from flying off and breaking your head neck on some rock.

"Faster!" Lagash called.

Ferran hupped again and this time gave Carrots a good slap.

Carrots broke into a faster trot, and it required all of Ferran's concentration to simply stay on.

They rode this way for a good distance, Itch riding on Lagash's lap. They came around a bend and saw a long stretch of road running across a wide meadow with tall grass in front of them. Running straight through the middle of it was a line that had been churned from the hundreds of hooves that had passed by earlier.

They followed the gash through the meadow. The ground here was much smoother, and the sled stopped bouncing as much. And then Ferran suddenly figured out how to move up and down in time with Carrots and started to feel secure and confident in his seat.

"I think I figured it out!" he called back.

"That's grand," Lagash said. "We'll notify the queen." And then the drag sled hit a bump, and Lagash groaned.

Carrots started to slow, but Ferran gave him a hup and slap, and they maintained pace. And with the fright of falling off lessening, Ferran began to think about their predicament.

"What are we going to do?" he called back.

"Ride."

"I mean with the band of outlaws."

The horse and sled passed by a swath of tall thistle with purple heads.

Lagash said, "The safest thing to do would be to run."

"You don't sound like you're wanting to run."

"Borros won't want to run."

"But there are only seven of us," Ferran said. "While the outlaws are all grown men."

"Don't let looks cow you."

"I'm thinking of their numbers. And what you told us. It's going to be easy for a mob of them to fix and flank the seven of us."

"It might not be possible to run. They're mounted. What if they come after us? Do you know when the largest slaughters take place in battle?"

"When they fix and flank?"

"When one side breaks. It's like wading out into a flock of geese with a stout stick. And if the enemy is mounted, the slaughter is even worse."

Ferran thought for a moment and said, "We'd have to escape before the battle then. Leave no trace."

"Borros isn't going to run away from twenty men."

"Because he can handle them on his own?"

"No."

This didn't make any sense. Ferran was willing to fight, but not when losing was assured. "So we're just going to die?"

"You have your sling."

"They have axes, spears, and swords!"

"Then today's the day we'll see what you're truly made of, Dog Boy."

Ferran knew what he was made of: flesh and bones and lots of other soft stuff that would not stand up to blades and murderous men.

"It's madness."

"Think," Lagash said.

What was there to think about? How could they beat twenty men? They couldn't. They could beat two. Or five. Or—wait. An idea rose in his mind.

"We don't fight twenty men," Ferran said. "We whittle them down instead. Fight little groups of them. Right? That way we can be the ones doing the fixing and flanking."

"Surprising," Lagash said. "You do have a brain. When facing a larger force, that's the goal. We can try to break them up. Or we can strike and run and whittle them down that way. The question is whether it's possible. We're going to have to see the lay of the land. See if we have any chance of actually doing this. You have to choose your fights, Ferran. You have to make your enemy fight you when and where you have the advantage. Always make your enemy do what you want them to do."

"And if you can't?"

"Then you run. And if you can't do that, you face it like a man, and you pray the gods are on your side."

Ferran did not want to face assured death for a bunch of cows. "What if it's not possible, yet Borros insists?"

"One of us might need to hit him on the head," Lagash said. "You up to that task?"

"Only if you give me a very long pole."

Lagash chuckled.

Carrots trotted into a wet part of the meadow, his hooves sucking, and the sled splashed through shallow marsh water.

"Gah," Lagash said. "Did you have to take the lake route?"

"I'm following the road."

"You could have skirted the wet part."

And then Carrot's hooves began flinging globs of mud.

"Where are you going?" Lagash said in annoyance and turned to look up the road. At that moment, Carrots churned up a particularly large glop of mud that sailed through the air and struck Lagash smack in the forehead.

He cried out.

"Sorry," Ferran said.

"I will remember that," Lagash said.

And then they were out of the marshy part and back up onto drier ground. Ferran began to think about fixing and flanking and making the robbers do what was to their disadvantage. He began thinking of ways they might draw little groups of them off.

He'd only come up with one option, when Lagash said, "We've got company."

Ferran turned. Back where there road entered the meadow, three riders trotted out of the shade of the trees and into the full sun.

"Recognize them?" Lagash asked.

Ferran did not. They were too far away, and he'd only seen Kohl-eye's group.

"What are we going to do?" Ferran asked.

"Do you want to fight them out here?" Lagash asked.

"Stuck out here on a mule with a drag sled? No."

"It looks like there's only three of them. They're probably the men with the fastest horses. Sent out as scouts. You sure you don't want to fight them here?"

"No."

"Wise choice. Let's find a better place. Let's lure them into ground that's better for us. Follow the road into the trees. Hurry now."

Ferran hupped and slapped the reins, and Carrots started into a canter.

The sled began to bump and bounce. Lagash cursed and groaned, but he did not tell Ferran to slow.

"Shouldn't you get out the crossbow?" Ferran called back.

"I want them to think we're weak," Lagash said. "I want them to see easy prey. I want them to come after us fast and hard."

The mule and sled neared the end of the meadow.

"And here they come," Lagash said.

The horsemen were maybe a third of a mile back, but they'd started to gallop.

Ferran urged Carrots forward. A few moments later, they rushed into the trees, the drag sled with Lagash and Itch trailing behind. They traveled a stretch, and then Lagash shouted, "There! See that large boulder up ahead where the road bends? Take us twenty or thirty paces beyond it. That's where we'll make our stand."

The boulder was huge and rose at least ten feet high, and the road beyond it was not visible from this side. A surprise, Ferran thought. An ambush. Originally, the road had been wide enough here for three wagons abreast, but the bushes and trees on the sides had grown up, and so it was now narrower. Ferran steered down the middle, following the trail of the cattle, and then they passed the boulder and went around the bend. About twenty paces beyond, Ferran brought Carrots to a halt.

"Tie the reins to a tree on the left side. Quickly."

Ferran leapt off, led the mule to a tree on the same side of the road as the boulder and tied a quick knot with the reins.

Lagash removed his crossbow from the sled. "Help me span this!" he called.

Ferran ran to him and, with some effort, drew it back.

He heard the galloping riders enter the woods.

"Get your sling and a number of stones ready. When they come around that corner, they're going to slow down just a bit. When they do, you nail the lead man. Then target the second. Then the third. Don't stop until they're all down. I will do my part. You do yours."

Ferran turned to Itch. "Sit," he commanded.

JOHN D. BROWN

Itch sat by the drag sled and wagged his tail, alert, wondering what they were doing.

Ferran removed his sling and selected two of the stones closest to the shape of an almond from his sack. Stones with such a shape flew truer and hit harder than rounder stones.

The men would be coming fast, bearing down on them. Lagash would only have the one bolt. Which meant Ferran had better not miss because it would only take a horse a few seconds to cover the distance, and then he'd learn what it meant to face a mouted charge.

Ferran placed the stone in the sling pouch, his hand shaking, and let the sling hang.

Lagash placed a bolt in his crossbow and raised it to his shoulder, grimacing.

The thudding hooves came closer.

Ferran's heart began to race, and he blew out a big breath to calm himself. Straight and true, he told himself. Straight and true.

The sound of the thudding gallops grew. A moment later, the three riders slowed and rounded the bend.

Lagash sighted down his bow and pulled the release. The bow slapped. The bolt flashed down the road and stuck one of the riders in the chest. He clutched at the wound, almost lost his balance.

Ferran whipped his sling around and loosed his first stone. But he was panicked and hurried, and the stone flew over the riders' head.

The riders reined in their mounts and milled around a bit.

Ferran fumbled a second stone into the pouch.

"Hit the one on the right," Lagash said.

Ferran swung and released. He missed the rider, but he did hit the man's horse in the side.

The horse flinched like it had been stung by a massive wasp. It bolted forward, bumping into the horse of the rider Lagash shot, almost knocking that rider to the ground.

"Keep your wits," Lagash said. "Hit the last man. Aim for his chest."

The last rider drew his sword. Then he spurred his horse forward and yelled.

"You've got him," Lagash said reassuringly. "An easy shot. You're one of the best slingers I've seen."

148

The blade of the sword flashed in the sun. One stroke could slice Ferran's head from his shoulders. Or cut his arm off. Or cleave his torso in two.

Ferran couldn't catch his breath. He slid the third stone into the sling's pouch, marked his target, and flung with all his might. He didn't notice the release. He didn't even see the stone.

But a moment later, the man's head jerked back, a bloody spot close to his eye. He dropped his sword, bounced hard on the horse, and then toppled right off. The horse ran a few more paces, kicked, reared its head, then slowed to a walk.

"Well done," Lagash said. "Strike the last man!"

Ferran slid another stone into the pouch and marked the rider who was struggling to turn his mount around. Ferran flung the stone. It struck the man high in the back of his shoulder with a nice thwap, and the man arched his back in pain.

Ferran slid in another stone, his confidence rising. He marked the same man and flung. This one hit him in the back of the ribs. He winced again, but spurred his horse away. Before Ferran could get another stone in, the man galloped back around the bend beyond the boulder and out of sight.

The man Lagash had shot turned his horse to flee back down the road and dug in his spurs. The horse surged forward.

Ferran marked the man and flung another stone. The horse shot back down the road. The stone streaked toward them, and Ferran thought it would miss, but it struck the man solidly in the upper arm. A blow to crack bone. The man flinched, and then he and his horse charged past the big stone and back down the trail.

The rider Ferran had hit in the face was trying to climb to his feet.

Ferran grabbed another stone, but Lagash walked past Ferran and waved him to put the sling down. With his good hand, Lagash drew his short sword and strode over to the rider.

The man heard him coming, rose up on one foot, and drew a dagger.

But Lagash was quick and ran him through the neck.

The man grasped at the sword, but he was clearly done for and fell to the ground. Lagash withdrew his blade, then wiped it on the man's tunic.

"Get his horse," he said and motioned at the man's mount.

The rider's mount was standing a number of paces down the road, looking back, its eyes a bit wide. It was a beautiful chestnut mare. Ferran slowly walked up to it with soft reassuring murmurs and picked up the reins.

"We don't have much time," Lagash said. "Get the man's sword, then tie his mare to one of the posts of the sled. We need to get moving."

Ferran picked the man's sword up where it had fallen, then quickly led the man's mount over to the sled and tied her to one of the cross posts. Lagash clambered onto the sled.

Itch barked and then whined, but he'd stayed put.

"Good boy," Ferran said and gave him a pet. "Good boy. Up on the sled."

Itch wagged his tail and took his place on Lagash's lap.

"Get this thing moving," Lagash said. "The rest are not going to be far behind."

Ferran untied Carrots, vaulted up onto his back, and gave him a hup and slap.

Next time, Ferran thought, I'll aim tighter.

23

BLACKMEAL

F ERRAN URGED CARROTS into a fast trot, and they followed the tracks of the cattle at a good clip with the horse trailing behind. Itch was happy to sit and bounce along with Lagash.

They traveled maybe a mile and a half this way, and then Ferran smelled the others. Or rather, he smelled the carcass of the korrog. The stench was strong and ripe. A few moments later the wagon with the korrog came into view. Winwalom was driving the wagon. Beyond him, Krov was at the back of the herd with a yellow flag tied to his spear. Caswal and Ranoc were managing the sides, making sure none of the cattle strayed into the woods. The lines of cattle stretched up and around the bend. Borros was nowhere to be seen.

Ferran whistled. Then whistled again more loudly.

Winwalom turned on the wagon seat. His eyes went wide at the sight of Ferran, and he shouted to the others, then pulled his wagon to a stop.

Ferran and Lagash caught up, and Lagash called the boys to him.

Krov walked up and eyed Ferran. "What's this?"

Lagash clambered off the sled. "Where's Borros?" he demanded.

"He's way up ahead," Winwalom said, "scouting."

Lagash shook his head. "Any of you know how to ride?"

"Ranoc does," Krov said.

Lagash shouted for Ranoc to hurry and then went to the horse they'd taken and began to adjust one of the stirrups to make it sit higher. By the time Lagash had adjusted it, Ranoc was there, eyeing Ferran suspiciously.

"You know how to ride?" Lagash asked and moved to the second stirrup.

"Yes."

Lagash undid the buckle, shortened the stirrup, and fastened it again. "Then take this horse, fly up the road, and catch Borros. You tell him that Drogan and a gang of twenty armed men are on our tail. Tell him he needs to get back now. And you give him this." Lagash withdrew from his vest something the size of a short fat sausage that had been wrapped in cloth and tied. It was the thing he'd removed from the false barrel bottom. "Upon your life you will not lose this."

"No," Ranoc said, his eyes wide with alarm.

"I'll put it here," Lagash said, then opened a saddle bag, slipped it in, and tied it up tight. "Now get up."

Ranoc took the reins and climbed up on the horse. Then Lagash swatted it on the rump. "Go!"

The horse jolted forward, and Ranoc bounced with it, holding the reins wide with both hands.

"I thought you said he knew how to ride," Lagash said.

"He does," said Krov.

And then Ranoc sorted whatever was going on with the reins, held them closer, and kicked the horse into a trot, posting in good fashion. He rode through the trees to the side of the cattle. Halfway down the length of the herd, a gap cleared, and the way to the road beyond opened up. Ranoc shouted, kicked the horse into a gallop, and raced down the road.

By this time, Caswal, who was far ahead, had seen the commotion at the end of the herd and was looking back.

Lagash waved for him keep moving. "Keep them going!" he shouted. "Keep moving ahead!"

Caswal turned and kept walking with the cattle.

Lagash surveyed the area. "This is not the place to make a stand." He motioned at Ferran. "Climb up that tree. Tell me what you see ahead."

Ferran ran to the tree, got a boost from Krov, and clambered up the branches all the way until the branches started to get thin and the top began to sway with his weight.

"What do you see?" Lagash called.

"Up ahead there's another small clearing. Then the walls of the canyon come closer. There are some steep cliffs there."

"How narrow?"

"I don't know. Pretty narrow."

"How far ahead?"

"Quarter mile."

Ferran turned and looked back the way they'd come. "I don't see any riders yet."

"After our surprise," Lagash said, "they're probably riding with a bit more caution. Going a bit slower. And that may help us. Get down."

Ferran clambered down the tree and jumped the last little bit to the ground.

"The woods here are a death trap," Lagash said. "There's no way to protect our backs. They'll just encircle us. But maybe we'll have a chance up ahead." He handed Krov his crossbow. "Span that."

Krov did and handed it back.

Lagash took the cocked crossbow and looked at boys. "You're going to run these cattle. You're going to run them this last quarter mile. And hopefully the narrows will give us some advantage we don't have here. Former positions with Dog Boy in the rear. And thank the ancestors we have Itch back. Go!"

The boys turned and began clapping and shouting and waving the flags on the end of their spears. Lagash tied Carrots to the end of the korrog wagon.

Krov and Winwalom ran up one side and shouted the new instructions to Caswal. Ferran gave Itch the command, and he started barking and running back and forth behind the herd.

The cattle began to bellow, and the ones in the rear hustled forward only to run into snags of cattle that were still walking. It was a loud mess, and then Caswal and Krov urged those in the front into a trot, giving room to those behind, and suddenly the knots of cattle loosened, and the whole herd streamed forward, Itch barking behind.

They jogged down the overgrown road, around a bend one way, then around another. About a quarter mile later, at the far end of the road, a sunlit clearing appeared. Beyond it the canyon did indeed narrow and the sides steepened. They continued down the road, the cattle bellowing, the boys shouting, and Itch barking. A few minutes later the cattle spilled out of the woods and into the sunny clearing.

"Tell them to get the cattle to the other side," Lagash said. "Quickly!"

Ferran shouted out the instructions.

The cattle were mooing in protest. A few clusters of them tried to spread out across the field and get away from the shouting, but the boys herded them back to the main group and kept them moving.

The road ran straight across the clearing and then into a narrow with a steep slope on one side and a swiftly-moving creek lined by thick willows on the other.

They herded the cattle across the clearing and maybe forty or fifty yards up the road, and then Lagash ordered Ferran to call the other boys back. He ran ahead and shouted at the others, then ran back.

When the boys had all hurried back, Caswal grimaced in distaste. "What are you doing back here?"

"Saving your worthless, flea-infested, manure-stinking hide," Ferran said.

Lagash held up an axe he brought from the wagon. "You," he said and pointed at Krov and Caswal. "Get up that slope and fell that tree. That medium-sized beech right there. I need it to fall right across the road and block it."

Krov took the axe, and he and Caswal ran up the steep slope next to the road.

"This is where we'll make our stand," Lagash said.

Krov and Caswal reached the tree. Krov chopped away some lower branches that were in the way, marked the line on which he wanted the tree to fall, then began to chop the trunk in that direction. The blows sounded off the canyon walls.

"What do you want us to do?" asked Winwalom.

"Get that wagon well past the line where the tree will fall. Then portion out the sling stones into five piles."

Ferran took the reins and moved the wagon well beyond the mouth of the narrow.

There was a silence for a moment as Krov and Caswal switched positions on the hill, and then Caswal began to swing, this time on the exact opposite side where Krov had struck.

Lagash pointed up the hill above Krov and Caswal. "Winwalom, get up to that outcropping. Keep yourself hidden, but whistle three times loudly at first sight of the men."

"Yes," Winwalom said and then he turned and began to scramble up the slope.

Krov and Caswal traded again, and the thock of the axe blows continued. Krov was an excellent woodsman and every bite of the axe seemed perfectly laid, but it was a broad trunk, probably as thick as a man, and it was going to take a number of strokes.

Above them, Winwalom reached the outcropping and peered back down the road. He searched, then looked down and shook his head.

Caswal tried to push the tree from the other side, but it was still too solid. Krov moved to that side and began to rain down his forceful blows, wood chips flying with each stroke.

A cow bellowed. Ferran turned to see what was causing the commotion and saw Borros and Ranoc riding back down the road through the cattle. A few moments later, they broke past the cattle and galloped to where Lagash and Ferran stood.

Borros pulled his mount into a stop, saw Ferran and scowled.

Lagash said, "He traveled twenty-five miles through the dark to warn us."

"Did he?" Borros said, clearly still angered.

"I didn't steal anything from you or Lagash," Ferran said. "Would I have risked life and limb if I had? It would have been much easier to simply let this band of killers take you and these other ingrates and give you your dues."

Borros narrowed his eyes and turned to Lagash. "It's Drogan?"

"Kohl eyes, tattoo, the works," Lagash said.

Borros spat. "How did those whoresons get away? They should be a jail somewhere. They should be missing a hand. Did those Mossby morons let them loose?"

Lagash shrugged.

Ferran spoke. "He said their leader and a number of men showed up in Mossby. They probably threatened the villagers to let them go."

Above them on the hill, Krov called, "Timber!" There was a loud pop and crack, and the tree tipped. And then it fell with a loud, shuddering crash of leaves and breaking branches. It was taller than Ferran realized, and its top crashed down through the trees on the other side of the road. When it finished, it lay across the road. A perfect barricade.

Krov and Caswal scrambled down the hill to where the others stood.

"What are we going to do?" asked Caswal.

"We're going to fight," Lagash said.

"How many are there?" Caswal asked.

"At least twenty men," Ferran said. "Maybe twenty-five or thirty. They're armed. Mounted."

"We did kill one and wound two others" Lagash added. "It's a good start."

"Thirty?" Caswal said in dismay. "We're only seven. And Lagash and Winwalom are injured."

"You signed a contract," Borros said.

"I signed up to drive cattle. And provide security. And I'm happy to do that. But I'm not going to run myself on a sword."

Borros looked at the others. "Is that what the rest of you think?"

The faces of the other boys were alarmed, scared.

"I'll fight for you," Ferran said. "That is if you have a plan."

"There are only seven of us," Caswal repeated.

Borros looked at him with disdain.

"Tell them," Lagash said to Borros.

Borros sighed, but said nothing.

"Then I'll tell them," Lagash said. "He was a grimsman. And his anointing has not yet faded. So we are six, plus one anointed with power."

"I'm sure he's a fearsome fighter," Caswal said. "But the anointing is nothing without the earthmeal."

"He has blackmeal," Lagash said and turned to Borros. "Ranoc gave it to you?"

Borros nodded.

"Did you take it?"

"I wanted to see what the situation was. It's old. Weaker. And the power rapidly fades. It doesn't last like new meal."

Lagash sighed in frustration. "It also takes longer for the earth might to rise. It's not like we have a lot of time."

"He has blackmeal?" Caswal asked in surprise.

The mages collected the power of the earth from graceseeps and turned it into godmeals. Such a meal allowed those who were anointed to suffuse themselves with power that they could then use. Blackmeal was the type most often given to those who had been anointed with strength, vigor, and speed. It was the meal given to warriors. It was the meal for battle. And it was forbidden for anyone but the queen's mages and their runners to possess or transport it.

Borros sighed, and then he pulled the wrapped object Lagash had given Ranoc out of his vest. He unwrapped it to reveal a dark brown bottle made with thick glass. He unstopped the top of the bottle and gently tapped out into the palm of his hand a little black lump the size and shape of a pea with a couple of thin spider strands of white running through it. He shook another larger lump out that was more of a dark brown color. And then he held his hand out sourly.

"That's blackmeal?" Ranoc asked, surprised.

"One variety," Borros said.

It was amazing. Ferran had never seen actual blackmeal. It was incredibly valuable. What he was looking at was probably worth this whole herd.

The other boys made small sounds of amazement.

"What's your anointing for?" Caswal asked.

"You've got a lot of questions."

"Will you be able to take thirty men?"

"No." Borros shrugged. "Maybe. But I'm not going to face thirty men."

Caswal looked confused.

"What we need to do is kill seven or eight of them. We do that, and the others will start to have second thoughts. We kill another seven, and they'll run."

"So we can take them?" Caswal said, his hope rising.

"No," Borros said. "Nothing is assured. There's a good chance we all will die."

"What we need to do," Lagash said, "is hold out until the earthmight rises in him. And then we'll see how the battle goes."

"We could run," Ferran offered.

"We could," Borros said. "But this lot will hunt us down. So if we're going to fight, we might as well fight in a place of our choosing."

"I'll fight," Ranoc said firmly.

"I guess I will too," Krov said, although he sounded doubtful.

"So we have no assurances," Caswal said.

"There are never any assurances in battle," Lagash said. "We might win the day but still lose one or two of us. Or three. One of us might lose and arm or finger or eye. You never know."

Caswal blew a breath out, wrestling with the idea. "Okay," he said.

"Good," said Lagash.

"How long?" asked Caswal.

"How long what?" asked Borros.

"How long until the earthmight rises."

"Twenty minutes. Thirty. Longer. This isn't fresh meal straight from the bowels of the mageworks."

But it wasn't ancient, Ferran thought. Blackmeal didn't last for years. From what he'd heard, it became rancid and unstable within a year. So it couldn't be that old. Furthermore, the various earth graces the mages created were strictly controlled, and, save for his drover's badge, Borros wore no official mark of any kind, which meant he hadn't received this through authorized sources, because he said he hadn't been a grimsman for years. That meant this blackmeal was stolen. Pilfered. Contraband. And possessing it demanded immediate execution.

And suddenly Ferran wondered if the droving and cattle were just a front. Maybe Borros wasn't really a drover. Maybe he was really a smuggler. And a very dangerous one at that.

"You look like you swallowed a fish," Borros said.

"It's nothing," Ferran said. "Just thinking about fighting thirty brutal men." And the fact that if an Inquisitor discovered the blackmeal, they would all hang. Unless of course, one of them were to turn Borros in. In that case, the informant might earn a huge reward. That was, if Borros didn't kill the informant first.

Ferran pasted a fake smile onto his face. What in the world had he signed on to?

"Okay," Lagash said. "We need to hold out for as long as it takes. When Borros joins us, your job will be to attack. Until then what we want to do is lure them out into the open where we can strike at them with our bow and slings without getting close to their spears and swords. They want to get close to bring their weapons to bear. We want to do the exact opposite. Never do what your enemy wants you to, not unless you have some trick up your sleeve.

"Krov and I will station ourselves behind the tree you just chopped down. The rest of you will climb up on that hill and hide yourselves. Don't go too far up. You need to be able to strike hard and accurately with your slings. And don't spread too far apart. Get a good spot with enough room so you can take a step and hurl those slings with your might.

"Krov and I will draw their attention and then retreat. Let them come out into the clearing to come after us. Let them get to the midpoint, then rise and sling your stones with all the accuracy and fury you can muster. If you can get a head or neck injury, take it. If you can only get the body, then injure that. If they're riding horses, strike the horses. Hopefully, the men will then turn to face you. And when they do, Krov and I will reappear and catch them with their backs to us."

"A cross fire," said Ranoc.

"And what happens if they charge us?" Caswal asked.

"Run along the slope above the road. Move up the canyon. You see that part of the slope that ends in a short cliff. That's your fallback. Stand behind the outcropping there and sling at the men who follow. If some come below on the road, pick up large rocks and thrown them down upon them."

"What if they overrun that?"

"We retreat up the canyon farther and pray that blackmeal didn't kill Borros."

"Kill him?" Krov asked in surprise.

"It's old," Lagash said. "It's close to the end of its life. And that's when it gets dangerous."

"Ancestors help us," Caswal said.

Ranoc got a wary look on his face. "I thought only mages and their runners could transport blackmeal."

"Don't be worrying about that," Borros said. "You worry about what's coming up the road."

"Get yourselves in position," Lagash said. "Each of you take one of those piles of sling stones. Fill your sling sacks, pockets. Put them in your hats. Don't leave a single stone here."

The boys hurried over to the piles and began to stash their sling stones, some larger, some smaller, some closer to the perfect shape, others less so.

From up the slope, Winwalom whistled three times.

Dread filled Ferran. He did not want to be in a battle, but he finished stuffing the stones in his pockets anyway.

"Hurry," Lagash said. "Get up there. But do it quietly. Tell Long Hair the plan. Get hidden. Go." He waved at them with his hand. "Go!"

The other boys stowed the last of their rocks, and then Caswal and Ranoc scrambled up the hill with their spears and stones. Ferran needed to take both his and Winwalom's pile, but there was nowhere to carry so many rocks, and so he pulled off his tunic, laid it on the ground, and pulled all of the remaining rocks onto it.

"Go!" Lagash said.

Ferran gathered the ends of his tunic up to make a sack, twisted it, then hefted it over his shoulder. Then he picked up his spear and ran up the hill in his bare feet, Itch coming right behind.

24

SHIELD, BOW, AND SLING

T HE SLOPE WAS moderately wooded with open spaces of grass or scrub here and there. Ferran kept to the wooded parts and raced up the slope with the stones and his spear as fast as he could while still being quiet. Itch ran with him. After a few stops to catch his breath, he joined the others up by the outcropping with Winwalom.

Caswal and Ranoc were huddled with him, peering through some brush at the road below. Their spears lay on the ground beside them.

Ranoc motioned for him to get down.

Ferran crouched and told Itch to sit. He was still breathing hard from his run. "How many are there?" he whispered.

"Just one right now," Winwalom whispered. "I think he's the scout."

"He's not wearing a helmet," Ranoc said.

"Probably to make it harder for us to see him," Caswal replied.

Winwalom's hair was short and ragged like he'd cut it with a knife. Long clumps of it lay on the ground.

"I see two more," Winwalom said. "By the road."

Ferran wanted to see what was going on, but the spot with the other boys was too crowded, so he positioned himself a pace away and slowly moved a branch of the bush to the side until he could see down. Two men were in the woods at the mouth of the road where it entered the clearing. "Where's the scout?" he whispered.

"You can just see his head," Winwalom said. "He's squatting about seven trees this side of the road at the edge of the clearing."

Ferran counted the trees and searched but couldn't see him. And then the man turned and signaled for someone behind him, and Ferran caught the movement. The man was crouched low behind some bushes.

"I brought your stones," Ferran whispered to Winwalom, and then he opened his tunic and passed the stones a handful at a time to Winwalom.

When he'd given him his share, he said, "We're a bit high here. I saw a good open space a little farther down the slope. There's a small flat part. It should be good for slinging."

"We should go now," Winwalom said. "Before more of them come."

Ferran moved to start descending the slope, but Ranoc stopped him. "You need to put on your tunic," Ranoc said.

"I'm fine," Ferran whispered.

"No. Skin shines. And it draws the eye. If you're bare-chested and bare-backed, you'll stand out like a beacon. Put on your tunic."

Of course he was right. Ferran pulled his tunic on, filling his sling bag and his pockets.

When he was set, Ranoc motioned for Ferran to lead the way. "Show us the spot you saw. And not a sound."

Ferran kept low and began to carefully move down the slope, reminding Itch to stay with him. A few moments later, Ranoc and Winwalom quietly followed with stones and spears. Caswal lingered a bit, and then finally abandoned the lookout to bring up the rear. The four boys kept themselves so low they were almost flat against the slope and quietly picked their way down until Itch and Ferran came to the shade of a stand of trees.

When the other three boys were with him, he pointed at the open, flat stretch that ran along the slope just ahead where the sun shone on the grass and low shrubs. The open area ran between this stand of trees and another a good distance farther along the slope. The flat part was maybe five or six feet wide, then descended in a steep drop to the clearing below.

Ranoc spotted a bush at the edge of this stand of trees, made a hand signal for them to move, and the boys crept in a line to it. They knelt in the dirt, placing their spears on the ground behind them.

Ferran looked through the leaves down at the clearing, and he realized this spot wasn't as far up as he thought. On the one hand, that was good because it meant the stones they slung would hit with more force. On the other hand, he didn't think it would take a man more than twenty seconds to crash through the brush at the base of the slope and run up to this position. He imagined having to face a charge of a dozen men up that slope, and his anxiety rose. He turned and looked higher up the slope but couldn't see a better spot.

"He's moving," Winwalom whispered.

Back down by the road, the scout began picking his way around the edge of the clearing, keeping himself behind the trees. He came to an opening in the trees that ran up the slope a bit, and instead of skirting round it, he crouched low and dashed across, taking up a position behind some tall shrubs right below the boys.

Maybe two dozen yards beyond him lay the tree Krov and Caswal had chopped down. Nothing moved there, and Ferran wondered if Krov and Lagash were actually there or had taken a position farther up the road.

Behind Ferran leaves rustled, and he turned, every sense alert. But it was only a squirrel that pattered across the ground. Itch moved to go after it, but Ferran shushed him and told him to sit.

Itch tracked the squirrel with focused attention but stayed where he was.

"He's a sitting duck," Caswal whispered. "Should we take him?"

Ranoc shook his head. "We wait," he said in a hush. "We follow the plan."

Caswal nodded.

The scout began to move again, stealing closer to the blocked road. Ferran tensed, still not believing he was about to take on a band of killers. He scanned the woods around the clearing, wondering when Borros would appear.

Below, the scout moved until he was just a few yards away from the fallen tree, and then he stepped out of cover. He peered through the leaves of the fallen tree, then signaled to the men on the far side of the clearing to advance. He turned around to proceed further, clearly having decided there was no threat, and that's when Lagash's crossbow thwapped. A dark streak flew out of the leaves of the fallen tree, struck the scout, and exited his back.

He cried out, clutched at his chest, and stumbled backward. Then Krov rose from the greenery of the fallen tree and did not sling, but hurled a fist-sized stone at the man. The stone hit him in the head, and he staggered one more step and fell to the ground.

Krov withdrew back into the leaves of the tree.

Suddenly bows on the other side of the clearing thrummed. Arrows raced across the open ground and snicked into the leaves where Krov had gone. They smacked into the trunk and branches.

A moment later Krov yelled in pain.

Ferran's heart raced. His anxiety grew. They hadn't expected men with bows. They hadn't planned for them. He looked across the clearing. Three archers had come to the edge of the clearing and taken position behind different trees. They held hunting bows, which, while not as powerful as warbows, would be more than enough to kill a bunch of boys because neither Ferran nor anyone else in the group had armor of any kind.

The archers released another volley.

Krov groaned loudly again. He was surely pierced in half a dozen places.

Fear gripped Ferran, urged him to run.

And then five men with helmets, knee-length mail, and big round shields moved out of the woods at the far end of the clearing. They stepped closer to one another and overlapped their shields to make a solid wall.

The crossbow thwapped. A bolt flashed across the clearing and slammed into the bottom of one of the shields. The man flinched, but it appeared the bolt had not hurt him. He gave an order, and the men crouched lower as they advanced to cover more of their lower legs.

Directly opposite the boys on the other side of the clearing, another three men suddenly ran out into the open by the creek and pushed through the thick willows. They splashed into the deep water, waded across the creek, and then into the line of willows on the other side.

Ferran knew what they were doing. The men with shields were fixing Krov and Lagash. The others, across the river, were flanking. The willows shuddered and moved, and then the men exited them, exposing their backs.

The crossbow thwapped again, and a bolt flashed toward the men, but there were some saplings in the way, and the bolt struck one and careened off into the bushes. Two more men suddenly followed the first group and splashed into the creek. Ferran figured they'd been waiting for that, knowing the crossbow would take time to span and load again, and before Lagash could target them, they were through the willows on the other side.

So that was five men who were moving to circle around. There were five more with shields below. Plus the three archers. Plus the scout who was lying in the clearing in an ever-growing stain of blood. That was fourteen. The man Lagash killed back on the road made fifteen. That meant there was still a sizeable number of men unaccounted for, including Kohl-eye and Big Beard.

Ferran eyed the slope behind him, but nothing was there. He realized he was anxiously stroking Itch's head for comfort and stopped.

"We should move," Caswal said in a hushed tone.

"No," Winwalom said. "Not yet."

Krov was groaning loudly somewhere in the mass of leaves. "Don't leave me!" he suddenly pleaded.

"We can't say here," Lagash replied just a loudly.

"Please. Don't leave me!"

A tree branch shook, and then Krov and Lagash rose and sprinted up the road in the view of the robbers.

The archers raised their bows and shot arrows, but Krov and Lagash ran around a curve, and the arrows missed them.

"He didn't have a shot in him," Ranoc said confused.

"Because that was all show," Winwalom said. "A ruse to draw the men forward. To make them think there's a third person lying wounded down there in the tree."

One of the soldiers in the shield wall shouted, and the whole line began to advance more quickly, shields up. And Ferran saw that he'd been mistaken before. Not all of them were wearing mail. Two of them looked to be wearing nothing more than a padded jacket. But they all had shields and helmets, which meant killing the men wasn't going to be like plunking rabbits.

"I think this is our cue," Ranoc said in a low voice, but he didn't move.

Ferran couldn't bring himself to move either, but then Winwalom rose to a crouch, and the movement gave Ferran the courage to rise as well. He chastised himself for his cowardice and the sickening dread he still felt. But the other boys rose as well, and it gave him more confidence.

And then Winwalom moved forward, and the others followed him in a line to the spot where the trees ended and the open space on the slope began. Winwalom removed his sling from his belt and took out two egg-sized stones. The other boys did the same.

Below, the men continued to advance in their line toward the fallen tree. They reached the middle of the clearing and passed it.

"Ranoc and Ferran," Winwalom whispered. "You're the better slingers. You take the archers. Keep them from shooting us to pieces. Caswal and I will take the shield men. And we'll all pray that Borros shows up before we're overwhelmed. Are you ready?"

Ferran and Ranoc nodded.

"Don't panic," Winwalom said. "Don't throw wild. Just aim and sling. Aim and sling like we're hitting posts at some competition back at home."

Ferran's heart was pounding like a galloping horse. His hands were shaking. How was Winwalom keeping himself so calm?

"Okay, you two first," Winwalom said and pointed at Ranoc and Ferran.

Ferran took a big breath, then slipped silently out of the cover and into the sun, Itch at his side. Ranoc came behind.

The boys quickly moved out into the open space in a line, making sure to give each other enough room to wield their slings.

Ferran marked an archer, and slipped a stone in his sling. But Winwalom was the first to sling. He spun his sling once, making a whumping sound, took a big stride, and released the stone. It sped down at the shield men, striking a man in the back of his calf.

The man cried out and faltered.

Ferran's spirits rose, and he slung his stone at the closest archer. It was a good shot, but just a tad wide, and missed its mark. He chastized himself. He was the best slinger here, and he needed to show it. He took a big breath and slipped in another stone.

The men and archers below were confused. They hadn't seen the boys yet.

Caswal and Ranoc slung a volley with Winwalom right behind them, making a small chorus of whumps. One stone hit a man in the back. Another nailed a man in his helmeted head. He cried out. And then an archer spotted the boys and shouted out their position.

The leader of the shield men gave an order, and three of the line below turned to face the new threat.

Ferran knew it was easier to avoid a stone if it arched high. It was much harder to see and avoid a stone that was thrown straight on. And so he sighted on the chest of the second archer who was raising his bow, whipped the sling around, and flung as hard as he could in a straight line.

His stone flew true. The archer raised his bow. Aimed. But then Ferran's stone struck him right by the collar bone of his bow arm. The archer twisted, released the arrow in a wide shot, and staggered back.

A thrill ran through Ferran. He grabbed another stone. Placed it. Saw the first archer aiming his bow. Ferran marked him and slung.

"Watch out!" Ranoc cried. "Arrow! Arrow!"

The archer released his arrow.

The other boys dove to the ground. Ferran stepped to the side of where he'd been, and watched the archer do the same, letting the stone sail right through the spot the archer had been standing.

Ferran placed another stone. He was going to nail that whoreson. And then he saw the second archer raise his bow. Ferran marked him, slung, and released. He didn't wait to see where the stone struck but pulled another stone out of his shoulder bag and placed it.

The other boys rose. A moment later came the whup, whup, whup of three more slings.

Ferran felt ecstatic. As deep as his dread had been, he was now filling with nervous excitement.

The third archer, the one Ferran had already hit, grabbed his bow and began to climb to his feet. Ferran marked his face, slung with all the force he could muster, and grabbed another stone.

The stone flew like a black messenger and struck the man right above the ear. The man wobbled, then toppled to the grass.

Ferran placed a stone. There was a frenzy on him. A euphoric joy. A sense of invulnerability.

Suddenly one of the shield men cried out and dropped his shield. He clutched at his back and turned, revealing a crossbow dart sticking out of his mail.

Lagash and Krov were back! One shieldman was injured in his calf and limping. The scout, an archer, and another shieldman were down.

"We're going to win this!" Ferran said. "We're going to beat these whoresons."

The slings of the other boys whirled and whupped. Stones struck shields and helmets. Ferran saw one of the archers stepping out to shoot and slung his stone at him.

"To the slope!" one of the shield men growled. "To the slope!" And they began to move toward the trees at the base of the slope the boys were on, seeking cover. A stone struck the top of a shield. Another glanced off a man's helmet.

The crossbow thwupped again. This time the bolt streaked toward one of the two remaining archers. Ferran loaded another stone and slung at a shield man who was holding his shield a bit low. The stone struck the front of his helmet with a pop and almost knocked it off the man's head.

Itch had been barking this whole time, but now he turned to face up the slope, and the pitch of his barks changed, became more urgent.

Ferran placed another stone looked for an archer to target, but couldn't find one, so turned back to the shield men. The two shield men facing the boys were now holding their shields up at an angle, covering both themselves and the men behind. But one of the men held his shield a little too high, leaving some of his lower leg visible. There was nothing protecting the leg. No padding, no mail, no leather or metal greave, nothing but trousers.

Ferran marked it. It was an easy target from this distance. He was going to crack that whoreson's leg bone.

Itch's barking became vicious and he surged a pace toward something up the slope from the boys.

A small alarm sounded inside Ferran's mind. He glanced up the hill.

Charging down the slope through the trees were at least another half-dozen men, axes and swords drawn, Kohl-eye and Big Beard among them. They were coming fast. Only a few seconds away.

25

THE BOY EATER

"**B**EHIND US!" Ferran cried.

Caswal and Ranoc slung their stones with a staggered whup, whup, but Winwalom turned. Saw the men.

There were too many trees between the boys and the men to give any kind of clear shot with their slings. And the men were too close anyway. They'd get off a stone each, and then the men would be among them, hacking and stabbing with sword and axe.

"Run!" Winwalom cried.

"Arrow!" Caswal cried and dove to the ground.

Ranoc hit the deck. Winwalom ducked. An arrow sped at them like a malevolent insect. It flew right above Caswal and snicked into the slope behind him.

"Back!" Ferran said and sprinted back toward the cover of the trees and their spears. The other boys followed. Itch snarled at the men coming down the slope.

The men shouted and roared, and Ferran poured on the speed. This position was no longer tenable. The boys had to get to the fallback position.

Ferran dashed past the spears lying on the ground, not daring to take a moment to pick any up. He flew past the clump of trees they'd taken cover behind and ran for the rocks where Lagash had said to make their second defense. He found a thin animal trail leading across the slope to the fallback position, and Ferran ran wildly along it in his bare feet.

Behind him, he heard two of the boys suddenly change course and run down the slope, cracking branches as they went.

"Get him!" a man roared. There were shouts from the men across the creek. Others from the clearing. Men crashed through the brush.

Itch galloped past Ferran along the animal trail.

Someone thumped along the trail a number of paces behind Ferran.

Ferran raced past a bush, then up and behind the outcropping, which wasn't more than three feet high. This was the fallback, which meant he was to turn and fight, so he turned, expecting to see at least Winwalom behind him, but none of the boys were there. Instead, two men charged along the animal trail toward him. They wore no armor, but both were carrying war axes.

Ferran grabbed a stone from his pouch, loaded the sling, marked the first man's chest, and flung. The man tried to dodge to the side, but Ferran had suspected he would and had aimed just uphill of the man. The rock struck the man a glancing blow on the jaw, and he tumbled to the dirt.

Itch stood up on the hill barking, and, seeing the man down, raced out with a snarl.

Ferran loaded his sling again.

The second man saw what Ferran was up to and darted for a tree.

Ferran marked him and flung, but the man was quick and dove for cover, and the stone flew high. But Itch changed course when the man ran and rushed to viciously snap at the man's face, and then bite his arm.

The man backed away and chopped at Itch with his axe.

Itch darted back, then snarled and snapped at his leg.

Ferran slipped in another stone, whipped the sling around, flung. The stone sailed right for the man's face, but he saw it, and brought his arm up to protect himself.

The stone struck the man on the inside of his upper arm.

The man cried out in pain, grimaced, and transferred the axe to his other hand. Itch snarled at him, and the man swung the axe at him.

Ferran slipped another stone into the pouch. Marked his target, whipped the sling about, and flung with all the accuracy he could muster.

The stone flew straight and hard and smacked the man in the side of the head. The blow knocked the man's head to the side, and then he simply fell over.

The first man rose, clutching his jaw, and ran for the trees.

Itch saw him and gave chase, snapping at his feet.

"Itch!" Ferran called and reached into his pouch for another stone, but he found nothing. He looked down and realized that the pouch was hanging sideways and the stones must have bounced out in his mad run. He shoved his hand in a pocket, felt a stone and grabbed it. He looked up to mark the man who he'd hit in the jaw, but the man was well into the trees, and any shot Ferran would attempt now would probably hit a branch or trunk.

He whistled for Itch to return, then heard shouting down on the road. It was Lagash with Krov and Caswal.

"Ferran!" Lagash shouted up and pointed at a clump of trees on the slope farther up the road. "There! Join us there!"

Ferran called for Itch, then turned and dashed along the animal trail. Below, Lagash, Krov, and Caswal raced up the road, heading for the second fallback.

"Help!" Winwalom shouted.

He was calling from behind. Ferran stopped and turned, only to see three men shove Winwalom and Ranoc down the last few feet of the slope to the road. They stumbled and fell to the ground, the men right behind them. One of them kicked Winwalom in the side of the head. Ranoc tried to rise, but another kicked him so hard in the gut that Ranoc doubled over and crumpled to the road.

Anger flooded Ferran. The men weren't that far back down the road. Maybe only twenty yards away. An easy shot with his sling, but there were too many tree branches between him and the men at his current position. He shuffled a number of paces down the slope and found a big opening. A perfect line.

A third man kicked Winwalom.

Ferran slipped a stone into the sling pouch, marked the man holding

Winwalom, whirled the sling, and let it fly. The stone struck the man right in the middle of his back. He flinched, stumbled forward a step, and cried out.

Ferran slipped another stone into the pouch, targeted the man beating Ranoc, and let his stone fly.

But the man saw the stone coming and dodged sideways. The stone sailed right past his chest, but Ranoc was free. He staggered to his feet and sprint-hobbled for the trees.

Behind Ferran, Itch yelped. But Ferran had another stone in his sling. He needed to nail the one who'd just kicked Winwalom again.

And then a branch broke up the slope from Ferran. He turned, only to find a man with helmet and shield rushing down the slope at him.

Ferran repositioned himself, targeted the man's face, and flung.

The stone flew straight and true, but the man simply lifted his shield a few inches, and the stone smacked into the wood of the shield and bounced harmlessly away. And then the man crashed into Ferran, hitting him with the metal boss in the center of the shield.

It was like getting kicked by a cow. Ferran reeled back, was airborne for a moment, and then crashed to the steep slope. He tumbled wildly, struck a rock, crashed through shrubs, then landed painfully in a cloud of dust on the road below. He tried to rise, but someone grabbed him by the hair and slammed his face into something hard.

Ferran's world turned white with pain for a moment. He fell to the ground, dazed and disoriented. A man growled. Another shouted, "Kill that little whoreson!"

Someone kicked him. Another blow cracked into his back. Ferran flinched and knew the next stroke would be a sword stab or axe hack.

"Stop!" a man with a deep voice bellowed. "Stop!"

Someone stomped Ferran's side, and a whole new pain shot through him.

"I said stop!" the man snarled. "If you kill them all, there won't be anyone to tell us where the quick tar is stashed."

Quick tar was a common name for blackmeal. How had these men known Borros and Lagash carried it?

Ferran looked up to see a huge, bull of a man. He hands were huge, big enough to throttle Ferran around the neck like a chicken. He was wearing leather gloves and mail and a helmet with silver worked into it, signifying his higher status. He had a dark beard and a scarred face and looked like he ate boys for breakfast.

"Get up," the huge man said.

Ferran rose, disoriented and in pain.

"They're heading up the field of scree," one of the men called.

"Get the archers on either side of them."

The men shouted out the orders, and it seemed there were robbers all over the place. They disarmed Ferran, Winwalom, and Ranoc, taking their slings, stones, and knives.

When they were done, Ferran looked up the slope and saw Caswal and Krov scrambling up the loose rock of a scree field toward a little rise of good ground between two runs of rock. It was a knobby projection of earth with three pines and some low brush growing thickly there. A few moments later, they reached the little stand of pines and slipped into the shadows.

Ferran wondered where Itch was, and then a moment later he appeared on a ledge above the road, barking.

"Somebody kill that dog," the boy eater ordered.

One of the bowmen turned.

"Scat!" Ferran yelled. "Scat!"

The archer nocked his arrow and raised his bow.

"Scat!" Ferran yelled again, and then someone slapped him upside the head and told him to shut up.

Itch hesitated. And Itch finally got the message and ran.

The bowman loosed his arrow. It struck the bushes just to the side of the running dog.

The bowman lowered his bow and said, "He'll come back. They always do. And I'll skewer him, and skin him, and put him on a spit over the fire. It's been a while since I've had me some roast dog."

Itch would not come back. Ferran had trained him to wait for his special whistle. He'd had to train him because a few years ago Itch had caused too many problems during the harvest, and the harvest master had threatened Itch's life if he didn't stay away. Of course, Itch didn't always obey.

Mind this time! Ferran thought. *Just mind.*

"Where's the drover?" the scar-faced boy eater asked.

"With them I think," one of the men said. "I saw that dark Sorosian disappear into those trees just before the boys did. He's the one with the crossbow."

"I'm going to enjoy killing that one," the boy eater said. Then he went over and grabbed Winwalom from one of the other men. Winwalom's shirt was torn and there was blood running out his nose. One eye was almost fully swollen shut from the beating he'd taken, but he was standing, and that's all the big man needed because he marched him down the road as a shield. When he got to the part where the scree field tumbled onto the road, he stopped.

"Borros!" he shouted up. "You should have left well enough alone."

Nobody replied from the little cluster of pines up the slope.

"Come down," he said. "Or we'll kill them."

"You won't be able to sell the cattle," Lagash shouted down. "They're marked with the queen's sign. Nobody will take them."

The presence of all that rock and the shape of the slope made him surprisingly easy to hear.

"Osson will take them," the man shouted back.

"Traitors," Ranoc muttered in surprise under his breath, and the man holding him punched him so hard in the gut that Ranoc doubled over and fell to a knee.

He could pound Ranoc all he liked, that wouldn't change the fact that they were filth who were willing to betray their queen and countrymen.

"Have the cattle then," Lagash shouted. "Just leave the boys."

"We want the drover," the boy eater said. "And we want his quick tar."

It suddenly hit Ferran that these men weren't just cattle thieves. They had known about the quick tar. They were coming for it. Which meant they weren't ordinary brigands. These were men that ran along even more dangerous roads.

"Quick tar?" Lagash shouted down. "The king's eyes, but you're a fool. Nobody in their right mind would carry quick tar."

"We rung the truth out of your source. That sniveling little silver smith in Faro."

There was a pause from up on the hill, then Lagash shouted down, "I don't know of any smith. If you want Borros, he's gone. Galloped away as soon as you came and left us behind."

"Then why is his mangy pony still here?"

There was no reply from the little cluster of pines, and Ferran wondered if that little stand of pines was where Borros had gone to wait for the earthmight to rise in him. And then Ferran began to wonder about what Borros had shaken out of the bottle.

"Give us the quick tar, and we'll let you go in peace," the boy eater shouted up. But there was no reply.

A robber with a weak moustache standing next to the big man said, "It seems he needs a bit of motivation. I'm thinking the sight of blood will help. Which one do you want me to kill?"

"This one will do," the huge man said and shoved Winwalom at him.

26

LAGASH

JUST THEN, UP the slope, the crossbow thwacked. It was a small sound but carried clearly down the rock. The robbers all ducked, and a bolt whistled past them and buried itself in the road behind.

The boy eater turned to his men. "I'm not going to waste any more time. Go get that dark piece of Sorosian filth and bring him here. Have Luz and the others with shields approach from the bottom."

The four men with the shields, helmets, and mail began to climb up the slope of scree, crouching behind their shields as they went. They didn't make a line but did keep close together and advanced without haste. They were clearly men who knew what they were doing, and Ferran suspected they were former soldiers.

The crossbow thwacked, and the men hunkered down. The bolt hit one of their shields and even broke through partway, but it wasn't enough to injure the man, and the group continued their ascent. Krov and Caswal slung stones, and while the stones struck the shields with plenty of force, they did not break through the wood.

Ferran imagined himself up in that little knob of pines, the men presenting hardly any target worth hitting. It was not a good place to be. What they needed were their spears. But the spears lay back by the clearing.

The men continued. One took a step and sent a little cascade of scree skittering down, and Ferran wondered why Lagash and the others didn't run now while they had a chance. But then he saw the bowmen in the trees on both sides of the scree field and knew that if Lagash and the others left the cover of the pines, they would be easy targets. They'd be stuck with arrows before they made it across the loose rocks.

Lagash and the others had been fixed, and now the men in shields were coming as the flank. Or was it the other way around? Ferran didn't know. All he knew was that Lagash and the others were truly trapped.

The shield men continued to advance, and when they were maybe only ten feet from the pines, the crossbow thwacked again. This time, at such a close range, the force of the bolt was strong enough to penetrate one of the men's shields. The man holding the shield cried out and stumbled back, although Ferran couldn't see if the bolt had also penetrated his mail.

But the other men took that as their cue and, with a roar, surged forward. It appeared this moment is what the men on the other side of the scree field had been waiting for, and the five of them streamed out of the trees with a yell and raced across the slide of rock to join the others.

There wasn't enough time for Krov to span the crossbow again, and so it was just the three of them against nine men.

Caswal and Krov tried to put up a fight, but the men entered the pines, knocking the boys down, kicking them and striking them with their feet and the butts of their spears, and then it was over. A few moments later, two of the men stepped back out onto the loose rock and looked up into the trees.

"Can you see anyone up there?" one of them called to the bowmen.

The boughs of one of the pines began to jostle, and shortly thereafter Ferran spotted one of the men climbing up the trees. He ascended another ten or fifteen feet and shouted to the men below him that nobody was there.

One of the shield men came to the edge of the nub of pines and shouted down the slope. "The drover's not here."

The boy eater cursed, then wrenched Winwalom's arm up behind his back. "Where is he?"

"I don't know," Winwalom said.

The man turned on Ranoc.

"He left," Ranoc said in fright. "I don't know where."

"You don't, eh? Well, we shall see." And he turned and yelled up the slope for the men to bring the others down.

Up the slope, the men hauled Krov and Caswal out of the pines and shoved them forward. The two boys began to descend the field of loose rock, but then one of the men kicked Caswal from behind and sent him sprawling. Caswal hit the rock hard, jostled some of it loose, and slid with a patch of it.

Other men brought Lagash out. He must have taken a beating in the pines, for he could barely walk. The men shoved him as well, and he descended haltingly, clearly in pain from his injuries.

The men harried Caswal, Krov, and Lagash down the rock field, shoving and kicking, one of them jabbing them in the backs with the butt of his spear. Krov, Caswal, and Lagash tripped, stumbled, and fell their way down the field of scree, the men jeering them from behind.

Ferran saw movement in the trees up the slope, and hoped it was Borros. But it was Itch, who simply looked down on the spectacle.

Good boy, Ferran thought. *Good boy. Stay away!*

And then Lagash and the others reached the bottom and were forced to their knees in front of the big man. He strode up to Lagash. "Where is he?"

"I don't know." Lagash's lip was split and bleedling. Blood was runing out of his nose and into his teeth.

The man struck Lagash in the face, knocking him to the dirt.

"Where is he," he demanded again.

Lagash pushed himself upright again and felt his jaw where he had been struck. "You must be Offa."

The big man hit him again, knocking him back.

"You can beat me all you want," Lagash slurred, "but we don't know where he went."

"Where's the blackmeal?"

"He took it with him."

"So you're basically useless to me," the big man said.

"Maybe he'll negotiate for our lives," Lagash said.

"Him?" he asked and barked a laugh. The big man turned and

shouted up the road. "Borros, you coward. You care about these worthless rots? We're going to start killing them. You want us to spare their lives? Then come down and talk."

He waited for a bit, but there was no response besides the mooing of a few cattle farther up the road.

Offa the Boy Eater turned back to the crew. "It looks like he doesn't want to negotiate."

"So what do we do with them?" Kohl-eye asked.

"Kill them. They're no use to us. And then we can focus everyone on finding that whoreson drover."

"Start with that runt," a short, thick man said and pointed at Ferran. "He broke Sim's jaw. Turned Hob into an idiot with a stone to the head. In fact, let me do it." He drew a long knife from the sheath at his waist and took a step toward Ferran.

Ferran's mind raced. They needed time. If Borros was actually still out there, then he just needed more time. If he wasn't there, if he'd abandoned them, or killed himself taking the old blackmeal, then Ferran would much rather die later because who knew if an opportunity might present itself for escape.

"I know where he hid it!" Ferran cried.

The big man turned.

"I know where he hit it!"

"Shut up," Lagash said.

Offa the Boy Eater held up his hand to stop the thick man coming to slit Ferran's throat. "It seems the runt has something to say."

"I know where he hid it," Ferran said. "It's in a brown bottle with thick glass. I saw him hide it. But I won't tell you unless you give me your oath you won't kill us."

27
RUSE

"WHERE IS IT?" Offa demanded.

"Not without your oath."

Offa motioned with his chin at the man holding Ferran, who painfully wrenched Ferran's arm behind his back.

"Where is it?" he repeated.

Pain shot up Ferran's arm and shoulder. "Your oath," he groaned.

The man continued to wrench until Ferran thought he was going to actually wrench his shoulder out of its socket.

"Your oath," Ferran cried out in pain.

Offa motioned for the man to stop. "Fine. I won't kill you."

The man let Ferran's arm go, and Ferran brought it around and cradled his shoulder. "None of your men can kill us either. Tie us up if you want, but you have to promise to leave us whole. Otherwise, I won't say a word."

Offa smiled, and Ferran knew his oath wasn't worth a flea's fart, but they needed time.

"Fine," Offa said. "I give you my oath. If you lead us to the black-meal, we will tie you up, but leave you unmolested."

"Don't take him there," Lagash said. And Ferran knew Lagash was playing along to make it seem like Ferran was telling the truth.

"You should shut up," Offa said and slapped him with his massive open hand. "The runt is saving your life."

The blow seemed to daze Lagash, who shook his head, trying to clear his wits.

Ferran said, "All of my crew comes. I will lead only you and three of your men. The others have to stay here."

"Four of us against five of you? I don't think that's fair. How about seven or eight? No, I think I need ten."

"Ten," Ferran agreed. "But no more." And he wondered how short this extension of his life would be.

Offa selected his men and told the others to remain behind, then motioned at Ferran. "Lead the way, rat."

Ferran figured the easiest place for Borros to find them would be on the road. He knew he couldn't go too far, but he figured he might be able to play it out for a quarter of a mile.

"It's back a ways," Ferran said, "but I know where it is. Just follow me." Then he began to walk back down the road. He played up his injuries and walked slowly, but it didn't seem slowly enough, for they quickly came to the tree they'd toppled across the road, skirted around it, and crossed the clearing. When they got to the other side, Offa said, "If you're leading me on a goose chase, I will hack off your feet and leave you for a bear to chew on."

"I know exactly where it is," Ferran said. "It's an odd brown bottle of thick glass. That's what you're looking for, right?"

"He showed it to you?"

Ferran caught a note of disbelief in that question, and said, "No, I caught him looking at it. I went to find him to ask him what we should do about you, and he was looking at these little lumps in his palm. One was black with a spidering of white through it. He didn't notice me. I came from behind and surprised him. He immediately closed his fist around the lumps and tried to act like it was nothing. But after I left, I glanced back and saw him burying the bottle and thought it odd. Who buries bottles in the middle of nowhere? I didn't know what it was then, but that has to be the quick tar, right?"

Offa grunted.

"I have your oath," Ferran reminded him.

"Oh, yes indeed, rat," the man said.

And so Ferran led the massive Offa and ten of his men back down the road, praying every moment that Borros would appear.

Kohl-eye was one of those that Offa had selected to come with him. He walked next to Ferran. "Well, well, well. If it isn't the boy in the dark. You should have run to Pencoy's."

Ferran shrugged.

"Warning them didn't do you any good, did it? It shows just how stupid you are. A stupid boy from a stupid little village."

Kohl-eye's skinny, tall companion walked on the other side of Ferran. "Maybe we can give his mother our regards. Give him a kiss from her son. Such a fetching woman needs some use."

He sounded like he'd seen her.

"He doesn't remember me," the skinny man said to Kohl-eye. "I'm offended."

"Last night was the first time I laid eyes on you," Ferran said.

"But that's not true," he said with a grin. "Such ingratitude. You were laden with a heavy burden, and I helped lighten your load. You don't remember? You and your little wheel barrow."

And then Ferran knew exactly who they were. "You," he said to the two men. "It was you on the road to Cor's Village."

Kohl-eye smiled. "It's coming to him."

Ferran remembered the men wearing grain sacks with slits for eyes. One had been taller and skinnier. "Did Caswal put you up to it?"

"Caswal?" Skinny asked.

Kohl-eye laughed and rapped Ferran on the head a few times with his knuckles. "They truly must grow them stupid in Buckle Hill."

And then Ferran knew.

"Hellum," he said. "Hellum tipped you off."

Hellum, that rich maggot of a farmer. Was he right now trying to pressure Ferran's mother into his bed?

"Hellum," Kohl-eye said, thinking. He turned to the skinny man. "Do we know anyone named Hellum?"

"I can't say that we do," Skinny said. "But then again, I can't say that we don't."

"Did he pay you?" Ferran asked in disgust.

"Now you're starting to see the light," Kohl-eye said.

"He paid you." Ferran's mind raced. Hellum had wanted mother poor and destitute so he could stroll in like some fancy savior. "Did he pay you to steal our original vessels from the cheese house? Did he pay you to poison our milk cow?"

Kohl-eye just grinned. "It looks like you've got a score to settle. So let's hope you're not leading us on a goose chase, because it's going to be mighty hard for you to give Hellum his just dues if you're missing your feet."

Hellum, Ferran thought. The whoreson. He'd orchestrated their downfall.

"I'm thinking," Skinny said. "If the rat here doesn't make it, maybe we should pay the cheese mistress a visit anyway."

"I like that idea. I'm sure Hellum wouldn't mind sharing her with us."

"Leave my mother out of this."

Kohl-eye just laughed. "Boy, if I were you, I wouldn't be worrying about cheese vessels and lusty farmers wanting to plow new fields. You've got your feet to think about."

Anger boiled up in Ferran. Hellum. That rotted blackheart. He was going to pay for this.

That was, if Ferran made it out alive. He peered into the woods on both sides, willing Borros to appear. But the big drover was nowhere to be seen.

Ferran continued walking down the road, playing up his injuries so he could slow the pace. Surely Borros would appear at any moment. But Borros didn't appear, and when they were some distance from the clearing, Kohl-eye said, "He's playing us."

"I'm not," Ferran said.

"You couldn't have seen him here," Kohl-eye said, "because I was following you when you passed this spot, and you didn't stop. You rode right on by, you and the dark one on the drag sled."

"No, it's up ahead," Ferran said.

"You saw them?" Offa asked Kohl-eye.

"They rode straight through. Look at the pole lines the drag sled made."

Offa looked at the road, then turned his terrible gaze on Ferran.

"It's up ahead," Ferran said and quickened his pace.

"Grab him," Offa said.

Skinny grabbed Ferran by a fistful of hair and yanked him back.

"You've got some spark, rat," Offa said. "I'll give you that. But you didn't put it to good effect. All you've done is wasted my time." He turned to one of his men. "Bring me that axe."

"I made a mistake," Ferran said. "The hiding place is back up the road a little bit."

Offa struck him and knocked him to the ground. The blow jarred Ferran, disoriented him. It felt like he'd been struck by a mountain.

"I don't want to hear any more of your lies," Offa said. "I made an oath, and now I'm going to keep it. I'm a man of my word."

Ferran was still disoriented, but he tried to back away, except one of the other men lowered his spear into Ferran's back. The point bit in, and Ferran stopped. Another man grabbed Ferran, shoved him to the dirt, and kneeled on his back.

Ferran struggled, thought he was going to suffocate, then finally found his breath and took a gasp of air and dust from the road.

A man handed Offa a war axe. He whirled it once, loosening his shoulder, then reached out and measured the distance to Ferran's leg. He said, "I would hold still if I were you. You don't want me to have to hack it twice."

Ferran struggled again, but the man kneeling on him struck him in the face. It felt like a hammer. The man struck him again. Ferran thought he blacked out. When he came to, someone was tying cords around his ankles. The man gave a signal, and the cords were pulled tight.

"No," Ferran said, his face in the dirt, realizing Offa truly was going to hack his legs off at the knees.

Suddenly Farmer Hellum's warning rose in Ferran's mind. *"You're going off with a strange man whose own crew turned on him. You're going into danger. Mark me, if you come back at all, you're going to come back empty-handed."*

It was all as Hellum had predicted and worse. Ferran was going to lose his lower legs and bleed out here on this lonely road to the Blight, many days from home, where nobody in their right mind would travel.

Nobody but vultures and crows would find his remains. And his mother or sister would go into bondage, wondering if he'd died or simply abandoned them.

He bucked, strained, tried to get away, but he could barely move.

Offa raised the axe for the chop.

I'm so sorry, mother, Ferran thought. *I'm so sorry.*

Ferran's heart sank under the burden of his foolishness. Why had he ever trusted Borros?

And then the road darkened. And something in the woods whispered. Something evil and hungry with long bony fingers and claws.

The hair on the back of Ferran's neck rose.

Offa paused, the axe still raised. "What was that?" he asked.

The voice whispered again. It was the voice of something that promised to keep Ferran and feast on his blood. Something that would pluck out his eyes and eat them like plums. There was a horror slipping toward them through the trees. A nightmare.

A number of Offa's men murmured and drew their swords in alarm and faced the woods.

The man kneeling on Ferran rose to one knee and drew his knife.

And then Offa groaned in sudden pain.

Ferran glanced up. Offa was standing there, axe in hand, but protruding from his chest was the bloody head of a spear.

Offa dropped the axe, which thudded into the dirt next to Ferran, and looked down at the blade that had impaled him, his eyes wide in pain and shock. And then he tumbled to the ground, heavy as a bull.

Something dark flashed past and struck the man kneeling on Ferran. He toppled over, blood streaming from a wound to his head that showed white bone.

Ferran saw the man's knife and took it to cut his bonds.

One of Offa's men shouted and charged Lagash with a sword.

Lagash lunged for the war axe lying on the ground next to Ferran. The man closed the gap. But Lagash dodged to the side, and with a grimace of pain struck the man in the back of the neck as he passed.

Ferran cut through his bonds.

"Get up!" Lagash yelled to the boys. "Fight!"

The woods whispered again. It was a creature a bone coming for them. A creature of death. Of darkness and torture.

Ferran rose, yanked the spear out of Offa's back, and whirled, looking for the nightmare in the woods.

Another one of Offa's men charged Lagash.

"He's come!" Lagash shouted, parrying the man's blow. "Fight, boys! Fight! Borros has come!"

Mists of darkness flowed out of the woods and onto the road. In the middle of it was a figure. The nightmare was upon them. Ferran's fear raged.

And then Borros rushed out of the darkening woods, sword in hand, the darkness emanating from him. He was the lord of bones. The lord of devouring. The lord of death.

28

BATTLE LINE

B ORROS STABBED A man. He whirled, swung his sword, and cut another man in the side. Wisps of darkness swirled about him as he moved.

Offa and three of his men lay in the road. Four others were fleeing, Kohl-eye and Skinny among them, but three of the men stood to fight, two with shields. They were hard men, anger in their eyes. One charged Borros with shield and sword, but the man exposed his flank.

It was a clear target, and Ferran moved, almost without thinking. See the target; strike the target. He lunged forward as they'd practiced, and the spear blade sunk deep into the man's side.

The man cried out and recoiled from the stab. And Borros finished him with a blade into the man's face.

Ferran pulled his spear out, horrified, and turned to face the other men.

The second man roared and raised his sword to lunge, but Krov was there and struck the man in the back of the head with a log. The man crumpled to one knee.

The final man saw his predicament, took a step back, his face a mask of horror, then turned and ran. But before he could take a second step,

Borros was upon him. He moved with terrible speed and might. His blade flashed, and the man fell to the road.

Borros turned and spoke. But it was Death that was speaking. "Where are the rest?" he asked, his voice full of a power that reached right into Ferran's heart and made him quail.

"There are a dozen or more back by the clearing," Lagash said. "Two archers, maybe three, others with spears, swords, axes."

"Face them. Fix them," Borros said. "I will go around behind." And then he charged into the woods.

The mists of darkness began to fade. Ferran's fear began to subside. He felt like he'd been hit by a huge ocean wave and slammed onto the beach.

"We must move quickly," Lagash said. "We have no idea how long the earthmight will last. Get a weapon! Move!"

Ferran had his weapon, the spear that had skewered Offa. Ranoc was taking a spear from another man's hand. Winwalom held a man's shield and spear, but he winced at his injuries. Krov stood with a spear and a sword. Caswal was on his knees, wide-eyed with fear.

Lagash kicked him. "Get up!" He shoved a spear at him. "Take this!"

Caswal looked at it like he'd never seen one before.

"Get up!" Lagash roared.

Caswal clutched it and rose, his face still showing the remnants of horror.

"Follow me," Lagash shouted, holding a sword and shield. "Quickly."

Lagash jogged down the road, grunting in pain. The others followed.

The horrible image of Borros still filled Ferran's mind. He'd never seen such power. Never felt anything like it. And for the first time in his life he realized the stories of the anointed didn't come close. He now knew why the meals of power were called godmeal.

He ran along behind Lagash as if in a daze. He remembered Itch and thought he should whistle for him, but then they arrived at the clearing and stopped. On the other side, the remaining group of robbers stood in a line. There were a dozen of them. The two original archers stood on the side plus another man who'd picked up the fallen archer's bow.

They sneered at Lagash and his little line of boys.

"Kill them!" one of the robbers shouted.

The archers raised their bows and drew their arrows.

"Get down!" Lagash shouted. "Crouch behind the shields."

Lagash and Winwalom knelt behind their shields. Krov and Caswal crowded behind. Ranoc and Ferran, seeing there wasn't room, dashed for the trunk of a fat tree.

The bows hummed. Arrows struck the shields. Another zipped into the trees where Ferran and Ranoc were.

The archers drew again.

"Forward!" the leader shouted, and the line of robbers began to advance. "I want all of their heads!"

And then Death whispered across the clearing, and the line of brigands faltered. The lord of devouring was here.

However, this whisper hadn't carried the power it had earlier. Whether that was because the earthmight was fading or it didn't have a long range, Ferran didn't know. All he knew is that while he felt the menace, his inmost parts did not quail as they had before.

"Forward five paces," Lagash said. And then he and Winwalom rose with their shields up and marched forward, then crouched again. Caswal and Krov followed their lead. Ferran ran out from behind the tree and crouched behind them.

A large stone flew from the trees behind the line of brigands and struck an archer, knocking him five paces back, and sending him to the ground.

"Behind you!" one of the archers cried. "Behind you!"

A number of the men turned to face the new threat.

"Wait for it," Lagash said.

And then the mists of darkness reached out again from the woods at the men.

"There!" one of the robbers shouted, and suddenly Borros raced out of that darkness and was among the archers, his sword flashing. He stabbed one, slashed another. The third archer tried to flee up the slope, but Borros caught him by the ankle, pulled him back, and skewered him.

"Battle line!" Lagash shouted.

The boys rose and moved into their battle line.

"Forward!" Lagash said and began to march forward. The boys lowered their spears and marched with him.

"Keep in line," Lagash said.

Behind the robbers, Borros yelled and the shout slammed into Ferran and passed through him.

"Get him!" one of the robbers shouted, and the battle line that had formed at the other end of the clearing dissolved. One man hurled his spear at Borros and missed.

Lagash picked up his pace to a slow jog. The boys followed.

"Keep in line!" Lagash ordered.

The boys maintained their line.

Borros charged into the men, his sword flashing. By this point, none of the robbers were paying any attention to Lagash and his crew.

"Find a target, then break it," Lagash said. "That's all you need to do. Get ready."

The men were shouting. The boys were jogging toward them. Borros struck a man, fled a few paces, struck at another. The men surged after him.

Ferran and the others closed the distance between themselves and the melee of men and swords and axes and spears. They were full-grown men. Strong men. Brutal. Kohl-eye, Big Beard, and Baldy were among them. Ferran's mouth went dry, and he tried to swallow, but found his mouth cleaving to the back of his throat.

One of the men turned, saw them, and shouted.

"Now!" Lagash roared and surged forward.

Ferran shouted a wild cry full of fear and bloody intent and the line of boys and an injured cook charged with blades into a disordered group of seven or eight men. Ferran looked for a target. Saw a man's back. Saw the line under his ribs where the kidney would be. He thrusted his spear. He felt it glance off bone and sink into the man's back.

The man cried out and fell to a knee.

Ferran yanked his spear out and struck the man in the back again. This time the man fell to the earth. Ferran looked for another target. Ranoc and Krov were fighting men to either side. Ferran looked at Ranoc's man, and then Skinny appeared in the gap between Ranoc's and Krov's foes, spotted Ferran, roared, and charged with an axe.

Ferran's attention snapped to Skinny. Find a target! Find a target! All Ferran could see were his eyes, and so he thrust the spear blade right at them.

Skinny turned, but the blade sliced open the side of his face. Skinny roared, fury and hate in every feature. Ferran pulled the spear back and thrust again, striking him in the chest.

Skinny recoiled from the blow and staggered back. And then Itch darted in, snarling, to bite the back of his leg. Skinny cried out and went down.

Ferran looked for another target. A man thrust his shield forward to block Ranoc's blow. However, when he pushed forward, he left his chest exposed.

Ferran lunged for the ribs and lungs underneath, but another man swung his sword and knocked Ferran's spear down, leaving Ferran's whole side exposed. The man stabbed forward with his sword. But Krov knocked the sword down with a fat branch, then slammed the man in the face with a two-handed swing.

What had happened to Krov's spear?

The man staggered back.

Ferran whipped his spear back up. Their battle line had broken. It was all now a jumble of men and boys.

"Find a target," he told himself and saw Winwalom on his back, holding his shield up to fend off the blows of a man hacking at him with an axe. The man's thigh was exposed. Ferran aimed for the middle and stabbed.

The man cried out and clutched at the spear, but Ferran yanked it back.

Then Ranoc slammed into Ferran from behind and sent him stumbling. And Ferran found himself on the ground, wide open for attack. He scrabled up, knowing a blade was going to slice into him at any moment.

A man thumped to the ground in front of Ferran's face, and suddenly the press of men was lessening. And the remaining robbers were breaking, running in different directions.

Borros flew at one man. His sword flashed, and the man went down. Caswal ran past Borros, chasing another man. Ranoc joined him. But Itch was faster than both of the boys and caught up to the man and bit him in the leg.

The man stumbled, and then Caswal rushed in and stabbed him in the back, sending the man tumbling. He stabbed him again, and a third time.

Three robbers backed themselves up to the slope. Kohl-eye was one of them. Krov and Lagash advanced on them, then Kohl-eye dropped his weapon and put his hands in the air. "Please!" he said. "I surrender."

Other men were running into the trees. Caswal and Ranoc ran after them.

Borros winced, then barked at Ranoc and Caswal. "Get back here! Get back!"

They didn't hear him.

"Ranoc!" Borros bellowed, and this time his voice slammed through Ferran as it had when Borros appeared.

"Get back!" Krov yelled.

This time Ranoc heard and turned and grabbed Caswal to prevent him from following the man.

And suddenly it was all over. The few remaining men were running through the trees. The rest were down.

Lagash ordered the men who'd surrendered to lie on their stomachs and put their hands behind their backs. Kohl-eye and Skinny were among them.

Ferran walked over and raised his sword to Khol-eyes face. "Just a stupid boy from a stupid village, eh?"

Khol-eye looked away.

Borros came up next to Ferran. "So I'm not the only one that has previous business with this one?"

"No," Ferran said.

Borros said, "Well you can be sure I'm not going to make the mistake I made last time."

"I can help you," Kohl-eye said.

"How did you get away from the headman at Mossby?"

"He let us go."

"You're lying."

"One of Offa's men was in the crowd when you delivered us to him.

The next day Offa was there with half-a-dozen men, and the headman let us go."

Borros shook his head. "Rot their bad sense."

Lagash ordered the other boys to bind the men. They did, and when they stepped back, Ferran looked around. All of the boys were alive. Lagash was alive. The others were bloody, their faces wild and distressed. Krov's arm looked like a butcher had been at it. Ferran looked at himself and found blood on his tunic and arms. He had a cut on his cheek that was bleeding that he didn't remember receiving. Itch came to him without a scratch, and Ferran fell to his knees and hugged him.

He and his were alive while all about them men were groaning and calling out. One was trying to crawl away, blood soaking his leggings.

Then Borros doubled over. He groaned and fell to one knee.

Ferran moved to help him.

"Stay back," Lagash warned. "Watch the woods! This isn't over yet."

"You should let us go," Kohl-eye said.

"Oh, we're going to let you go," Lagash said. "You can count on that."

Ferran and the others turned to watch the woods. Behind them, Borros twisted in pain, then toppled to the dirt, gritting his teeth, growling, the pain wracking his body.

"The earthmight is leaving him," Lagash said, scanning the woods. "Normally, it's not like this. But that's what happens when you take hog-farted Gorlander blackmeal that's a day away from going rancid. Keep your eyes on the woods, boys. Don't let the rotted whoresons sneak back. The last thing we need is to have our backs turned when they counterattack."

But the men didn't sound like they were coming back. It sounded like they were running away as fast as they could, cracking branches and tumbling rocks as they went.

A moment later Borros relaxed only to groan and writhe again.

"Do you think they'll gather and come back?" Caswal asked.

"I think they've just had the fright of their worthless lives," Lagash said. "But some men are idiots. You never know."

"I pissed my pants," Ranoc said.

"You're not the only one," Krov said.

Ferran checked his own pants and found them dry, but his heart was banging away like it wanted to jump right out of his chest. He couldn't catch his breath and had to to put the spear down and take a knee.

Winwalom's face screwed up, and he suddenly bent over and vomited in the grass.

"It's the fear washing out of you," Lagash said. "It will pass. Stand up. You're going to be fine."

Borros arched again in pain, but this time it was shorter. He grunted and rolled over on his back, taking in huge gasps of air.

They all watched him in shock.

But then he finally got his breath back and sighed. "The king's eyes," he said, exhausted. "I'm too old for this." And then he flinched again. But that soon passed as well.

"It took you long enough to arrive," Lagash said. "We almost lost Dog Boy."

"The thief?" Borros asked.

"I'm *not* a thief," Ferran said. "At least not since I joined you."

"Dog Boy saved our hides," Lagash said. "If it wasn't for him, we'd all be dead."

Borros groaned again, but it was clear whatever had taken him was passing, and he rolled over and pushed himself up onto his hands and knees. He stayed there for a moment, then climbed to his feet. He wiped some blood away from his mouth.

"How many of them are left?" he asked.

"Five or six," Lagash said.

"Rotted traitors," Borros said.

"What do we do now?" Ranoc asked.

"Strip their bodies of everything of worth. Take their mounts. I'll question these to see what we can find out about Osson so we can inform the queen."

Lagash turned to Krov. "Let me see that arm."

Krov held it out. The skin was laid open for almost the whole length of his forearm. It was a big slice with the pink and bloody flesh underneath pushing out.

"Oh," Winwalom groaned in revulsion and retched again.

"Get that bound," Borros said and motioned at Krov's arm. "And put some honey in it. That's begging for corruption. Anyone else?"

There were other cuts and bruises, and an arrowhead that had actually penetrated Lagash's shield and poked his arm, but there were no other wounds like Krov's. So Lagash and Winwalom set to finding something to bind it with. Although they might have to forego the honey because it was back with Lagash's wagon.

The other boys rounded up twenty-four horses that had been tied in the woods. And then they went to remove anything of value they found on the men. They found their slings and stone sacks and all of the knives but the one that had belonged to Caswal.

They also found boots, additional knives, swords, spears, helmets, two war axes, and four hunting bows with sheaves that contained nineteen fine arrows. They added to that coins, rings, gloves, a necklace with a fine pendant, a comb made of turtle shell, and two pair of bone dice. They brought it all back and put it in a pile. Ferran found a pair of boots that were a little too big, but he stuffed the toes with some cloth and put them on. The were dead men's boots, but they were boots.

Four of the wounded were still alive. One was so far gone, Borros didn't bother asking him anything. One was an archer who had broken his leg falling down the slope after taking a blow from Borros. Another was a man in mail who'd been stabbed in the chest. The fourth was Baldy. He had tried to flee up the road toward the cattle, but his wounds had overcome him, and he'd settled himself behind a tree, hoping they wouldn't find him.

Ferran looked for Big Beard, but he wasn't among the fallen. He'd gotten away.

Borros interrogated all of the men about their arrangement with Osson: when and where they met, who had been the go between, and the names of all involved. He asked them pointed questions about numbers and ships and many other things.

Queen Conwenna, may the ancestors bless her, had refused to back the new king of Osson as high king. So he was coming to put her down.

"Where were you to take the cattle?" Borros asked.

"To a spot on the Shaver's Coast," Kohl-eye said.

"That's Duke Rannel's land," Borros said.

There were five dukes in Akken. Rannel was probably the most powerful.

"There's no way you could take a herd this size across his lands without him noticing," Borros said.

"Notice?" Kohl-eye asked. "He's the one that employed Offa. Which means you have just made yourself a powerful enemy."

"Rannel," Borros said in disgust.

"Sounds like he wants to supplant the queen," Lagash said.

"It makes sense," Borros said. "He's wanted the crown for a long time. Now is his chance to join with Osson, slaughter the queen and her army, and set himself up as the new king of Akken. One that is willing to bow to Osson rot."

"The mage queen won't win a war against Osson," Kohl-eye said. "It's not just Osson coming. Gallas the high king has called the armies of Norsson, Bergon, and Drochia to join him. Domania as well. Armies from five kingdoms. Akken cannot stand against them. The queen was foolish to rebel. But you don't have to follow her in her foolishness. Take these cattle to Rannel. Spare our lives, and we'll help you."

"I hired you once before, and that didn't turn out so well, remember?"

"Now we'd be on the same side.

Borros drew his sword.

"Rannel will need men like you. You could rise far."

"Rannel is a weasel turd."

Kohl-eye motioned at Lagash. "He promised to spare me."

"And we shall. We're going to spare you a long torture."

"I know where you can get blackmeal, bonemeal, redmeal."

"Oh?"

"Yes. I could lead you there," he said earnestly.

"I already know about the Serpent Circle," Borros said. "And you'd be leading us to our deaths."

"I could ease your way in."

"How did you find out about the silver smith?"

"It wasn't me. I didn't touch the man. It was Offa."

"How did you find out about him?"

"That quick tar wasn't the smith's to give," Kohl-eye said. "It was Offa's. It was stolen. And he was simply taking it back."

"You didn't answer my question."

Baldy spoke up. "Offa tracked down the thieves. They were the smith's men."

"But Offa's gone now," Kohl-eye said. "You could step in his place."

Borros looked at Kohl-eye in disgust. "You're a maggot, Drogan. Do you really think I would trust you? Or that I would want to join you? You have allied against the queen. You've invited Osson filth to plunder our lands and rape our women and make us all thralls. I am a queen's man. A war is almost upon us, and you selected the wrong side." And with that he killed Kohl-eye, and then proceeded to kill all of the others.

29

OATH

FERRAN WAS SHOCKED by the brutality. He was shocked by all the dead bodies, the flies that were already buzzing about them, the gore.

Borros saw him and said, "You look a little pale, Dog Boy."

"I thought we accepted their surrender. I thought—"

"Are we in any shape to watch prisoners? Do we have so many men we can tend to the wounds of our enemies?"

"No."

"This is but one battle, Ferran. There are traitorous men still out there. Was this their whole band, or did they only bring a part? Are they right now feeding their rage and convincing themselves to take revenge because we killed a brother or cousin?"

"I don't know."

"No, you don't. If I let these go, they would only join them, and add their numbers to those that might attack us again. Maybe even go and bring back men loyal to that slime Duke Rannel. If I kept them, we'd have three traitors in our midst, looking for a way to get the advantage and betray us. We are two men, five boys, and a dog. Most of us are injured to some degree. They chose death when they attacked us. Did you forget they almost hacked off your legs?"

"No," he said and looked down at the dead men.

"Battle is a bloody business," Borros said. "But better bloody than dead. And now we need to get the cattle to the next steading."

Ferran nodded. The men who had chased them were indeed not only outlaws, but traitors. And he suddenly began to wonder about Hellum. He had hired these men. But how had he known who they were and how to get in contact with them? Was Hellum himself part of their network? If so, did that mean he was supporting Rannel? And was Rannel the only one that had turned against the queen? How many enemies did she have in her own kingdom?

"What's the Serpent Circle?" Ferran asked.

Borros looked down at him. "It's a dark society that stretches across multiple lands. It's a tainted vine that only produces poisonious fruit."

"A criminal society?"

"Yes. They're like a disease that rots and cankers whatever it touches."

"And Offa and these men were part of that?"

"Offa was part of it. He came back from the wars with Soros and became a thug. And these men followed him."

"And your silver smith had some association with them?"

Borros saw where Ferran was going with this line of thinking and shook his head. "No, the smith was as good a man as you could find."

And yet he was a criminal, for it was illegal to possess, transport, or sell godmeal.

"I know what you're thinking," Borros said. "But he was a good man doing good. Sometimes the mages are blind to the needs around them. Men like the smith help rectify that."

Ferran nodded. A good man who just happened to be in the black market for goods that were forbidden.

"There are people who risk their lives and fortunes trying to help others. And then there are the vipers in the Serpent Circle. Men, and some women, who'd kill their own children for a bit of gold or position."

Lagash spoke up. "I think we need to get going."

"How close were you to fixing that wagon?" Borros asked.

"With the help of a couple of boys, I can have her back on the road in a jiffy."

They packed the loot they'd won on two horses. Then all of them rode back, except for Lagash who preferred to rig another drag sled. They brought all the horses with them plus carrots and the mule pulling the korrog. They wanted to leave nothing for any man who might have circled around or lingered in the woods.

Ferran hurt all over, but he was glad that was the extent of it. He was astonished he was not dead. Astonished that he had fought in a battle line and not died.

And now that he looked back on it, it seemed that it had been over in a flash. It had been a flurry of panic and stabbing, of men shouting and grimacing and roaring as they faced the demon that was Borros and the little band at their backs.

But of course it hadn't been just that. For the voice of death had fought as well and smitten the men before a blade had touched them. It had darkened the very air, and Ferran shuddered. thinking about what the voice had said.

When they reached the cook's wagon, they found the barrels and boxes scattered about. Lagash located his little hogshead of wine and took it to wash Krov's wound. When he'd finished that, he told him to drink some, and then drink some more. And when the wine had dulled Krov a bit, Lagash stitched up the huge gash on his arm with a bone needle and linen thread, the skin tugging with almost every stich. Krov gritted his teeth and grunted in pain, but when Lagash was done, the wound was closed with meticulous stiching. Lagash smeared honey on it, then a layer of oil, then wrapped it with a clean cloth and tied it tight.

"That's going to leave a nice scar," Borros said.

"Let's hope that's all it does," Lagash said. "Lesser wounds have corrupted and killed."

"Should I have a hundred years to contemplate a face as fine as thine," Krov said.

"I think you gave him too much to drink," Borros said.

"No," Krov said. "It's the first line of my poem."

"Very nice," Ferran said. "What happens if you have a hundred years?"

"I don't know," Krov said stumped.

"Well," Lagash said, "make sure you include the fact that you fought a battle and took that scar just so you could gaze upon her fair beauty once again."

"She might swoon at that," Borros said.

"A swoon would be a definite possibility," Lagash said.

"Scars?" Ranoc asked. "Women like scars?"

"The right kind, they do," Borros said.

Ranoc looked himself over and held up his finger and pointed at a little scratch. "That's all I've got."

"Better luck next time," Lagash said, then turned to repairing the wagon. With the help of the others, it was fixed quickly, and they traveled back up the road to the clearing.

Somehow it didn't feel right to leave the bodies of the fallen men to simply lie where they were, but Borros wasn't going to waste any time with them.

As they rode through them, the small korrog appeared and circled high overhead.

Borros waved at the creature and shouted up that it was welcome to feast.

Winwalom said, "Do we really want it getting a taste for human flesh?"

Borros shrugged. "Didn't I tell you they were like crocodiles?"

They dragged the fallen tree out of the way and proceeded up the road with their new treasure of horses.

They came upon the cattle maybe two hundred yards farther on. Ferran dismounted and worked with Itch and the others on foot to herd the cattle out of the trees and then up the road. They did not hurry the cattle, but maintained a slow, plodding pace. And that suited everyone fine because all knew they were approaching the blight.

A few miles later they came to a dilapidated steading that had an overgrown paddock and an old, one-room cabin that was sagging, but still sturdy enough. However, swallows had made dozens and dozens of mud nests in the rafters, and the floor was spattered with their droppings. They let the cattle and captured horses into the paddock, then set about repairing the fence as best they could. By early evening, they finished.

All of them went to the creek to wash themselves and their bloody clothes. Ferran scrubbed his trousers and tunic in the cold water with sand until all the blood was gone. When they came back, they started a fire, and Lagash put on a batch of porridge. Lagash added a different set of spices this time, including a large quantity of dates.

"We need ale," Borros said. "After battle a man needs ale."

"Did you forget your lecture to the boys? We are not out of danger yet. There are murderous men out there who might decide to follow us, and in following us they might talk themselves into a foolhardy courage that might lead them to attack. And even if they don't, we're on the doorstep of a blight. This is no time for ale. It's a time for vigilance."

"It's a time for roast meat then," Borros said and he ordered Ranoc and Caswal to find something succulent that Lagash could cook and salt.

"It's the earthmight," Lagash explained to the boys. "Some men are sickened by the thought of food after wielding such power. But not our hero Borros."

"I wish we had eggs," Borros said.

Lagash rolled his eyes.

Ranoc and Caswal returned with five squirrels, which caused Borros to protest mightily. But the two boys claimed that's all they'd seen. However, Ferran wondered if their proximity to the blight had spooked them, and they had not hunted as far and wide as they might have otherwise. Still, he was glad of the meat. They all skinned the squirrels, then cooked and salted the meat and ate it with the date-sweetened porridge.

Borros then asked Lagash to review the battle. Lagash told the tale in a matter of fact manner. He asked the boys to share their stories in the same way. When they were all done, Borros nodded. "You did well," he said to the boys. "You almost died, but that's to be expected. What impresses me is that you fought despite the fears that led some of you to soil your pants. What did you learn?"

Ferran said, "I learned it's nice to have Krov at your side."

"You weren't so bad yourself," Krov said.

Ranoc said, "I learned that we needed someone on the lookout.

When we were on the hill, we were all so focused on the men in the field that we allowed the other group to flank us."

"Good," Borros said. "What about you, Caswal?"

"I don't know," he said.

"Nothing?"

Caswal had been withdrawn and silent the whole evening. "I don't know."

Ferran tossed Itch his last squirrel bone, which he happily munched.

Winwalom said, "Surprise can turn the tide. Krov and Lagash surprised the scout. We surprised the shield men. Their flankers surprised us. And I think we all were surprised by Borros."

"Deception and surprise," Borros said and nodded. "That's how battles are won. What about the shield lines? You were outnumbered when you crashed into them."

Ranoc said, "They were in disarray."

Lagash said, "Remember that. We beat a force more than twice our size because we struck as a unit."

"What about you, woodsman?" Borros asked.

"Well," Krov started then hesitated. "I," he started and again and faltered.

"What is it?"

"That voice. The mists of darkness," Krov said, glancing up at Borros. "It was not natural. It was as if a demon had been brought to battle."

It was a bold statement, for who knew if mentioning the creature would draw its attention. And who knew if Borros would lash out at such impertinence.

The statement hung in the air, then Borros said, "They used to call me The Mangler. They used to call me The Body Cleaver. They used to call me Death."

Ferran believed it. And he suddenly feared Borros. He suddenly wondered what he was. Was he man? Was he demon? Ferran's mouth went dry and he tried to swallow.

"You look a little pale, Dog Boy," Borros said.

"I just..."

"Out with it."

Ferran didn't dare.

"Do you control a demon?" Winwalom asked. "Or do you serve one?"

The implications of the second question sent Ferran's mind reeling. He'd never thought Borros might serve such a creature. What would a man do who served such a being? What deeds would such a lord require?

Ferran could see some of the other boys were as surprised by the thought as he. All eyes turned to Borros.

The fire crackled.

"Did you see a demon out there?" Borros asked.

"No," Winwalom said. "Yes."

Borros looked at the boys, slowly rubbing his hands together, then came to some decision. He said, "I don't say much about my anointing. Tell an enemy your strengths, and he'll be able to prepare. Keep them hidden, make him think you're just a fat old man who likes his beef, and he'll leave himself open. It's smart to keep such things hidden. But I will tell you this. More than one gift was woven into my anointing. It was bestowed upon me by a difficult and cantankerous mage who was probably the last of his kind. It was a unique blessing."

"And did it involve demons?" Ranoc asked.

The question was so impertinet, but stated with such innocence, it made Ferran smile.

Borros smiled wryly. "I was anointed as one of the king's grimsmen. I was anointed to protect the realm. I was anointed for battle."

Caswal said, "He was anointed to be a thief."

Everyone looked at him.

"He was anointed to rob men of their courage."

And Ferran realized that this is probably what had been troubling Caswal, for he remembered Caswal frozen like a rabbit with fear when the voice had first reached into them.

Borros smiled. "Take a man's courage, and the battle is won."

Ferran imagined facing an army and then hearing that voice come from their terrible ranks. He said, "How did any armies stand against you? And why aren't you in the queen's service now?"

"You ask a lot of questions for a thief."

Ferran's hackles rose. He was not a thief!

Borros continued, "The mages are cunning, and there are ways to fight such dread. But I did not think any of those bandits would possess it. As for not being in the queen's service, what do you think I'm doing with these cattle?"

"Well, right," Ferran said. "But anyone can be a drover."

"There's a price to be paid with an anointing. Sometimes a steep price. And that is why many of those who are anointed do not have the blessing renewed, but simply let it fade until it loses all power. I filled my oath. And I would like to extend my days upon the land. I have fought many battles. And if the queen requests it, I will fight more. But there are others she has raised. It is the way of the world for the old make way for the young."

Ferran wondered how long it would take for Borros's annointing to fade until it granted him no powers.

"Don't let him fool you," Lagash said, a knowing look in his eye. "He finds retirement boring."

"Not when Lady Patience is around," Borros said.

"Lady Patience?" Krov asked with curiosity.

"Yes, a great lady with vast estates," Lagash said with a grin, emphasizing the word "estates." There was some joke there, for Borros grinned, but Ferran couldn't fathom what was so funny.

Borros said, "There's something else that's rather important that you boys are missing."

The boys looked at him expectantly.

"We may yet meet others on our journey with criminal intent. If you want us to be able to surprise them, I need you to keep your mouths shut about any blackmeal you may or may not have heard about. You will not speak of it to anyone or where anyone might overhear. Can I trust you?"

The boys nodded.

"Let me hear it from your lips."

Each of the boys said yes.

"That's good. It's also going to protect your own hides for another reason, because if the Inquisitors found out about our little battle, they would consider you suspect. They would assume you all had a part to play. And they would torture you until you confessed it."

Ferran had heard many tales of the Inquisitors. They were an order of mages to be feared, and he had no desire to have them notice him at all.

"If people hear about what happened and know you were involved, they'll know they can turn you in to earn a nice little reward. So if you want to save your own hides, it's best to keep your mouths shut. Are we agreed?"

Turning Borros in would earn a bigger reward, but Ferran didn't think now was the time to point that out.

Borros looked at them.

The boys nodded and said yes. And as the word passed Ferran's lips, he realized he had just made some criminal pact. His mother had always told him that it's best not to take the first step on a forbidden path because one step tends to lead to another, and before very long, you're so far down the path that it becomes difficult to find your way back. Ferran wondered if they had all just set their feet to one of those paths. It seemed this job was filled with forbidden roads.

"Good," Borros said. "Feel free to talk about the battle, and when you come to my role and surprise, just tell them I was one of the queen's grimsmen. An outright terror in my days."

Lagash groaned. "Oh, here he goes."

"Tell them that, and they won't think twice. Tell them that, and you won't have to fear me."

The boys eyes widened a bit, and they all nodded agreement.

Borros smiled again. "Good. You boys did well." And then he turned to Ferran. "Now to you."

Ferran braced for an accusation.

Borros said, "I'm quite certain we would have been murdered to a man had you not turned back. And that means we are, all of us, in your debt."

Ferran waited, but no recrimination followed those words, and he realized Borros was thanking him. Everyone looked at Ferran, and the collective gaze made him uncomfortable. "I, yes, well, I suppose," he stammered and then gave Itch a scratch.

"Why did you return?" Borros asked.

"Because I kept thinking of them cutting all of you down and knew I couldn't live with myself if I just let it happen. Anyone would have done the same."

"No," Borros said. "That is not true. I've seen men do just the opposite. Especially when they felt wrongly accused. But you made a great effort, at night, in this wild place."

Ferran shrugged, not knowing what to say. It was true, he had indeed saved their skins. And suddenly he felt himself brimming with a warm pride.

Borros said, "Even so, we still have not settled the matter of the stolen items."

Ferran had been thinking about how to solve the issue. He said, "Why not trust me this time and set a trap?"

Borros nodded and looked at Lagash for his opinion.

"I think a trap is a splendid idea," Lagash said.

30

TRAP

B ASED ON THE past thefts, they decided that the thief wasn't
looking to enrich himself. Instead, he was trying to survive. A bow
would be useful for that purpose, but the thief had already passed that
up. Probably because the crossbow needed bolts, and what would he do
once the supply of them was exhausted? So the bow wasn't practical.
But a horse and saddle was. And Borros now had more than twenty of
them.

And so they stacked the saddles and bridles on the wagon with the
korrog. They assigned Lagash and Winwalom the watch. The rest of
them made their beds in the shadows of the trees. But instead of sleeping, they stuffed their beds and used their hats to make it look like they
were sleeping and then positioned themselves in the darkness.

They figured the thief would steal a bridle and saddle first, then lead
a horse out of the paddock. And that's what happened. The thief came
when Lagash and Winwalom were at the far end of the rounds they
made around the camp and field.

He was wearing a dark cloak and ghosted silently from shadow to
shadow. He quietly removed one saddle from the wagon and carried it
down the road a few dozen paces to the darkness under some trees that
wasn't visible from the camp site. He waited for Lagash and Winwalom

to return and begin another round. When they were at the far end again, he came back, took a bridle, and crept over to the split-rail fence surrounding the paddock. He crept through the split-rails and into the paddock, and that's when Caswal and Ranoc stood from where they'd been hiding with the cattle.

"Hello," Caswal said.

The thief startled and sprinted back for the fence. The boys shouted an alarm and gave chase. The thief vaulted over the fence and landed nimbly on the other side only to find Krov, Borros, and Ferran waiting for him.

He charged in Ferran's direction, obviously thinking it would be easier to get by the smallest of the three. But Ferran had played ragball and knew how to tackle a man far larger than himself. It was done by taking the legs or the head. Ferran liked the head.

The thief darted to the right, and Ferran sprang onto his upper back like some large cat. He quickly wrapped himself around the thief's head. The weight pulled the thief off balance. He stumbled and tried to throw Ferran off, but that delay simply allowed Borros and Krov to catch him. A moment later Borros tripped the thief and threw him to the ground.

The thief tried to scramble away, but Krov jumped on him and took him in an iron hold. The thief struggled agaist Krov, tried to throw his head back into Krov's face, but Krov had been wrestling forever and knew that trick. Men came from miles around Buckle Hill to wrestle the woodsman and his sons. This thief, though persistent, was a piker.

"Stop your struggling," Borros said.

The thief struggled and groaned.

Borros knelt and felt around the thief's waist and came up with a knife. Borros yanked off his boots, but there were no weapons inside there either. Satisfied that they'd disarmed him, Borros rose and said, "Let's get him back to the camp fire where we can get a good look at him."

By now, everyone was there, and they hauled the thief up and marched him over to the fire.

Borros held the knife up. It was Lagash's knife with the fox inlaid in silver.

"Hold him," Borros said.

Krov had one arm up behind the thief's back. Caswal held the other. Borros grabbed the hood and pulled it back. The thief's face shone in the firelight.

"Well, I'll be," Borros said.

The others were taken by surprise as well.

"A girl," Winwalom said.

"A Mashad," Lagash said and pointed at a tribal scar on her cheek.

Mashad? That was one of the main tribes in the Nahav, the great desert out west. Hundreds of years ago the Nahav had been the center of the world. And then its massive earthseep dried up. Without that, its power crumbled. It was now nothing but a shell of its former self. A place of sandy ruins, rock, goats, and bandits. What was a Mashad girl doing here?

Borros turned to Ferran. "Is this your thief, or is there another one out there?"

Her hair was cut in short, ragged clumps. She was tall, probably in her later teens, and fierce. She was also beautiful in the way of the Nahav. When Ferran had seen her before, she had been hidden in shadows, but this was the same hair, the same angular features. "It's her," he said.

"You sure?"

Ferran nodded.

"Can you speak Corom?" Borros asked.

The girl just gritted her teeth and glared at them.

Borros tried a few words in the desert tongue, but she did not respond.

"What's that on her arm?" Lagash asked.

Krov held her arm out and pulled up her cloak and tunic to reveal the marking of a slave.

"A runaway," Caswal said.

"A rotted lizard," Ranoc spat. "I say we turn her in for the money."

There was no love lost between Akken and the tribes of the Nahav. They very frequently raided the western part of Akken. And Ranoc's brother had been working as a courier for the old lord when a war band had come and killed him. Ranoc hated the tribes. It's part of why he wanted to joing the Queen's Rangers, so that he could go kill some of them.

"He wants to sell you," Borros said. "But I'm willing to listen."

The girl looked at them, then said, "Let me go."

"You've stolen from us."

"I will repay."

"What are you doing out here on this road?"

"Is this not the road to Broniss?"

"It is."

"I know the way back from Broniss. And so I am going to Broniss."

"Back to your clan?"

"Yes."

"This road was closed years ago. It's a forbiden road. We're heading into a blight. It's not a hundred paces down the road. Did you know that?"

She narrowed her eyes in concern, then shrugged. "I need to get to Broniss. My people will pay you well for my return."

"So you were taken and sold."

She nodded. "To Ogthan."

"Ogthan?" Borros asked. "That turd slime?"

"Who is Ogthan?" Krov asked.

"A petty lord in Gorland that deals in slaves. A sneaking, lying, disgusting turd of a man."

"Let's sell her back to him," Ranoc said.

"Ranger Boy doesn't like you," Borros said.

"I don't like him," she said.

Borros said, "You still have the coin?"

"Yes," she said.

"You'll give them back and work off the other things you stole?"

"Yes," she said.

Borros nodded. "Let her go, boys."

"What if she runs?" Caswal said.

"She won't run," Borros said and looked at her. "Will you?"

"No," she said.

"No, because she wants our protection."

"Protection?" Ranoc asked indignatly. "Why should we give a lizard any protection?"

"Because maybe some day you'll be somewhere in the Nahav and want protection from her clan. And they will give it to you. And because Ogthan is a slimy pus. So let her go."

Krov and Caswal let her go. The girl brought her arms forward and rubbed one shoulder.

"She looks hungry, Master Cook. Can you find her something to eat?"

"Yes," Lagash said. "You want a single portion or double?"

"Double," Borros said. He turned to the girl. "You know the spear?"

She nodded.

"Bow?"

She nodded again.

"Knives?"

"Yes," she said.

The Mashadians were said to train all their children in war because the various bands were constantly at each other's throats.

"Good," Borros said and smiled. "Let us make an agreement. What is your name?"

"I am a warrior. My name is Sura Man Killer. Hora's Daughter."

Sura the Man Killer. Now that was a name. Ferran raised his eyebrows and looked at Krov and Winwalom.

"I am Borros of Three Hammers, Sura. And these are the queen of Akken's cattle." He pointed to the scarlet badge on his hat. "This is the offical badge."

"A cattle herder?" she asked.

"You did not see the battle?"

"I saw."

Which meant that she knew Borros was not simply some herdsman.

Borros smiled. "Make an agreement with me, and the queen will be pleased. And you'll be in the queen's employ should any slave hunters come along."

She nodded. And Ferran wondered how far she'd run and how she'd evaded the hunters to this point. He also wondered what she was worth.

They discussed their agreement while Lagash made another batch of porridge. When they were done, Borros said, "Well, Dog Boy, it appears you were indeed telling the truth."

Ferran nodded. "So I'm hired again?"

"At full wages."

"What are we going to do with a girl?" Ranoc asked.

"We're about to pass into the blight," Borros said. "I'd think you'd welcome another person who can fight."

Ranoc glared at her, then looked away. But Ferran did not want to stop looking at her. She was unlike any girl he had ever seen.

She glanced at Ferran, scowled at him and the other boys. And then Lagash came with her hot porridge. She wolfed it down, then wiped her mouth. And then she reached into the neck of her tunic and pulled out a small leather purse that had been tied to a cord. She pulled the cord off her neck and held it out to Borros.

Lagash grabbed it. "I believe that is mine."

"Is it all there?" Borros asked.

Lagash opened the mouth of the small purse and dumped the coins out into his hand. And then he nodded.

"Thank you," Borros said to her. And then he turned to the boys. "Time to take watch and get some sleep. Tomorrow we enter the blight."

Krov shook his head at the prospect. It was clear all of the boys were worried.

"Cheer up. You'll be mounted. You'll be riding in fine style."

"I haven't ridden much, Sir," Krov said.

Winwalom corrected him. "He hasn't ridden at all. Only Ranoc knows anything."

"Well," Borros said. "Now's the time to learn. Think of that, Lover Boy, riding up on your very own horse to regale that lass with your drippy poetry."

"You're giving me a horse?"

"In battle, you split the plunder. And all here attest to your lively smacking about with your stick. So I'm not giving you anything. You earned it."

"I own a horse?" Krov said in surprised delight.

The other boys looked at each other.

"Us too?" Ranoc asked.

Borros looked at Lagash. "Scrappy, but not too bright, is he?"

Lagash chuckled. "All of you share."

The boys looked at each other in wonder. Ferran couldn't believe it. A horse! That would pay a sizeable part of their debt all by itself. And if it was really fine, it might pay all of it. A horse! He'd only ever dreamed of owning one.

"There are twenty-four of them," Caswal said. "Does that mean we each get three and a half?"

"Don't get uppity," Borros said. "We share, but we don't all share equally. The lord always takes a larger cut. Followed of course by his cook."

"His cook?" Lagash asked flatly.

Borros shrugged. "Maybe the lord and his cook share equally."

"Maybe the cook shares sixty-forty," Lagash said.

Borros ignored the comment and said, "You will each get two horses and your fair share of the mail, swords, axes, coins, and other things."

Ferran couldn't believe what he was hearing. Mail was often worth more than a horse. As was a good sword. He was going to not only be able to pay the debt, but he'd be able to buy his own plow. Buy oxen to go with it. Or maybe he'd learn some other trade.

After a number of exclamations of joy, the boys made their beds. Sura made hers on the other side of the camp fire. Ranoc wagered a birdseye that she would run in the night. Ferran took him up on the bet.

Ferran and Winwalom manned the first watch. As Ferran waited for Winwalom, Borros came over.

"Well, Dog Boy, three more days and we'll be through the blight. When we come out on the other side, you'll be at Kog's Pass. The whole valley will stretch out before you. In the distance you will see Broniss shining on the river."

"I can't wait, sir."

"You did well."

Ferran swelled with satisfaction. "Thank you, sir."

"I want you to know that I'm in your debt. And I repay my debts."

"Yes sir." Ferran thought about him coming out of the woods. He could still feel the echoes of that voice. He thought of their talk of demons and felt a bit of apprehension being so close to Borros.

Borros clapped him on the shoulder. "Stay awake. Make sure you yell loudly if some monster comes charging out of the blight."

"Yes sir," Ferran said and gulped. He certainly hoped there wasn't any monster.

Borros walked back to the camp. And then Winwalom returned.

"What was that about?" Winwalom said.

"Oh, he was just lauding my greatness and splendid abilities."

"Sure he was."

Ferran gave an exaggerated sigh. "It's true. What can I say? You just can't keep good breeding down."

"Oh brother," Winwalom sighed.

"The korrog ate your fish on sticks," Ferran said.

"It did?"

"The fish were gone and its footprints were all around."

Winwalom nodded in satisfaction. "Next time we try hares."

"I don't know if hares will do the trick," Ferran said. "Not if it's back at that clearing, feasting on the livers and hearts of men."

"Maybe it will think that's a gift as well."

And then the whole battle came back to Ferran and made him feel the anxiousness, triumph, and revulsion all over again.

"It's too bad it isn't tame," Winwalom said. "It would come in handy in the blight."

Ferran looked at Winwalom. A korrog would indeed come handy. And he suddenly saw what Winwalom was doing in a different light. "It's said that Old Blood could bond with animals."

A heartbeat passed.

"Yes, that's what's said."

Ferran nodded and thought that if he were Old Blood he could do worse than bond with a korrog. Bear or wolves would be good. But a korrog—that would be a mighty partner.

And he couldn't believe he was thinking such unholy thoughts. Life had been so simple in Buckle Hill. And now it was all jumbled up with grimsmen and outlaws and Old Blood and korrog and black tar smugglers. But it would soon be over.

He clapped Winwalom on the shoulder. "Borros says it's three more days, and then we'll be marching into Broniss. You'll start your apprenticeship to the felter. I'll get my family out of debt."

"Not just three days," Winwalom corrected. "But three days through the blight."

"Well, we've got boots and real spears."

"And a wild woman from the deserts."

"And Borros," Ferran said, "who may or may not be a demon."

"A demon?" Winwalom said and laughed at the notion, and then his laughter abrutly died. "Oh, I didn't think of that."

"Yeah."

"No," Winwalom said, rejecting the idea.

Ferran shrugged. Who knew what was going on with Borros? "Either way, it's nice he's on our side."

"That's true," Winwalom said.

"So this should be a breeze, right?"

"Indeed," Winwalom said.

Itch gave Ferran's hand a lick, and Ferran gave him a scratch around the head. And then they began to make their rounds. The crickets chirped in the darkness. Above the dark trees, the stars twinkled in the night sky. A slip of moon shined bright.

Broniss was three days away. Just three quick days through the blight.

DEAR READER

I hope you enjoyed this installment of the tale of Ferran, Winwalom, Borros, and the rest.

If you did, please leave a review on Amazon.

A line or two not only helps your fellow readers, it also helps ye doughty author bring you more books.

ACKNOWLEDGMENTS

I want to thank the following individuals. For accurate reports of their beta reads: **Alexandria Wall, Eadie Ogilvie, Eric Allen, Gary Ogilvie, Jared Johnson, Justin Wall, Kassandra Brown, Kristin Westergard,** and **Lilia Brown.** The report each shared helped me make this tale better. A heartfelt thanks also goes to **Dixon Leavitt** for his help on the cover. A huge thanks goes to the excellent **Nellie Brown** for helping me see a better ending.

ABOUT JOHN

John D. Brown is the bestselling author of the The Drovers series, Dark God series, and Frank Shaw series. He loves loading his stories with action, adventure, suspense, and characters you want to cheer for. He lives in the hinterlands of Utah where there's lots of fresh air, many good-hearted ranchers, and a red tailed hawk that likes to occasionally dive bomb him on his hikes.

Learn more about John at his website: www.johndbrown.com.

To keep up-to-date on his releases and receive exclusive bonus content, join his newsletter.

If you liked this book, please take a minute to leave a review. A hearty huzzah will not only help your fellow readers, it will also help the author bring you more books.

www.ingramcontent.com/pod-product-compliance
Lightning Source LLC
Chambersburg PA
CBHW031223260626
47169CB00007B/2165